One Tree Hill

Kevin Davies

Order this book online at www.trafford.com
or email orders@trafford.com

Most Trafford titles are also available at major online book retailers.

Note for Librarians: A cataloguing record for this book is available from Library
and Archives Canada at www.collectionscanada.ca/amicus/index-e.html

Printed in Victoria, BC, Canada.

ISBN: 978-1-4269-0994-8

*Our mission is to efficiently provide the world's finest, most comprehensive book publishing
service, enabling every author to experience success. To find out how to publish your
book, your way, and have it available worldwide, visit us online at www.trafford.com*

Trafford rev. 10/12/09

 www.trafford.com

North America & international
toll-free: 1 888 232 4444 (USA & Canada)
phone: 250 383 6864 ♦ fax: 812 355 4082

To my brother Barry who lived the same experiences, has his own memories and his own stories to tell of those boyhood years,

and,

to Warren, Party, Bobby, Carl, Mathew, Frank, Stretchy, Jim, Mum, Fernsy and Pommy...and all the kids in the Boys Home... ...what fun we had!

Acknowledgements

While I sweated over this collection alone, I received help from many people and wish to thank:

My writing group: John, Brad, Louise, Antonio. You listened to new stories each session, giving suggestions and guidance for improvement. Your encouragement over the years was essential to my writing process and development.

Rebecca, my editor, a real guiding star. You wrestled with the collection as much as I did and influenced me greatly. You were the teacher and I the student. Thanks Rebecca, for your time, patience and care.

Friends who supported me over the years it took to complete this project. When asked to read selections you suffered in silence and gave me back helpful advice and encouragement. I understand completely if, after all these years, you might feel that there is no book and I have just been faking it.

My wife Claudia who put up with my total distraction in the process of writing 'One Tree Hill'. Even on the worst days you gave me support. Hours were spent together reading, discussing, and analysing. Your questions, patience and love, kept me on track. Thank you Claud, for being my favourite critic while encouraging me at the same time.

The boys of the Home at 109 Mt Smart Road, Onehunga, Auckland, New Zealand. You are the family I think about still; the ones involved with me in the fun and sadness of my boyhood. You have the same stories, told in your own voices. To all of you and the staff, thank you

Contents

Introduction

I found it very difficult to write 'One Tree Hill' but it was eventually finished after 4 years of hard work. Upon completion of a Life Writing course, I launched into the project fearlessly but with little idea of what I wanted. I was inspired to write; exactly what, was yet to be discovered.

In my writing group we discussed memoir. I read my notes, books and boldly set about getting the process started. Immediately I was taken back to those years from age 5 to 13 in post-war New Zealand, (1945 - 1954) and was confronted by memories and recollections. I wrote draft after draft about my early years. At first, none of it was satisfying. Some stories had the ring of truth, but not a lot I felt, would be found interesting by readers. I struggled to find my voice in the process.

Questions arose: Who was my audience? Which events should be the ones to write about? Would my writing sound authentic? On the advice of my wife Claudia, I decided to focus on the one passage of time in my life which would likely be seen as the most interesting, even if I had avoided admitting to that, all my adult years.

That's what I did. I went back to those years in the Boys Home Orphanage in Onehunga. Photographs from my mother, old letters, conversations and personal memories became my reference materials; thoughts, impressions, recollections and imagination, my tools. These are what I have relied on, sometimes knowing they were accurate and sometimes flawed. I wove the real events into stories. That was the easy part. Other times I could not recall facts, sequences, characters or outcomes. That was the difficult part and where I drew heavily upon my imagination.

As the stories began to emerge, I struggled, confronted by the dilemma to use real names or not. Eventually, with development, the characters emerged. They are the boys I grew up with, the ones who were a part of my family for all those years. I found my voice at the same time as they found theirs.

This is the first time I have spoken at length about my life in the Onehunga Boys Home; the first time I have told my story to an audience. The stories are true in part and fictional where I couldn't recall real-time events. I have stayed loyal to the short story form I hope, but found sometimes that my own life broke out and interfered. I wanted to tell what happened and I wanted to write stories. I hope I have been somewhat successful on both counts.

For the most part the memories of my time at the Boys Home have been positive. In fact, for years I struggled to recall any negative incidents. During the writing of this collection however, I was brought face to face with the good side and the shadow side of life in the orphanage. The stories have helped me face this period of my past with greater courage and understanding. Mostly, they were a lot of fun to write. The process has certainly been cathartic for me.

Here then, are the boys of the Onehunga Boys Home, portrayed as brothers, friends and companions during this difficult but strangely happy time of my life.

Kevin Davies
April 17th, 2008
Vancouver, BC, Canada

Kowhai Glen

"Kevin is a sissy, Kevin is a sissy, Kevin is a -"

"You cut it out, Gwen," said Mairie, "he's not a sissy, he's just a young kid."

"He's a bloody sissy, Mairie. And you don't have stick up for him. He's got to learn to do that for himself," said Gwen glaring at her sister. "For God's sake he's a boy and he needs to toughen up and not be such a baby. He's a bloody sissy Mairie and you know it!" After another horrible day at Otira School I wasn't feeling good about listening to any of this; feeling pretty miserable in fact. We had left on the bus early in the morning and all the way to school I felt lonely and scared. School was not my bag right from the beginning. I hated it. I knew I had to go because other kids did. My brother Barry had already started and he was fine, so Mum told me. But I wasn't.

Mum was waiting around to be accepted to a staff position at the Presbyterian Boys Home in Onehunga, a suburb of Auckland. Meanwhile, we were staying on a farm near Warkworth, north of Auckland, with my Grandmother's sister

Aunty Mag, Uncle Jock and their daughters, my cousins Gwen and Mairie. It was important for us to be near Auckland so that Mum could begin the job as soon as she was required to. Mag and Jock were only too happy to help out and so we began months of farm-life which were to change to Auckland city-life when the time came.

In 1945 in Wellington when I was about 4 years old, without any warning, my Dad left us just when I was getting to feel more of a boy and less of a baby; just when I was looking toward my Dad for fun and activity in my life; just when I was learning to love him more and more. There were no clues that could've warned my brother Barry and me that something huge was about to blow. When Dad left he threw a wrench into our family life. One day he was there, the next day he was gone taking all that father-love with him. I was left standing in my four-year-old's play clothes looking for my playmate each day but he never showed, and I never understood why. I never understood what it was that drove him out of our door and away from me. I lost my Dad and that hurt me deeply. Life can be hugely disrespectful sometimes.

We moved away from Wellington, away from all my relatives. Where did they all go to? Why didn't they visit any more? Where were the cousins I played with? Each day I felt my Mum's pain. I watched sometimes as she stood staring out the window crying, standing there with the tears running, trying to stifle the sobs but not being able to. In my small-boy way I knew why she was so upset because I felt like how I imagined she did inside. In my brother's silence I heard anger and confusion. I tried hard to stem the tears I sensed he wouldn't like and to keep my feelings inside. It didn't help to watch Mum fall apart and to lose herself in sorrow. Maybe it helped a little bit when she gathered Barry and I together in her arms, held us tight and spoke through her sobbing, "Barry and Kevin, now boys, we have to be strong. We have to look after each other. Your Dad's not going to be around any more to help us, so we all need to help each other."

Having said all that, it was a very tough 'ask' to expect a young mother with two boys to step out into this 1940 New Zealand world and cope successfully. Sure the country had come through the depression of the 1930s and the Second World War which followed, but it would be a while before New Zealand with it's small population, would gain a higher living standard that other countries were well on their way to achieving. Women all over New Zealand who found themselves without their male breadwinning mate, found it extremely hard to bring up their children, find a job, keep it and pay the increasing bills to afford even a semblance of a reasonable life. The next years were going to be hard on Mum and she knew it.

I felt that she wanted to be a strong and capable mother in the face of so much and it made me feel that I wanted to be strong too. Too many tears just would not do. She wanted to say more, to cling to us more and sometimes she did and it was at those moments that my brother Barry couldn't stand the tension and tore himself away from her, and me. As he grew older he turned to us less and less. That's how he dealt with his pain and sorrow I guess. Mum seemed sad all the time and our house seemed sad too. Life changed irreversibly for me without a father. The person who helped me find excitement and fun in my life had turned his back on us and walked away. I don't think I ever fully recovered, but I did learn, unfortunately, to keep the tears inside.

Soon after my Father had left us my mother had to re-think how she was going to support herself and her two boys. One day she received a letter from her friend Gertie Williamson. Willy, (my Mother's affectionate nickname), said she would soon be leaving her job as the sub-matron of an orphanage in Auckland, housing thirty boys, and wondered if Mum might be interested in working there.

"You'd be a natural at this job, Joyce," Willy wrote. "Oh, and there are lots of other staff as well. You won't be the only one of course."

Mum, who had never done anything like this in her life, jumped at the suggestion. She loved kids and agreed that this would be just the ticket for her.

"You know what, Willy?" she wrote back, "I'm going to do it. I'll apply for the job. The lord knows I need a different direction in my life right now. Now that Jack's gone I have to find a job that will pay enough money for the three of us and allow us to stay together as a family. Maybe this is just that opportunity."

Besides, it would get her away from her awful Wellington memories and out of the clutches of her relatives who meant well in their desire to keep the family together, but couldn't help themselves in their constant urgings.

My Grandmother said to Mum one day soon after my Father had left, "now, you know Joyce, this is the time to rely on your family for help and to trust in the Lord that he will bring you through. You are being tested right now and we can help you pull through this, you know." To my Grandfather and other family members, Nana said, "we have to help poor Joyce right now. It's a terrible thing Jack has done, walking out on her. Joyce has never been very strong in a crisis and she will fall apart if we don't gather around. You all know what she's like, so very fragile I'm afraid."

"Let's pray to the Lord, Ethel," said Grandpa. "He will show us the right thing to do."

This was not a time for too much thinking by Mum. Urgent action was called for. She needed to move quickly to gain some much needed separation and independence; to move to a place where she could begin to think clearly without the noise of interference. Mum sent off a letter of application, travelled up to Auckland for an interview and was told in a letter a few weeks later:

.....*indeed, Mrs Davies, the Presbyterian Orphanage Society would be pleased to employ you in the position of Sub-Matron at the Onehunga Boys Home. However, you'll have to wait until your youngest is at least four-and-a-half to place him here. We advise you at this point that it may be to your advantage to place your oldest*

5

boy in The Home as soon as possible which will serve to definitely reserve a place for you and your youngest. If you like, you can make arrangements with us to wait for the next six months to go by and start the job then when he's old enough. Yours faithfully........

We waited out the time on the farm at Warkworth until I was old enough. Barry was placed in the Home soon after our arrival in Auckland so that our position was secured. This must have been a tough decision for Mum to make. I'm sure this separation affected Barry emotionally and that he suffered a certain amount of trauma. Like lots of young kids who have had similar experiences, he learned to deal with it by suppressing his feelings. He must have been hurting terribly from the rejection and abandonment he felt from our Dad leaving. I know I did. Then, before he had time to cope with his grief over that, he was separated from our Mother and from me. Mum was caught between a rock and a hard place. Reality told her that she needed to secure a place in the Onehunga Orphanage. The opportunity of a job with a regular wage offering a place to live and be supported was too important to let slip. This position at the Presbyterian Boys Home would provide the stability she felt was threatened at this point. It can be said that when it all boiled down to the bottom of life's saucepan, Mum placed Barry in the home because she just simply could not cope and by doing so secured herself and her two sons a future with at least some prospect of protection.

Mum's new life, Barry's and mine, was about to begin.

On top of the trauma of Wellington, the new demands and experiences coming my way, life on the farm with my cousins Gwen and Mairie was enough of a shock, but having to start school was way over the top for me. I couldn't handle it well at all. From the time I became aware that my Dad was not around any more to the time I saw it was just me, Mum and Barry, was only a few months of my young new life. The only way I knew to deal with my own hurt while watching Mum cope with hers, was to keep a lid on my crying, stuff my feelings down inside and get on with things. I hung around Mum trying to make her feel better but that didn't work. Barry tried his best to look after me when our mother was obviously having trouble coping, but his own sorrow and anger boiled over and often got in the way. His occasional ear-pull or tea-towel flick on the back of the legs were the kind of thing he'd do to let off some steam. I probably cried at that and he probably grinned and walked off. It was all too much for young boys to deal with and even too much for Mum who had gone through many difficulties already in her life even though I didn't know about any of that at the time.

Pretty soon we moved into Auckland City somewhere in the Mt Eden area and stayed with some other relatives. They had an outhouse which was fairly common in New Zealand homes in those days. Indoor toilets were becoming more popular with people who could afford the plumbing but most still had the outdoor 'dunny' as it was affectionately known to Kiwis. They were small, cold, practical sheds in the single seat or two-seater style. Some were painted, most left unpainted, not yet at the point where people put up pictures and left magazines in an attractive basket on the bench. As I remember it, ours had the usual resident spider in one corner and a roll of toilet paper hanging from a string loop nailed to the wall.

I made good use of our dunny one day when Mum had taken me off to Kindergarten on a particularly dull and wet Auckland Monday. I felt exactly like the weather, or under it. I did not want to go to this school even if it did have a nice name like Kowhai Glen Primary School.

"It'll be fine once you start Kev," said Mum. "Barry's at his school and he loves it. He's already in the footy team. Once you get to know the teacher and some of the other kids you'll have fun, you'll see."

Well, I didn't see. That very first day of kindergarten I left at playtime, ran out through the front gate and all the way home in the rain. I hid in the dunny until I thought it would be safe to go inside and see Mum. This seemed like hours to me.

"Oh Kev, you're home early," said Mum as I entered the door, "I was just thinking about coming up to the school to meet you. I've made some nice soup for you. Your favourite...tomato soup."

"School was over early today Mum," I lied, "so I thought I would walk home and maybe meet you on the way."

"Did they say why it was out early, Kev?"

"No, the teacher just said we could all go home, so I did."

That was the first time but definitely not the last time I skipped out of school early and hid in the dunny to pass time before going home. Mum never discovered my ruse and before she had time to find out, we were on our way to Onehunga and a big change in life.

Mum was contacted by the Presbyterian Society and told that they were ready for her to take up her position as sub-matron at the Boys Home in Onehunga.

"109 Mt Smart Road, Onehunga, Auckland is the address, Mrs Davies," stated the letter informing her about her new job and when we could finally move in. I had been missing Barry terribly. He had been gone now for some time. This was the first time he had been away from us. Now we were finally going to see him and this was exciting.

"Will Barry be waiting for us, Mum?"

"I'm pretty sure he will, Dear. He'll be just as anxious to see us as we are to see him."

Everything happened quickly after that. We moved into the Boys Home within a week. It was a sunny day when Barry met us at the front entrance and as we approached I could see many other boys there too.

The Onehunga Boys Home

Barry wriggled quickly out of the hug Mum laid on him. He reached out to me and gave me a warm but shy hug. That felt good.

"Hello little brother," he said ruffling my hair and pulling one of my ears. "You're gonna like it here, Kev. I've made lots of friends already. There's plenty of kids."

"Yeah, there's thirty of us altogether, Barry," said the good-looking boy standing next to him.

I looked up at Barry with a grin. He was my older brother, taller than me, physically much larger and always with a warm grin on his face. I felt safe when he was around and now after such a long absence that feeling was right back where it should be. I was the little kid and as far as I was concerned he was the adult. I depended on Barry for help and the occasional bossing around, *"just what big brothers are supposed to do,"* I thought.

"Kev, this is my friend Mathew. We do lots of stuff together. Mathew and I can show you around later. It's a big place. Matt's been here longer than I have but I've been here a long time too. It's good to see you and Mum again."

"Hello little Davies," said Mathew towering over me.

I had no idea at the time, but that name was going to stick with me all my years at the Home.

Mathew said, "I'm looking forward to showing you around, mate. Wait 'til you see our cow-shed and our cows. And there's chooks too and pigeons in coops."

"Don't forget the footy field, Matt," said Barry. "Kev's going to like that. He likes footy, doncha Kev?"

Mathew smiled at me and put his hand on my shoulder, which made me feel accepted. Looking shyly around the front entrance I saw kids all over the place hanging out of the big windows, standing and sitting everywhere. They seemed friendly enough but they looked so big.

Our bags and stuff were unloaded and taken inside. "Come on you boys, help Mrs Davies by carrying her bags into the lounge," said a tall, thin woman who I later learned was Miss Sylvia Ferns, the Matron of the Home. I spent the next hour going from this room to that listening to many instructions and loads of information being shared between Ms Ferns and Mum. Soon Barry arrived to take me away from the adults. I felt small and very nervous. I was young too, nearly five years old... well, four and a half going on five.

Barry and Mathew spent what seemed like a long time showing me everything at the Home and of course afterwards

I couldn't remember a thing that they told me. But it was fun being with Barry again and I knew he liked it too because every now and again he would put his hand on my shoulder or gently ruffle my hair. He didn't say much. He didn't have to.

Young Kevin & Brother Barry

It did feel like I was in some kind of home. I wasn't sure if this was going to be a home like my Wellington cousins lived in or whether it was going to be some giant camp-like home with all these boys.

This is going to be alright, I thought. *I sure like the idea of having all those kids to play with.*

I stood alone in my thoughts now, mulling over *what was in store for me ?*

School Daze

From the beginning I hated school; getting ready to go in the morning, walking to it and being there during the day. The best part was the bell at 3pm and the walk home when a sense of freedom washed over me like a warm shower on a cold morning. I believe this distaste had less to do with academic difficulties and more to do with my inability to come to terms with leaving the nest. Fear of flight was a real threat for me but eventually I did fly the coop and ironically, when the time came for a career choice, I chose to become a school teacher.

After my kindergarten initiation at Otira and Kowhai Glen, Te Papapa Primary School in Auckland was my first full school experience. I didn't want to go and sabotaged any attempt to get me there. Illness, often feigned, usually worked. I was never averse to seeking out a variety of measures to help with subverting yet another day in my academic career.

On one typically warm rainy day in Onehunga, after delaying my departure from the Home with excuses of a sudden ailment, I set out for school to my mother's great relief. I was on my own that day as all the other kids had done the normal thing and left at the usual hour. In the downpour I walked along Mt Smart Road and arrived at the first intersection where there was a corner grocery store with a porch-front covered by a nice old curvy-corregated-iron overhang. It was an old building and had seen many years of weather. The rain was coming down in buckets and pouring through rust holes and rips in the overhead gutter. Without a thought I moved beneath the largest stream and stood there. Pretty soon I was soaked through. *This is exactly the trick,* I thought. *This is my way out of school today. For sure I can't go now.* Just to be on the safe side I stayed under the stream a while longer until I felt the water running down my back letting me know that I was thoroughly soaked to the skin.

School being out of the question at that point, I sloshed my way back to the Home where Mum met me at the front door. She had seen me coming in through the gate and, before I had finished telling her, "gee Mum, I couldn't find any shelter anywhere," she found a set of dry clothes, fitted me into them and buttoned up another raincoat.

"Hey Mum, this one's a bit too big for me," I said walking toward the front gate. As I turned to say "goodbye," she held me by the arm and said, "it's alright Kev, I'll walk with you all the way." With no chance of avoiding the issue further, I realised that as much as I hated it, this was going to be a school day for me after all. I cringed, my stomach tightened and that certain kind of childhood stress came over me. But there was no way out of this. My shower trick under the spouting had back-fired.

Before long we arrived at Te Papapa, Mum having done her duty and me feeling growing fear. All the classes were in session as we entered the school. Mum talked with my teacher Ms Barrett. I looked on but didn't listen closely to what she or Ms Barrett were saying. It probably amounted to something like, "yes, well, I'm terribly sorry Kevin is so late, but he had a problem making up his mind about going to school today. I decided to walk him here to be sure he made it alright. He seems to have taken a dislike to school from the start and I do so want it to be different for him at Te Papapa."

"Don't worry, Mrs Davies," replied Ms Barrett, "I'll keep an eye on him and see that he starts to enjoy himself a little. He'll soon make friends here."

I missed the exchange of knowing-smiles between Mum and the Teacher because I was nervously peering around the classroom.

Mum left saying she would see me when I got home after school. " 'Bye, Kev," she said, "have a good day at school dear. It seems like a lovely school. Your teacher seems nice and friendly," she added in a whisper. Not for a moment did I think that any of this was difficult for her, or that she was alarmed at the intensity of my dislike of school or my inability to get through even one day trouble free. Everything she had done and said so far, seemed quite natural to me. I fully expected her to do what she was doing. She was my Mum after all. She left me and walked off into the rain without a backward glance, which is always tough to do!

"Come on Kevin, let's go and meet the other kids." Ms Barrett took me inside, helped me hang my coat in the hallway and we entered the classroom. She was a tall, athletic woman with attractive dark hair. I especially remember her lipstick which was the same as my Mum's, when she allowed herself to wear any. Ms Barrett had glasses which suited her and all the time she looked at me she had a warm welcoming smile. If nothing else, that smile helped to calm my fears. All the same I was very nervous as she showed me to my desk. As she turned away she said to me, "Oh, Kevin, morning break will be coming up soon and I'm going to need you to ring the bell for me. Please see me at the end of the class, that's a good boy."

The class went by in a blur and I don't recall anything about the rest of the day except that I rang the bell not only at morning break but lunchtime and afternoon break as well. I had to admit to myself, I was pleased to be doing such an important job. I smiled as I hung on with both hands and shook the shiny brass thing. By the time school was over for the day I had stood on the step outside the classroom three or four times with the kids filing past me, some saying, "good ringing, good ringing! Wish I could do that, Kevin." It surprised me that some of them even knew my name.

The next few days went by sort of foggy-like. Each morning the teacher came up to me and said, "don't forget Kevin, you are on bell duty again today. You're the best bell ringer we've had for a long time!" How could she know that a simple little job like ringing the bell would have the effect of hooking me into her class and giving me something to look forward to? If nothing else I learned that break times and lunchtimes were important moments in my life...and still are!

As I walked toward the school gate each afternoon of that first week I looked back and saw the teacher wave to me from the classroom step and, with some relief, I waved back. I know now that it took that small amount of caring by that individual teacher to help me break through my fear and loathing of the daily school routine.

When I got home each day that first week, Mum could hardly contain herself. Once Monday and Tuesday were over, her obvious nervousness transformed into genuine excitement. Was it possible that I might actually make it through to the end of the week without a crisis?

"Hello Kev, how was school today?" she asked nervously at first.

"It was alright Mum. I rang the bell four times."

"Four times dear? The Teacher must like you doing that job."

"I think so Mum," I said, "she said I can ring it for the rest of the week."

The look on Mum's face by the time Friday rolled around told me that she could hardly believe that I had lasted this first week out at Te Papapa without any more attempts at sabotage. All because of a small brass bell!

I did last the week out and lots more after that. Pretty soon I was like any other kid in the class looking forward to the activities and lessons that the Teacher had for us. I played footy with other kids on the school field and walked to and from school each day with my friends from the Home. I was even ready on time each morning, although I did have Miss Ferns on my case now and again calling, "come on Kevin Davies, tuck your shirt in. My, my," she shook her head as she said this, "but you are the slowest kid to get ready Kevin Davies!"

Five Homekids Ready For School

I wasn't the slowest kid when it came to having fun on the way home from school though. The route back to the Home took me past some houses that had fruit trees growing in the front and one particular place had a small orchard next to it. One afternoon, after being in the Home for about a year, I walked back to Mt Smart Road with Warren Francis and Robin

(Party) Partridge two kids from the Home who had become my friends. We stopped by this house and looked over the fence at the apples and gooseberries dangling from fully laden branches. It was a familiar sight, a scene we had checked many times before.

Warren said, "I'll lay my coat over the barbed wire, Kev, so you can scuttle over and grab a few of those apples. I'll be right behind you."

"Me too, Kev," grinned Robin.

I was small and agile and pretty soon I was in the field on the other side of the fence. Not waiting for the others, I headed straight for the nearest gooseberry bush and filled my pockets with the delicate little fruit. Ahead was an apple tree and just after I had stuffed three or four apples into my shirt I was startled by a shout, "You bloody kids get out of my field and leave my fruit alone!"

An old man with whispy grey hair flying about came out of his backyard with a stick in his hand and a dog at his side.

"You little bastards are gonna feel my stick when I catch up with you," he yelled. "Go, Foxy, go," he growled at his dog, "get in there and bite their bums. Teach you a bloody lesson to steal from my trees," he bellowed.

I ran like crazy toward the fence and saw Warren and Robin on the outside with wide grins on their faces. Without a thought to safety, I flew over the fence onto the road outside. Warren grabbed his coat as I wiped some blood off my leg which I had snagged on the barbed wire.

Robin yelled, "let's get out of here."

We ran as fast as we could with the dog barking after us and the old man swearing in the distance. By the time we reached Mt Smart Road and saw that we were safe, we slowed to a walk. Sucking in a large breath I looked at the other two and said, "Nice friends you two are, leaving me in the field to face that crazy old coot."

Party grinned as usual and said, "Aw Kev, mate, don't be mad. Warren and me were just about to get over the fence when we saw the old man coming out his back door. Nothin' we could do, Kev, but stay there and see that you were safe. Didn't want the dog to get you mate."

"Yeah, Kev, me and Party would've stuck up for you, mate," said Warren. "Now how about some of those gooseberries!" I was too busy enjoying the delicious fruit to notice the grin going back and forward between my two so-called friends.

Eventually it was time for me to leave Te Papapa and begin Standard One at Onehunga Primary School where Mr Black was the headmaster. I remember that his hair was jet black so I thought that was how he got his name. He was pretty good to me even considering that I spent quite a bit of time in his office for a variety of escapades.

Onehunga Primary School

I was older now, a bit bigger and had been at the Home long enough to form friendships and bonds. Us Home Kids stuck together and backed each other up in all situations. Like the time when we knew that a group of bigger kids were walking around the games of marbles going on in the school grounds and stealing other kids' alleys by stepping on some which had been misfired and picking them up in their toes.

One day after we tired of watching these bullies, a group of us Home Kids surrounded them and ordered that all the marbles be dropped on the ground in front of them. Pretty soon a big crowd of kids gathered to watch and see what would happen. For quite a while nothing did happen. It was a standoff with the bullies eyeing us and refusing to empty their pockets. We pushed the circle tighter and made threatening sounds. Then, just as

21

somebody hissed, "teachers are coming," the alleys were dropped, the standoff was over and we had broken through the bullies' bravado. The kids they had stolen from were now grinning as they collected up their marbles.

During a footy game another day, when a couple of big kids booted me hard after I was tackled at the end of a long run, a fight broke out and I joined it at the back of Bobby Parata and Carl Newman. Mr Black banned footy for a week after that and ordered all the Home kids involved in the fight to pull out convolvulous creepers from the hedge that ran along one side of the field. We felt sorry for ourselves at the time because of this injustice but turned up each day to take our punishment with other kids looking on and laughing.

A year later in my standard three class at Onehunga, the 'Blackhawk Gang' was formed. We named ourselves after the hero Blackhawk, in our favourite comic. He was the best pilot in the air force and his men were particularly loyal to him. There was no fight they would back out of once 'Blackhawk' gave the order. Criminals, Nazis and others up to no good in the world, were hunted down and dealt with. Unfortunate victims of crime and evil, those caught in disasters who needed rescuing and people in all kinds of nasty predicaments needing the Gang's help, got it... and quickly. It was no accident that among all my heroes, Blackhawk, Robin Hood and The Phantom ranked high. They knew how to deal with injustice. Our own Blackhawk Gang at Onehunga School turned up at all sorts of situations in the playground helping to solve disagreements and taking the side of the wronged and the underdog in fights.

The crunch came one day when the Blackhawk Gang rescued some young kids who were trying to defend their marbles after a game had just finished. We grabbed the three bullies who were already pocketing the alleys, tied them hand and foot with flax leaves and left them on the lower field near the gorse bushes so they couldn't move. Then we rushed off to class as the bell went. All would have been well except that the three were discovered missing from their classes and after Mr Black had located them he called the Blackhawk Gang to his office.

"Alright boys," he said in his fairest tone, "let me hear your story, one at a time. Kevin Davies you start."

I mumbled about bullies picking on young kids who couldn't defend themselves, unfairness, and how we wanted to help.

"But don't you know, Master Kevin, that making sure kids are well behaved at Onehunga is NOT YOUR JOB? IT'S MINE!" said Mr Black, glaring at me through what I was sure were two black glass eyes. Other kids then put in their two-pennies worth, but I could tell that it was going to make no difference to our headmaster.

"I'm telling you boys from the Home once, and I'm telling you clearly," he said sternly, "you will not behave like this at my school. The Blackhawk Gang is to be disbanded after this and I do not want to hear about it ever again. Is this understood? Kevin Davies? Warren Francis? Robin Partridge? Carl Newman? Bobby Parata?..... No more Blackhawk Gang!"

We had nothing to say to that but Mr Black added, "now line up outside my office boys and wait until I call you in. You are to be punished for this event. Enough is enough!"

One by one we were called into the The Head's office where Mr Black laid on four of the best to our hands. Nobody said a word... until later.

"I didn't cry," said Carl, "did you Kevin? I thought you were crying when you came out."

"Just a bit," I said, "but it wasn't the strap, it was because I'm sad we can't have the Blackhawk Gang anymore."

Party grinned and said, "It didn't hurt. How about you Warren?"

"I didn't feel a thing," said Warren. "Take more than that to make me cry."

"I didn't cry," blurted Carl.

"Hey, but Carl, if you didn't cry mate," asked Bobby, "then what are those wet streaks on your cheeks?"

"Liar, Parata, I never cried! I never cried. Stop trying to make out that I did."

"Oh, sure then Carl, I believe you, I believe you, but thousands wouldn't."

We turned then and went off back to our classes, red hands in pockets, the sting of Mr Black's strap lasting for the rest of the afternoon.

In my final year at Onehunga School before I made the jump from Standard Four to Form One at Manukau Intermediate School, I achieved something really special in my life. My teacher announced one day that the school was offering a competition for a written essay with the title of: "The Person Who I Look Up To Most In My Life." All that week I thought about this and talked to my Mum.

"I'd sort of like to write this Mum. I think I can do it."

"I'm sure you can dear," she said, "you always get comments from your teacher about how good your stories are. Why don't you give it a try?"

"I even know what I'm going to write," I said, "and I'm going to keep it a secret until I've finished."

"Go for it, Kev," she said. "I know you can do it."

So, I did. I wrote about my brother and how I felt that I wanted to emulate him in my life. I looked up to Barry very much in those days and now that he was at Otahuhu College and doing big kids work and playing footy in the 1st XV and preparing himself to become an engineer my admiration for him was strong. I poured over this essay during the following week, rewriting it many times until I felt satisfied I was saying what was in my heart. I submitted it early and waited anxiously for the results of the competition that came two weeks later. I can still feel my pride at the moment that the teacher announced in the class, with Mr Black standing just inside the door that, "the winner of the essay competition is Kevin Davies. Congratulations Kevin. Now class, I'd like to read out Kevin's essay and you will see why it was chosen as the winner." I beamed right through my curly hair.

At the end of year ceremony I walked on stage to applause and was handed three brand new books as my prize. Mum and Barry were there and I was extremely proud of myself. For a long time after that I thought about the essay and how much I had enjoyed writing it. I felt that I could write lots more and as time went on I did . I drew cartoons and pictures all through my two years at Manukau Intermediate too, letting this creative side of myself emerge and gaining immense pleasure in it as well.

The February following my writing triumph at Onehunga I began Form One at Manukau Intermediate School. This was the 'Big-Time' for me and certainly felt like a version of what I imagined highschool to be. There was more of everything: woodwork, cooking, art lessons and classrooms opening out onto a huge blacktop playground with playing fields spreading beyond that. A dental clinic even occupied a corner site of the school and it was there that I began my life-long fearful affair with dentistry. I sensed in my first few weeks at Manukau that these teachers and the Headmaster viewed school far more seriously than I did. In the first two weeks I had my knuckles rapped for mispelling words I had neglected to learn, a clip or two on my ears for failing to keep my woodwork bench tidy and was embarrassingly thrown out of an art class for fooling around with paint. I realised quickly that these people meant business. If those of us from primary school thought we could continue to take our time about maturing, the staff here would speed the process up considerably.

It was early days yet at Manukau and I was feeling nervous about my new school. Each day at three I met up with some of the Home Kids and walked back to Mt Smart Road. One day

I was outside the front gate when Dennis McKenna walked by with his bike.

"Gee Dennis, that's a beauty bike," I said.

"Thanks," he replied.

I had met Dennis the first week in my Form 1 class. He wasn't a Home Kid but was from the Onehunga community. He was friendly from the start which was unusual because most community kids steered clear of Home Kids if they could. Dennis was different. He was taller than me too and stockier. His face was a mass of freckles and his head was thick with wild red hair. It's a wonder that he didn't have 'Ginger' or 'Bluey' as a nickname. I liked Dennis enough that he and I spent time with each other at school. Strangely that never transferred to out of school times except for the few times he walked with me homeward down Manukau Road.

"Just got it, Kev," he said. "It was my birthday on Saturday and my Mum, Dad and Grandparents all chipped in to buy it for me. My Dad and Grandpa were both bike racers when they were young."

I was attracted by the newness of the bike. The red paint, the chrome and the black tires and the lettering were dazzling.

"What type of bike is it, Dennis?" I asked.

"It's a Raleigh Racer, made in England," he said, "and you can tell it's a racer by the handle bars curving down. It's really light. Lift it, Kev."

I did and was amazed at how much lighter it was than the old blue clunker I rode around the Home sometimes. I had never seen a new bike before and certainly never been this close to one. New things didn't often come my way. It was just the way things were in my life. Christmas time and the occasional birthday sometimes brought a new toy or a book but mostly the gifts were practical things my Mum thought I needed like a new pair of shorts, a fishing line or a Bible. Nothing as desirable and luxurious as a bike. Not that I thought about it very much and it certainly didn't mean I was not attracted to bright new shiny things like I was now to Dennis' bike.

"It's a beauty Dennis. I bet you can go fast with those gears," I said showing my knowledge of bike technology even though I had never seen a bike with optional gears before. Nobody at the Home had one.

"Why doncha try it, Kev. Have a ride to the end of the road and back."

"Are you sure Dennis?" I asked. "I don't wanna crash and damage it."

"Come on mate," he said, "you know how to ride. Give it a go."

I did, gingerly at first, carefully steering and pedaling slowly. Pretty soon though, the exhilaration of riding a new bike made me feel like seeing what it could do. I pedaled faster and gripped the handlebars tighter. When I squeezed the brakes at the end of the road I felt like one of the bike racers we watched going fast down Mt Smart Road on the occasional Saturday morning.

I turned and rode back to Dennis a little bit relieved when I dismounted. I had not crashed or damaged his new Raleigh.

"Jeez, thanks mate," I said. "What a great bike. I can feel how new it is."

"Yeah I love it," he said proudly. "My Grandpa says if I ride it a lot he'll show me a few tips about real bike racing. My Dad says I need to build my confidence first, 'cos it's not like an ordinary bike."

At Manukau I made other new friends. In Form Two I met Warren Gargan and we became best mates. Warren and I played in the Manukau School rugby team and were both selected for the local rep team. There were also a few other kids I hung out with at Manukau. I even learned to talk, rather shyly, to some girls. Living in the Boys Home was a sheltering experience and we were a tight family, very close in our friendships. Through our loyalty and bonds with each other, I think we inadvertently created a fortification against outside aquaintances. I felt the need for the first time to branch out at Manukau. It was the right time for me, and safe, because if the new friendships didn't work I had the Home Kids to fall back on.

I loved to draw and I loved the whole art experience but unfortunately the art teacher at Manukau was more concerned with a tidy classroom than she was encouraging the creative process. So I often spent time drawing in my other classes when the teacher wasn't looking. Even though I was older now I was still no better at my schoolwork except for writing and drawing. Often during a math class I would draw and sometimes Warren Gargan would grab the page and start it circulating around the classroom.

"Hey Kev, give me that mate," he'd say, "that's a beauty."

"What d'ya think of this one Warren?" I asked one day.

He took it and laughed. Pretty soon it had gone the distance around the room without the teacher detecting it, even though several kids laughed out loud. My sketch showed a huge pile-up of rugby players in the middle of the classroom. There were faces, fists, knees and boots sticking out at all angles from the pile of bodies. Dust, flies, birds, books and pencils were flying everywhere. I had set out to make it funny and was more than pleased when it had the desired effect.

"Hey that's funny, Kev, "said Warren, "you should draw more like that."

Not much else was done during my classes over the next week and certainly not during my homework time later in the evenings.

Leaving Manukau was difficult for me. I had to go because Mum had made the decision to move to Wellington and my time at the Home was coming to an end. Saying "goodbye' to Dennis McKenna and Warren Gargan was not easy.

"Give me your address Warren and I'll write to you," I said.

In a letter from Wellington a few weeks after I had begun school in my new city, I told him of some of my new experiences.

"I'm in the footy team mate and we've already had one game on Athletic Park. Oh yeah," I continued, "we have a two-way intercom in each classroom so we can hear announcements and the teacher can talk back to the Headmaster. That's pretty good don't you think?" I wrote.

Warren replied and left me hanging with, "who cares about your fancy intercom. You never thought about that when you were at Manukau. I bet our Manukau team can beat your team any day, even if you do play on Athletic Park and there are some All Blacks watching!"

I wrote a few more times but Warren didn't reply. Neither did Dennis. I guess both of them could let go easier than I could. I learned the hard way. Perhaps their lives were full even without me, whereas they were a bigger part of my life than they knew. There was no upheaval and disruption of life for them but I found it a difficult and wrenching thing to leave the Home, school and friends I had made. It was not easy to put that part behind me. It was all I had and knew for the past nine years. I reached out desperately to those friends in the letters I liked to write, re-learning the rather sad lesson, now at an older age, that the one who leaves is often the one who is affected most.

Best Mates

In the early years at the Home on Mt Smart Road I became friends with Warren Francis. He seemed to like doing the same things as me and we had a similar measure of fearlessness about us. Warren and I connected from the moment he came to live at the Home. We were both about six years old at the time and ended up in beds side by side in the Lane dormitory. We even had our lockers together in 'the Front Room' at the Home where we kept our stash of toffee and other valuables for the annual Xmas trip to Camp. Once a month when the truck arrived and dumped a new load of lumber on the wood pile in the paddock we built our hut together along with Party and Bobby. Sometimes we even let Carl help, but with Carl it was usually that we wanted to have some fun at his expense. He could be really goofy at times.

During the years following on sunny Saturdays, Warren and I made our sleds out of scrap wood and trudged together up One Tree Hill to spend hours sliding down the dangerous, steep, old volcanic grassy slopes. We were older by then, able to withstand greater rough and tumble games and activities and certainly more daring in our approach to life. Later, on Wednesday evenings, we both climbed the trees in front of the Home to smoke a cigarette in defiance of all the rules before we slipped away together to Waikaraka Park for the weekly sports meeting. Warren and I were both fast runners and always featured in the 100 yard dash, later sneaking off to smoke in the cemetery nearby. I guess that at our young age we emulated the adults by coughing and spluttering our way through the occasional contraband smoke.

Warren had regular contact with his older brother Malcolm who was a fireman and he stayed with him in his flat some weekends along with Malcolm's girlfriend. Warren came back with tales of his brother's love life. Over the week he would feed me tiny morsels of titillating tales about noises in the night and blushes in the morning. I admired this connection Warren had with the outside world that, to me and the other kids, gave him an aura of being worldly-wise; well, the world we thought existed outside of the Home anyway.

Warren was a good talker and I sure liked listening to him weave his tales, personal or otherwise. Sometimes if I closed my eyes when he was into a story I could imagine that he was actually older than he really was because his stories sounded so grown-up. One Saturday when he and I were walking back from the State Theatre after the weekly Hopalong Cassidy serial, we fell into talking about ourselves. Warren began,

"About 1939 at the start of the 2nd World War, my Dad enlisted in the army and went off to North Africa with the New

Zealand Battalion to fight against the Nazis who were all over those parts."

"Hey, 1939. My brother Barry was born in 1937 so this happened to your Dad two years later," I said. "So, then, what did your Mum do, Warren?" I asked.

"She stayed home and looked after my older brother Malcolm and me, later of course, when I was born. She had a part-time job that she went to a couple of days each week. One day when she had just come home from work some army men came to the front door of our house and told Mum that my Dad had been killed."

"Boy, that's sad. Your Dad killed! What happened?" I asked. "Did he get shot in the war?"

"No, nothing like that. He wasn't a big hero or anything, just an ordinary soldier in the war," he went on. "It was an accident. My Dad and his gun crew were loading the shells into the big gun. One of the shells jammed, overheated and exploded. Three men and my Dad were all killed because they were so close."

"I guess they didn't stand a chance," I said.

I looked at Warren at this point, trying to gauge how upset he was. I sure would have been if my Dad had died like that but he didn't even go to the war being a conscientious objector and all. Warren continued with his story.

"My Mum was so upset about it and she couldn't get over it, so she quit her part time job that gave her the money to keep our house and to buy food. The Government gave her a little bit of help but not enough to keep the house and look after us. She got lots of advice from her family and eventually she decided to place me in the Home here. She felt that she was forced to do something."

"What about your brother Malcolm?" I asked.

"Malcolm was in the Home a few years ago but he left after he finished high school. He got a job and rented a room at my Uncle's house in Remuera."

"What did your Mum do after she put Malcolm into the Home?" I asked.

"Well she tried to get a another job so she could get money to rent a house for herself and me. She really wanted to have me and Malcolm live with her again, you know, keep our family together."

"So then what happened?" I asked.

"She couldn't get a job 'cos they weren't hiring older women, or something like that. Or, when she did get one she had to quit soon after," Warren added. "That's what she told me anyway."

I noticed that he had become nervous talking about his Mum, so I didn't push it. He took a deep breath before he went on.

"To tell you the truth, Kev, my Mum started drinking quite heavily after my Dad was killed and she couldn't stop or pull herself together. She just couldn't seem to keep a job. The government stepped in and persuaded Mum to put me in the Home so at least I would be cared for and be able to see Malcolm on the weekends. That's the real story."

He looked at me nervously watching my reaction to this very personal information.

We were silent for a second. I was taking this in.

"Wow, mate, " I said. "That must have been tough for your Mum to do. I bet she's upset and sad. I bet you and Malcolm are too."

"Yeah, well, Malcolm's used to it now 'cos he's working and he rents his own place and that seems alright for him. He's just applied to become a fireman."

D'you think about it much, Warren?" I asked.

"Yeah, lots," he said.

"D'you get to see your Mum very much?"

"Once in a while at my Uncle's place mostly, when I go to see Malcolm, but not a lot. She seems to spend a fair amount of time in the hospital. The doctor says it's the way for her to get better."

"That's sad mate", I said and fell silent again because I didn't know what else to say. My mind flitted over the time, long ago now, when my own Dad had left us; no warning either, just up and left. Sadness flickered through me as I remembered. I wanted to tell my story too but it wasn't my time right now. I felt that Warren's situation was probably worse, his Dad being killed and all that. There was no warning for him as well. At this moment I didn't compare or judge. This was Warren's story so I just accepted the state he was in. He sure had to, pain and all.

We carried on walking in silence. I turned to him and tried to find some words to say that I thought would make a difference but instead I punched him on the shoulder because I didn't know what else to do. That sort of did it because pretty soon we were talking about Hopalong Cassidy, 'quick with the rope and the gun' and currently our hero.

One Saturday after spending a lot of time building a hut in the field, we proudly entered, sat on sacks inside on the floor and began looking for cracks in the roof letting the light in. Outside, other kids were building their huts as well and the various structures reflected the energy and abilities of the boys involved. The wood available was off-cut material from building sites mixed with old previously-used timber from demolished houses and buildings. It was suitable only for fuel for the Home furnace and to feed the fires under the copper kettles in the laundry washhouse but we always managed to salvage the best boards and pieces for hut construction. Building skill played a big part in the final architecture of each group's structure, but so did imagination. Most of the huts were the familiar four wall and roof design but it was the interior where the greatest variation occurred and that's where I shone as an 'ideas-guy' coming up with different suggestions to many of the other kids.

All the huts were built in the part of the back field (there was a front field at the Home as well) nearest to the woodpile close to the furnace at the back of the laundry building. The paddock stretched two hundred metres away down toward the road which defined the Home boundary. We were aware of houses outside our fence-line but paid no attention to the people living in them. They were outside of our world. Trees, and there were many of them, spread around the corner of this part of the field all the way up to the front of the Home and to the boundary of Mt Smart Road. Many were native varieties like rata, kahikatea and puriri. Large oaks spread out all over too, and in a line beside the fence at the side of the building, three or four walnut trees spread their foliage wide.

Cowshed In The Paddock

The paddock was large enough for us to build our huts and lay out a rugby field for our games. In the center stood a milking shed for the cows which roamed the pasture. Sheep would graze on the grass during the growing season and keep it short. It was a place for us to play and work, a safe area which sometimes became a noisy space during a footy game, tree climbing and the perrenial acorn wars. At other times it was a quiet sanctuary for tending the animals, collecting walnuts, walking among the trees or just sitting in the grass on a sunny day.

Carl was the last one in through the entrance of our newly completed hut and as he sat down in the corner we noticed that he had been crying.

"E tama Carl Newman, what're you blubbin' for this time?" asked Bobby. "Every time we do something a little dangerous mate, you get the waterworks going."

"My foot hurts Parata, OK?" said Carl. "I stood on a piece of wood that had a bloody big nail in it. Went right in. Hurts like hell."

"Hoo, that's gotta hurt alright," sympathised Bobby and then added in a decidedly unsympathetic tone, "but what are you gonna do about it, Carl, other than cry and call for your Mum?"

I looked sharply at Bobby, Party dug him in the ribs and Warren mouthed "shuddup!" All of us caught this bit of unusual meanness in Bobby's voice and felt that not even Carl needed that.

What the heck was eating Bobby? I thought.

"Yeah, well, I would get my mother to help me but she's not around is she and that's too bad 'cos she'd fix my foot right now and put a big bandage on it. I wish she was here." He looked thoroughly miserable.

Carl Newman was always getting cut or stubbing his toes or being involved in one accident or another. He loved to get attention and to have a bandage or plaster on his body somewhere. We often kidded him about this but not too much because he'd had a tough time and he had no problem telling us how much he missed his Mum. This was a clue to the amount of sadness he felt inside, which all of us could relate to. Carl drove us all to the edge of distraction sometimes, and we often felt like giving him a hard time. We didn't though, as we all had our own pasts to face up to and our own ghosts to deal with . Cutting down someone else like Carl was a bit like doing damage to yourself. Like Carl, we needed each other for support and friendship. Anything less would have been unthinkable.

We sat quietly waiting for Carl to tell his story, if he felt like it that was. We wanted to know what happened to him in his early life and how he got to be here. It was like this with all of us in the Home, this curiosity about where we came from and what had happened along the way to bring us into this big family of boys. Nosiness wasn't a part of it. Knowing about each other created an intimacy leading to the close family bond we felt. This knowledge of personal history led us to our depth of liking for each other and the friendships we developed. The more we got to know each other, the more our loyalty grew.

Pretty soon Carl began talking. He must have felt safe enough at this moment. "I miss my Mum," he began.

"Yeah," he hesitated as he looked around at us, gauging his safety, I guess. "I miss her and I wish she was around, 'specially at these times. You blokes know what it's like, 'cept you Kev 'cos your Mum's here."

"I know Carl, but I don't see her much mate," I said hoping this would make my personal situation more acceptable.

"My Dad's a bastard," Carl continued, "and I don't care if I'm not 'sposed to say that. He's got a really bad temper and he used to hit me and Susan."

"Who's Susan, Carl?" asked Party.

"My sister and you know I miss her too. Anyway," Carl continued, "my grumpy old Dad didn't like any of us. He hit my Mum lots, even more than my sister and me."

"Jeez mate, I wouldn't have liked that," said Bobby. " 'Probably would've run away."

"The worst thing," Carl continued, "was that the bastard used to come home drunk all the time. That's when he usually hit my Mum."

"That dirty bugger'd laid a hand on me," said Warren, "and I would have---"

"Yeah, I felt like it too but he was strong as well as being mean and nasty."

Carl looked around the hut at all of us. His big eyes wide open behind his glasses in the gloom. I could see the tears brimming as the light caught him now and again.

"One night I remember Dad came home late and he was in a real shitty temper. Mum was a bit behind with the dinner because she had been helping Susan who had hurt her leg playing at school. He walked in and I could tell right away he was drunk. He looked at the table. He looked at Mum and before you knew it he hit her so hard she fell back, hit her head on the shelf and was out cold."

Carl's Dad said, "Stupid bitch, can't do anything right. I've told you lots of times I want my dinner on the table when I come home. You just don't get it."

We sat looking over at our friend. looking really sad in the corner. Bobby said, "tutae kuri. What a bastard!"

I whispered, "he can't do that. You can't hit people."

This was the first time I had ever heard of violence in a family and it shocked me. I thought of my Mum. There was silence in the hut. Then Party asked,

"Jeez, Carl, what did you do?

"I ran at him, screamed at him, "you bloody bastard, you leave my Mum alone you bully. She's much smaller than you."

"What happened then?" I asked.

"He punched me. The bastard punched me. Broke my glasses and knocked me flat."

"E tama, that dirty piece of---," said Bobby.

"What about Susan," asked Party, "was she alright?"

"No. She was standing in the doorway crying loudly."

"What the hell are you snivelling about?" growled her Dad, "stop it now! Shuddup and keep out of my way."

"Susan turned outside and ran next door to the neighbour's house," said Carl. "I guess she said something like Dad was about to kill Mum, because pretty soon Mrs James our neighbour came running in."

There was an eerie silence in the hut. We were stunned by Carl's story. No kid should have to go through that kind of stuff.

Carl, coughed and wiped his hand across his eyes.

"The police and the welfare people arrived. Then an ambulance came and took Mum off to hospital. She was holding her wrist. I think that it was broken and her face was really swollen too."

"What about your Dad?" asked Party.

"The police took my Dad off and charged him I think and I haven't seen him since then. Thank Christ for that. What a bastard."

"What about you and Susan?" asked Warren. "Where did you two go?"

"Our neighbour Mrs James had us stay with her. She was really nice. After a few days Mum came home with her wrist in a cast and stitches in her face. She must have broken her cheekbone when she fell after he punched her."

"What happened then, Carl?" asked Party.

"We stayed with Mrs James for a while," said Carl. "The welfare lady visited and talked to Mum and one day they called Susan and me into the living room."

"Carl and Susan, I need to talk to you about what's going to happen," said Carl's Mum. "You kids know that welfare has threatened a few times to take you away from me because of your Dad, right? Well this time kids, they mean business."

"What do you mean, business, Mum?" asked Carl.

"Carl, you and Susan are going to have to stay in a care-home for a while until this mess gets sorted out. Your Dad and I can't stay together that's for sure, not after what he's done. But you two are going to have to be strong while I try to find work and find a place for us to live."

"What do you mean by a care-home, Mum?" asked Carl.

"The welfare lady said there's a nice Home with other kids in it not far from here. She can get you in there."

"Can we take our stuff?" asked Carl.

He wiped tears from his eyes and by this time his face was just a big dirty mess. I wanted to laugh, to break the tension I guess, but of course I didn't. There was nothing funny in Carl's story.

"After that I don't remember much. Susan and I both stayed in that Home and shortly after she went to a girl's Home and I came here to Mt Smart Road. It all happened so quickly. I'm still waiting for Mum to call one day to tell me she's got a job and a house and we can all go home again.

"Glad you're here, Carl, mate," said Bobby.

"Yeah, me too," said Party, Warren and me at the same time.

Carl wasn't the brightest kid in our group. He was forever doing or saying silly things that were often not very funny. Warren thought he was a complete idiot at times. Out of all of us in our group Warren was the most dismissive of Carl. He simply tried to ignore him but this didn't seem to faze Carl at all. In fact I'm certain that he thought Warren really liked him.

For sure Carl could be really goofy but I often felt sorry for him. He wasn't a kid I warmed to easily and I surprised myself that I hung around with him at all. But I did and I found that in his own peculiar way, Carl was a good friend and even funny at times. He grew on me and I learned to like him just for who he was. He was a slightly pathetic character, even a little out of place, and carried an aura of sadness and helplessness about him. He could just not help himself in certain situations it seemed.

Party, as he did always, just grinned and said, "awww Carl Newwwwmaaannn." Bobby, with lots of patience, had many reasons to become angry with the stupid stuff Carl often said and did, along with the many unfounded accusations of Bobby stealing his things. But to my knowledge Bobby only flipped out once on Carl and that was this time in the hut just before Carl told his story. Bobby counted Carl as one of his best mates in the Home. I'm sure that Carl knew all this and felt safe. If nothing else he felt a kind of warm security in our group making up for the coldness of his own family situation.

Warren was a good storyteller. There was no doubt about that. Lying in our beds at night in the dorm, Warren would often launch into his version of a movie he had seen while staying over with his brother. And sometimes he would re-tell the story of a movie we had all seen at the matinee on the Saturday past. I couldn't help listening, so drawn-in was I to his re-telling. He had a phenomenal memory for details and facts and an ability to bring a movie alive again whether we had seen it recently or not. At night, in a half-sleep, with Warren's story sounding out like a radio serial, it was the most magic of times for me; times which increased my admiration for him; times which made our friendship deeper.

Where I come from, friends are 'mates', you know, best pals. These are the kids you want to hang out with because you learn that all the best things happen when you are with them. They are the ones who stick by you in the tough times like when you are sad and sometimes have to cry. They'll stick up for you in an argument or a fight and they'll tell you their personal story right after you've finished telling them yours. They are your mates and mates stick together, wait for you after school and share stuff. As well as Warren at the Home, I was friendly with all of the kids and close to quite a few. But my best mates were Warren, Party, Bobby and Carl although, as I said, Carl was 'off and on' as a friend because now and again he did something so incredibly goofy that I had to keep away from him for periods of time to let the dust settle, or something like that.

Years later, when I had left the Home and was into my teenage years I felt an inexplicable sadness for the separation from these friends of mine. I never did recover to replace them or allow myself to draw that close to others in my life to the same extent as existed at 109 Mt Smart Road. Everybody there found their place....perhaps some kids didn't....and most kids had real mates they could count on. We were all quite dependent on each other and out of this dependency was born a realisation of our large group as family, even if it was a surrogate one.

The Ghost of Peter Griffen

I love a good story and one I held in common with all the kids at the Home was the story of Peter Griffen. Peter is part of a legend, with me to this day, but back then he was a tragic memory made real during my years growing up in the Home. Peter was a kid like the rest of us, but had spent all of his life in orphanages after having been left as a baby wrapped in an old bedsheet on a front doorstep of one. As he grew older he gained the reputation of being an 'original' and developed the charisma of a natural-born leader in any of the various homes he lived in. At 109 Mt Smart Road he was popular with all and involved himself in every game and adventure that happened... exactly like this one handed down over the years...

One Saturday, Peter, looking particularly menacing in his warpaint and flax skirt, was speaking to a group of excited warriors. He was the chief of the Seminole Indians and was exhorting his men to be brave in the upcoming attack on the

Iroquois, who were slinking behind every tree at the front of the property relishing the prospect of the skirmish up ahead. Peter's warriors had spent the last half hour after their regular Saturday morning chores, finding old clothes and bits of material, anything really, that helped to create the image of the kind of warrior they imagined themselves to be. Lastly, around at the furnace room, the final touches of charcoal smudges were being smeared over some pretty fierce looking faces. This was the stuff of all boys' imaginings.

There was the usual whooping and hollering and thumping of home-made spears as the tension in the Seminole camp rose, each warrior reaching for the courage he knew would be needed that day. As Peter led his group, crouched low and hidden from view by the big hedge separating the lane from the front lawn, he paid no attention to the strong wind which had sprung up out of the morning breeze. The Seminoles had a job to do: nothing less than the defeat and capture of the Iroquois was on every warrior's mind. The Chief would not tolerate any distractions or deviations from this purpose. Peter's men were silent by now and ready to do everything he commanded. They rounded the hedge at the top of the front lawn unseen by the Iroquois, and Peter Griffen, hereditary Chief of the Seminole Nation, let out his most hair-raising scream and led his men into the forest to do the business they were born for.

The battle was fierce. Wooden spears found their mark. Painted faces cried out in death screams. Bows made that day fired arrows that flew true. And all the while, the wind, having risen swiftly to something approaching a gale, blew ferociously and added to the noise and eeriness of the battle scene. During the whole chaotic action, even though the Iroquois put up a brave fight, it became apparent that the Seminoles were achieving the victory they knew they must have as more and more of the enemy seemed to turn tail under the onslaught and run screaming back toward the dormitories or scuttled as fast as they could around the back of the Home, some scooting as far away as the cowshed. The rout of the Iroquois, it seemed, was soon to be realised.

Seminole Chief, Peter Griffen was last seen dashing at the head of four or five of his bravest men toward the place where the Chief of the Iroquois stood protected by a circle of his finest warriors. Capture of the Iroquois Chief would mean the end of the battle and certain victory for the Seminoles. Peter and his men were confident in their charge on this small protective band. At ten paces away both groups of warriors locked glares, with the defenders standing tall and firm. Peter and his men raised their weapons, yelled aloud the Seminole war song and ran swiftly toward their mark.

Their whooping and screaming however, did not drown out the sound of a sharp crack, loud enough to distract the warriors from their charge. Both chiefs heard this ominous sound and looked overhead to the tree tops. All stopped in mid-attack and watched horrified as a huge kahikatea branch smashed it's way down landing uncannily, but directly, on top of Peter Griffen, proud Seminole Chief, knocking him crushed to the ground. At first there were cheers from the Iroquois in their realisation that fate had saved them from certain defeat. A few of the warriors carried the charge through and locked in battle. But when Peter did not rise from under the branch, reality set in. The whole group, friend and foe alike, froze in mid-action staring open-mouthed at the body of Peter lying prone under the largest branch they had ever seen. Everybody at the battle scene became aware of the ferocious wind blowing in from Mt Smart Road and whipping branches in all directions.

The sound at that moment was not the sound of mighty warriors fighting for their lives. It was the sound of Seminoles and Iroquois becoming very scared and frightened boys once again. Eyes on their friend widened with fear and confusion. Peter, not moving at all, was now the focus of the scene. Nobody moved because nobody knew what to do next. It seemed an age before one of the senior kids came through the trees leading Ms Pomeroi toward the place where Peter lay. Confusion reigned. More staff arrived. Kids stood fixed and quiet and some began drifting towards the scene from where they had been engaged in the battle, walking carefully and keeping their eyes on Peter. A few fearful ones stepped closer and looked on with one question on their lips: "was he... was Peter - ?"

An ambulance arrived. A stretcher was laid out, and Peter Griffen's body, so recently indestructible, was slid into the vehicle that disappeared swiftly up Mt Smart Road on its way to the legendary Greenlane Hospital. There was a furious but measured buzzing among the boys for the rest of Saturday afternoon. Apprehension was in the air knowing that their favourite had been seriously hurt but not knowing how serious. The events and details of the battle so recently cut short were repeated, examined and sorted through. Boys told and retold their versions. The boys with Peter on the final charge of the Seminoles, spoke excitedly how they had seen him stop at the sound of the breaking branch and look up. They felt that at that moment he knew his fate was sealed. They heard it in his voice. Their last sight was of Peter standing strongly and pointing up at the falling branch.

When the dinner bell finally rang later that evening, the boys filed quietly into the dining hall and took their places. There were none of the usual complaints about the food as the trays and saucepans were brought in and set on the serving table up front. They were together now where they all needed to be. In fact afterwards, nobody could remember if the dinner had included tripe or spinach, equally despised by all. Even the insipid blancmange for pudding was forgotten as each boy was served his meal by a staff member equally upset. Where tables were usually buzzing with conversation and energy, there was an awkward silence in its place. All heads bowed low at the saying of grace by Frank Bickerton. The eating of this dinner by the thirty boys of the Home was done in a strange and unusual atmosphere of uncertainty and fear.

Ms Ferns the Matron, ('Fernsy' the boys called her), appeared at the head table and called for attention. "As you all know," she began, "Peter Griffen met with a terrible accident this afternoon." Fernsy paused to catch her breath. She looked around the dining room at the boys with every eye glued on her and right then decided to be as direct as she could in giving the information she had only just received. There was no other way. This was not the time to add to the boys' confusion.

"We have just had very bad news indeed from Greenlane Hospital that Peter did not survive the ride in the ambulance. He died before they could do anything for him at the hospital."

A staff member at the head table must have asked a question, because Fernsy answered for all to hear, "Yes, it was the branch that fell on Peter that killed him. He was knocked unconscious and stayed that way until he passed away. He had many bones broken and was bleeding a lot inside. Nobody could live through that."

She paused and looked about, sadness in her eyes.

"I am so sorry for Peter, boys," she went on, "he was your favourite and the staff's as well. Let's bow our heads a while right now and think of our friend."

The older kids always passed on the legend of Peter Griffen to those kids newly arrived at the Home. He had lived in the Home a long time before I got there they said. In fact there were only a few older kids, possibly Stretchy, Jim Palmer and Frank Bickerton, who actually lived at Mt Smart at the same time as Peter Griffen. They said he was killed while playing a game. Something about trees falling, a dark night and a storm. Over the years the story had become the stuff of legends passed down by word of mouth as all good legends are. And as legends go, this one was made up of some truths and some half-truths, some facts and some imaginings. Among thirty boys it couldn't be any other way.

The senior kids said, "Peter visits once in a while. He's probably lonely and likes to come back to where he spent time as a kid. This was the only home he knew and the kids were his only family."

"Will he come into our dorm?"

"No. He likes to stay outside."

"Is he dead?" one of us asked.

"Will we see him?" a small voice piped up.

"Does he make sounds?" I asked.

One of the seniors, Stretchy I think, said, "Look you Lane Kids, we don't know exactly when he'll come. He likes the dark, and he likes it when it's very stormy 'cos Peter Griffen's...... a ghost."

"A GHOST!?!"

"Yeah, a ghost. Are you little twerps scared yet?"

"Nah, Stretchy, we're not afraid of ghosts!"

I'm not sure if it was the night after or the night after that, but it doesn't matter. All of us little kids in the Lane dorm had been thinking of Peter Griffen constantly since Stretchy and the senior kids from the Balcony had visited. We were asleep and then suddenly we were wide awake. My bed at least was partially bathed in light from outside. It was a particularly wild night out there. Party was at the windows looking out and beckoning us to join him.

"Hurry up you blokes," he whispered, "hurry or you'll miss this. Jeez!"

Fifteen or more pajama'd bodies jumped up on the beds by the windows and squinted eyes into the darkness.

"Shshshsh....." shissed Party. "He's up there in the trees."

"Who?" someone asked.

"Who else? Peter Griffen you goon," he whispered.

"I'm scared," said the Lee brothers.

"Shuddup!" said Party. "Watch the trees. Listen!"

I was never sure exactly what I saw, but I know what I heard...and felt. A low moan came to us through the night and grew louder and louder. It was all around us it seemed. I heard whimpering next to me.

Then..... a hiss from Bobby Parata, "ssss.....there!"

A smoky white form appeared among the trees across the lawn and drifted up by the road.. disappeared... appeared... gone again... there it was...

"Where?"

"There!"

All through the trees the white form moved sometimes in sight, sometimes not, but always eerily.

"Was that a glow coming from it?"

All around us were moaning and growling sounds.

The hair on my neck rose. I glanced nervously at the Lees huddled together. I moved closer to Bobby and Party. Warren was right next to me. All of us stayed glued to our window places with eyes wide open. And all that dark night it seemed the ghost drifted in and out of sight and the moans seemed to grow ever more frightening.

"Wow, Stretchy was right," I whispered.

"But how do we know it's real?" somebody asked.

"It's real alright. Look at that."

"What if it's really one of the senior kids trying to scare us."

"Don't be silly, look how it moves. That's him alright."

"Who?"

"Peter Griffen," said Bobby, "anybody can tell that."

I heard feet crossing the floor and the squeak of beds as if someone was getting back in.

It's the Lees, I thought.

For what seemed hours we stayed at the windows cold and very afraid. Then one by one kids flopped into beds and fell fitfully asleep.

As Bobby went back to his bed he said, "Hey Partridge, what's that smell? You must've filled your pants!"

Some under-the-covers laughing and a snort from Party was heard faintly. Then, a whisper, "I've gotta pee. Kev, will you come with me?"

"I'm not goin' out there, Carl. Are you nuts? Pee in your bed," was all I said and all I remember as the night closed in and a sort of fitful sleep came over me.

My dreams that night were dreams of searching for Peter Griffen. How had he been killed? Where was he when this terrible thing happened? Who was there and what effect did it have on people? Could his terrible death have been avoided? Was he in pain when he died? Did he blame Home Kids for his death? Would he hurt us if he came into our dorm?

The unanswered questions followed me into my troubled sleep and I woke the next morning with the same questions buzzing in my mind. At some point I would talk to the other kids about my thoughts, maybe on the way to school or in the cowshed at milking time or on our way to One Tree Hill on Saturday afternoon. One way or another, I needed to talk about this.

Depending on your age at the Home, you were stuck in a particular dorm. There were three: 'The Lane' for the really young kids, where I was with Warren, Bobby, Party and Carl, for the first couple of years when I first arrived; 'The Courage' for kids about ten to thirteen; 'The Balcony' for high school kids and older teens who were known as the seniors. Pillow fights were a regular event because they were exciting, a little bit dangerous if you were very young, and nothing but fun unless you got hit full in the face by a pillow with a book in it. Now that was dirty, but it sometimes happened. Often in the middle of an attack, the alarm would sound that Pommy, Fernsie or Mrs Davies... (my Mum)... were on their way and in a few seconds everybody scooted back to their dorm, slipped under the covers and faked being sound asleep as if nothing had been going on. It was always risky doing things after 'lights-out' in the dorms. Even talking. Pillow fights usually resulted in an unwelcome visit to the 'Pink Seat' to receive Fernsy's regulation straps on a hand or the bum as punishment.

Once in a while if no staff appeared, we'd fall into talking very quietly. Sometimes it would be Warren making us laugh with his recounting of the latest Bob Hope classic and other times one kid or another would launch into his life history after a few probing questions. There were no interruptions during life stories, only a quiet listening. We all had our own story to tell and we respected each other's.

"So Party, how did you get to be at the Home mate?" asked Bobby Parata.

There was silence for a while before a reply. Robin was thinking about whether he was going to get into his story. He was a quiet and rather shy kid. I knew what made him tick.

"I was dropped off. I came from another Home," he said quietly.

"Which one?"

"Ahh.. 'nother Home out at New Lynn," he said, hesitant to get into details that were very close to his heart. "When I was a baby somebody in my family wrapped me in a blanket and put me on the steps of the orphanage for girls in New Lynn. The next morning when the staff opened the door, there I was and they took me in and looked after me. I was no trouble when I was a little baby."

"Not like now," laughed Carl.

"Cheeky bugger," said Warren.

"Were you allowed to stay in the Girls Home?" asked Micky.

"I found out when I was much older that the church and the courts came to some agreement that I would stay in the care of the staff at the Girls Home and would be transferred to the Boys Home when I reached the right age."

"What age is that Party?" asked Micky.

"You can't come here until you're at least four and a half," I responded. "I know 'cos that's when I was allowed in."

"What about your Mum, Party," asked Warren, "did you find out anything about her. Did the staff at the girls home know anything?"

"Nah," said Robin, "they didn't know her, but they did tell me that my Mother was pretty young when I was born. Her family was poor and often there were babies in those families. It was fairly common in those days."

The local rumour mill in the community had generated the story that Robin had been born to a very young teenage girl. Because there already were other young kids in the family to care for, it was decided that another mouth to feed was just too much. Her father threatened to put her out on the street, "and I will," he said angrily one day during her pregnancy, "if you don't give that kid away or put it up for adoption so people with more money than us can raise it. There's too many kids around here as it is."

And so, the story went, Robin's Mum gave birth to Party at her Aunt's house where all precautions were taken for an uncomplicated birth to secure the health of the baby and the mother. The Aunt was a midwife operating outside the law in those days. "You'll be safe here my dear and you know I'll do a good job. I've had lots of experience at this and everything's going to be as clean as a whistle. I might be illegal but I'm clean and I'm good at this baby stuff," laughed the Aunt.

"One thing's for sure," she added, "you don't need to be around your crabby old father. He was a pain in the backside when we were growing up as kids so I know what that brother of mine can be like."

"What happened after you were born Party?" I asked.

How 'im I s'posed to know that Kev?" answered Robin, "I was just a baby."

He went on, "but I do know a little bit 'cos the staff at that home told me. My Mother was forced by her father to wrap me up in a blanket and to go to the Girl's Home late at night and leave me on the front steps."

"Why d'ya think he said to leave you at the Girls Home?"

"Probably 'cos he knew that when the staff found me they wouldn't be able to resist a baby and he knew they would want to look after me. And that's how it turned out I guess."

"Oh yeah," he added, "she stuck a note to the blanket telling them my name was Robin Partridge."

"Jeez, I thought it was Party," said Carl, " didn't your Mum know that?"

"Well," said Party, "she was just making sure I wasn't gonna be named Carl Newman or some other goofy name."

That raised a laugh all 'round the dorm.

The irony of their belief and action was most likely lost on Party's family. However, as it turned out they did the right thing by the baby in some respects and likely continued living with a clear conscience. No doubt they lived their lives out with full knowledge of what they had done and a confidence that it was the right thing. Robin, meanwhile, lived his life in a cloud of mystery as far as his origin and family were concerned.

Party, as we came to know him, grew up knowing as little about his mother and his beginning family as they knew about him. He was about the same age as myself and while I recognised a certain eccentricity about him, I loved him as a true friend. He said very little until he knew he should and when he eventually did speak it was always relevant, spoken in the gentlest of manners and often with warm humour. Party was very funny while at the same time having a serious reserve about him. His blond curly hair and constant smile masked the pain of the tragedy he must have felt about his birth and the rejection by his maternal family. In life, Party was a 'watcher'. There was little that went on around the Home that he did not know about. He was completely trustworthy and a very loyal friend.

Years later, whenever I thought about the ghost of Peter Griffen, I thought about Party as well. There were similarities in their early childhood. Both had an air of tragedy about them, were loved by the boys they lived with and respected for their loyalty in friendship. Tragically, and I learned this about Party later in my life, both he and Peter died early in their lives in accidental circumstances. Some incidents become legends and are fixed firmly in memory with a lasting effect on those of us who are left to remember.

The Pink Seat

It was standing room only outside Ms Ferns door on the night when all of us in the Courage Dorm were caught in the act of raiding the small kids in the Lane Dorm. It really was a fair cop. We were out of our beds tip-toeing in the hallway with pillows in hand when Pommy came out of her room and nailed us with a laugh.

"Ah-ha!" she stared at us, holding her door open. "Not quiet enough eh, boys! Nothing else to say is there? You know the rule about raiding another dorm. Now, off to the 'Pink Seat' the lot of you. Miss Ferns is not going to like this!"

Ms Sylvia Ferns was the Matron of the Presbyterian Boys Home all the time that I lived there. Fernsy, as we all called her - not to her face though - was a tall, thin, bony, severe looking woman. Without some personal experience with Fernsy as we had, one could be forgiven thinking that her sharp and serious outward demeanor indicated a similar personality. After being in the Home for a while I knew that Fernsy could also be friendly and cheerful. In spite of her seriousness I knew her to be fair in her dealings with me and I base that on numerous visits to the

Pink Seat. She could fix you with her eye, give you the 'Ferns Lecture' or nail you with a few of her best on the bum or the hands.

Ms Sylvia (Fernsy) Ferns, Matron

In the waiting area beside the door to Fernsy's flat was the 'Pink Seat'. It was a padded bench-type seat with a wooden back upon which four boys could perch at any one time. The seat itself was covered by a worn brocade-stitched picture of birds flying across a forest, a pink forest. In the minds of thirty small boys raised on the fear of being sent to the Pink Seat, there was no doubt of its colour. But in actual fact, and for all I know, 'pink' might have been a reference to the colour of collective boys bums as they left Fernsy's front room holding their rear-ends in pain, some shaking their heads defiantly and others with shoulders stooped holding back the tears that flowed afterwards when they were alone.

The waiting room was at the end of a narrow hallway, past the staff lounge on the left and the sick bay on the right. A doorway from the outside let you into a small waiting area with Ms Ferns' entrance door in one corner. Adjoining this was a tiny storage room and the few times I was in there I always went right to the box containing half a dozen pairs of 3-dimensional viewers. These were the kind, first produced in the early 1900's, which had a wrap-around visor with two glassed-in eye holes. You held the viewer in place by a handle that dropped down from the visor. Protruding straight out from it and parallel to the floor, was a rod with a moveable wire frame on it, something like a miniture sheet-music holder. In this you placed a card on which there were two identical photos and then slid the frame until the picture came into focus for you. The magic of it was that the two photos became one with a 3-dimensional quality. It was amazing to look at a scene of London City with people walking about quite detached from their backgrounds. Each photo became a reflection of scenes from real life. I never tired of looking at the huge menacing gorilla eating in the forest, Groucho Marx hitting Harpo over his head with a club, mountain goats leaping across a chasm high up in the Canadian Rockies or Al Capone shooting his tommy gun at a car full of pursuing cops. In the box with the viewers were dozens of these cards with photos ranging from a scene out of sweet Swan Lake to a silly little girl in a frilly frock trying to blow out her birthday candles .

Predictably, the older kids started a rumour that there were also pictures of nude women in the box, but after searching for them many times, I decided that either this was a myth, or the older kids had probably taken the cards to hide in their lockers so they could leer over the images at their leisure. Of course I was most likely way off the mark because if the truth were known it was Fernsy who had removed the 'filth' in her Presbyterian quest to protect her boys from moments of temptation and a further slide toward the sinful side of life.

The 'Pink Seat' had such a legendary reputation at the Home that no staff member, my mother included, would send you there unless it was for a good reason. I wasn't afraid of Fernsy but I was occasionally wary of her, especially if I was doing something I knew to be a little suspect. She never shied from her responsibility to mete out punishment as she saw fit but at the same time was mostly concerned that we understood the error of our ways. Our understanding of right and wrong, the moral aspect of any incident, was a foundation of Fernsy's attitude to discipline. She also never held a grudge. Once you had served your time at the 'Pink Seat' and taken your punishment, Fernsy let it all go and never mentioned the misdemeanor again. This endeared her to us in a peculiar way. She might have been a serious Ms Ferns, ready to punish a 'Pink-seater' at the drop of a hat, but, she was our Ms Ferns!

Four of Fernsy's best was the most I ever suffered and I felt each one stingingly after Robin Partridge and I were fingered by some kid who told one of the staff, "I saw Robin Partridge and Kevin Davies throw their spears through the wire mesh windows of the cream- shed." That was a real let-down especially after Party and I had been fanatic members and loyal soldiers of Spartacus' army fighting the Romans all afternoon. After one particularly cunning ambush, we were seen throwing our deadly spears at two fleeing Legionaires and watching in horror as they flew over the victim's heads only to tear sickeningly into the soft protective wire mesh screens covering the cream shed windows. We saw in a flash that there was no way to repair these ugly gashes so we decided to end the game right there and disappear. Before dinner that night the whole of Spartacus' army of grubby rebels was overflowing outside Fernsy's door and the 'Pink Seat' awaiting the worst.

Through years of dealing with such events and with a deftly honed skill, Fernsy eliminated the non-guilty boys quickly and left Party and me sitting on the 'Pink Seat' while she decided our fate. The wait only served to intensify the punishment when it came about an hour later. Four of Fernsy's hardest, a lecture, and an additional humiliating order to go straight to bed without dinner, reduced us to the small boys we really were and cemented that misdemeanor in our minds forever. To rub salt in the wound, the next morning we were summond again to the 'Pink Seat' where a still irate Ms Ferns explained to us that we would be spending the next four of our scheduled playtimes helping the workmen to repair the damage that we had so callously inflicted on the cream shed windows.

"And don't you forget, Robin and Kevin," she added menacingly, "otherwise you'll receive the same punishment all over again!"

Punishment, when it came, was sure. You could spend an anxious amount of time waiting on the Pink Seat for Fernsy to appear with her summons, so that when she finally did, suspense had worked it's way thoroughly into your nervous system. I wouldn't accuse her of being sadistic by making us wait, but it did get to me now and then.

Fernsy actually had great patience with all of us and the hijinx we sometimes got up to, but she had a firm line which, if crossed, meant a visit to her for sure. Leaving the Home grounds without permission was punishable. Fooling around in Church, a felony. Defying a staff member unforgivable. Lying, bullying, failure to complete a scheduled job, stealing, smoking, swearing and a list of other objectionable boyish behaviours were all met by Fernsy at the Pink Seat. We were clear about the line she had drawn and whenever we stepped over it we knew that the punishment would come. Keeping thirty boys in line at the Home was Fernsy's responsibility and she used the 'Pink Seat' to great effect. To balance this though, she was equally interested in our moral development and while that meant she could be insufferably 'churchy' at times in her lectures, this form of sanctioning was less severe than the renowned pain inflicted by a taste of Fernsy's leather strap.

Believe it or not, there was a time that I paid a visit to the waiting area outside Fernsy's door and did not occupy the famous 'Pink Seat'. Mum came to me one day and told me that, "Miss Ferns would like to see you Kev."

"Oh, d'you know what for Mum?" I asked, a little wary.

"Not really. She didn't say what except that she had a job for you. Why don't you drop 'round to find out."

So I dropped what I was doing at the time and nervously made my way through the Pink Seat waiting area to Fernsy's apartment. "Come on in, Kevin," said Fernsy at the door, "I've got something to show you."

I went into her room which was some kind of lounge area. She took me over to a door, which she opened a fraction very slowly and pointed to the window in the wall to the outside. I could see that it was Fernsy's bedroom and felt a little shy about looking in. But there on the floor all hunched up like a little ball of fluff was a blackbird. All around it were small feathers and little turds of white bird droppings. This little fella was clearly frightened, it's chest heaving rapidly in and out.

"I left the window open yesterday while it was sunny and I guess it flew in and couldn't get out again. It's been flying about getting all frightened and banging into the window that I had to close from the outside. I don't know how to get it out but I must because as you can see it's making a terrible mess in there. I thought you might be able to help me Kevin. Your mother said you are good with animals."

Now that I knew the purpose of my visit to Fernsy, any nervousness I felt had left me. I thought of a solution to the bird situation right away.

"I'll just open the window, Miss Ferns, and the bird will eventually fly out if we leave it."

"Hmmm..... not good Kevin. The window is stuck shut after I closed it. I must have slammed it too hard...... Mmmm, your Mother said something about you being able to catch birds using a box. Can you really do that?"

"Oh yeah, Miss Ferns, a box, some string and some bread. I can do that and it'll probably work too because the bird will be hungry by now."

"Well good for you Kevin. Why don't you wait here while I go and get some string, a stick, a box and some bread from the kitchen if you think that's all we need."

She was back in fifteen minutes with all the right stuff and while she watched, I set it all up in the room with the bird and trailed the string out through her door where we closed it enough so we could see the bird but it couldn't see us. I had done the same thing many times at the water trough near the cowshed when we tried to catch seagulls.

"I think this will take a while, Miss Ferns," I said.

"Take all the time you need, Kevin," she said bringing me a cushion to sit on and surprisingly, a glass of milk and two biscuits.

I was all set for the time it was going to take to catch this little blackbird which had hopped nearer the window and seemed more frightened than ever.

Once in a while I got up and looked around Fernsy's room with the curiosity of a kid feeling a certain amount of comfort and security. I was captured by a sketch of a large fat man on a horse leading a troop of odd looking characters through a forest clearing.

"Oh, that's my Chaucer sketch," said Fersy noticing that I was looking at it. "He wrote Pilgrim's Progress. Have you heard of it Kevin?"

"No Miss Ferns, but I like the drawing," I said.

"Well, what about this one then," she said pointing to a large drawing of some bloke with big muscles pushing against the columns holding up an entire building.

I liked it right away.

"Do you know who that is?" she asked.

"No Miss Ferns," I said again.

"It's Sampson, Kevin, you know, from the Bible, and he's pushing the columns down to destroy the temple because God told him to do it."

"It's a good drawing Miss Ferns. I like the way there's shading on Sampson's body showing all his muscles. That's hard to do."

"Oh, I forgot. You like to draw don't you Kevin?" said Fernsy. "Perhaps you could draw me a picture one day."

"Yes Miss Ferns," I said.

Back at the bird I could see that it had moved more toward the centre of the room and closer to the box. "Won't be long now," I thought, " it's getting interested."

So, I waited, looked around, ate my two biscuits and drank the milk. I heard a noise from the room and saw the bird had got to its feet and was hopping about on the wooden floor. It hopped to the box and then away from it. To, and from. Forward, and back. And then it seemed to make up its mind walking toward the box in a cocky fashion moving from side to side like birds do sometimes. It stopped at the box, cocked its head to look at the stick, saw the bread and walked right in. I took a breath, held it and waited for the bird to start eating.

It didn't take long, a few pecks in fact. I tensed, pulled the string sharply and "bonk" down came the box trapping the blackbird inside. I knew what to do next.

"Miss Ferns, I've caught the bird, but I need a sheet of cardboard to slide under the box so it won't escape when I pick it up."

"Cardboard? I've got just the thing Kevin," she said. "My, but you were quick. I'm very impressed. Do you think you can get it outside alright?"

"Yes Miss Ferns," I said, "It'll be safe outside pretty soon."

Fernsy ducked back out into her lounge while I kept my weight bearing down on the box so there was no chance of escape. She returned quickly and handed me the cardboard which I slid under the box. A quick flip and I had the box in my arms with the blackbird trapped securely inside.

"I'll let it go out by the walnut tree, Miss Ferns."

She came with me and watched.

"There it goes Kevin. Look at it fly! Probably as pleased as punch to be free outside as I am to be free of it inside my room. Thank you for doing such a good job Kevin. I couldn't have done that myself. You have been very helpful and kind."

Fernsy paused.

"Perhaps I should have sent the blackbird to the 'Pink Seat' for some punishment," she said with a twinkle in her eye. "It certainly was a naughty bird don't you think?"

I looked at her and she looked at me. She struggled with a smile and was waiting for my response. I struggled through nervousness to naturally enjoy the joke.

"The 'Pink Seat' Miss Ferns?" I gasped, "oh, ah, the blackbird would've just made a big mess on that. It's way better off outside.

I walked out of Fernsy's apartment and along the corridor until I found my way outside. I sat in a sunny spot on the step of the back verandah where the budgies in their cages were squawking their usual racket. My head buzzed with the events of the past two hours. I had been right on the edge of nervous tension yet somehow, now, I was feeling pleased with myself. When I had first gone to see Fernsy it was a bit like visiting the Pinkseat for a punishment. Anticipating the worst, I had a hard feeling inside just like the last time I was sent there. But now that edginess was gone. Sitting on the step in the sun I felt calm and content. It occurred to me that Fernsy sometimes had that effect on us kids. If it was punishment you were in for, she could be as cold and hard as the Pinkseat itself. But when it came to general contact in the course of any day, Fernsy was often kind, friendly and soft in her approach to us boys.

This contrast was not confusing to us at all. There was no unpredictability about Ms Sylvia Ferns. We knew what to expect from her in any situation. Consistency in adults behaviour towards us was important for small boys like myself. A visit to the Pinkseat for our 'just-deserts' was just that, and I accepted it, rough as it was. When moments like this bird incident happened, I was able to separate Fernsy the Matron, from Fernsy the friendly person who liked me and wanted me to help her. The squawking budgies in the backgound didn't distract me from feeling a large amount of satisfaction in recognising this difference. At that moment on the back step in the sun, life was pretty good for me.

Gravel Rash

Do you remember the first time you tried to ride a bike? I don't mean using training wheels or anything as easy as that. I mean getting on, riding, falling off, getting back on until you found one time that you could go for longer and finally longer again. At the Boys Home we learned to ride just like that. The older kids would start us at the top of The Lane, push us about half way down and then let us zoom straight on until we either hit the work shed wall at the bottom, fell off or just froze with fear. The Lane was surfaced with gravel made up of small sharply-edged, reddish stones. If you landed on it you were guaranteed a major gravel-rash down your leg. We found out that it was part of the process of learning to ride; a sort of 'badge of courage'.

The Lane Drive

Getting ready for the event, which always seemed to be on a Saturday morning after jobs, filled us all with a nervous energy.

"Hear this, hear this you kids," Stretchy called out. "Bike lessons are about to begin in The Lane. Be there to learn from the best teachers. If you don't learn now, you'll never learn! Hear this.... Hear this...."

The young kids, who hadn't yet learned to ride, rushed there because we wanted to get a good bike, not that many of them were very good especially as nobody could keep one looking new for long in a group of 30 or more boys. There were actually very few available bikes as they were not something many people owned in those days. The ones we had in the Home were antiques from years past and the senior kids had ownership of the lot.

By the time we arrived at the top of The Lane the older kids were riding up and down, circling and showing us younger kids how it was really done. From that distance it seemed a long way down the narrow driveway to the cream-coloured shed wall at the bottom. The thought of the bike getting faster and faster as it was pushed was frightening. It probably scared some of the older kids too, but they kept their fear in check. The chatter and excitement of the group kept us all from focussing on how nervous we really were. Falling off was a certainty, and most of us novices had permanently skinned legs marking us non-riders. Our stomachs tightened, anxiety was a knot in our chests, but we lined up because our desire to ride was greater than our fear of falling. The atmosphere was full of the tension and excitement of a major sporting event. Bike riding was seen as mark of achievement, a milestone along the way from being a small kid with limited experience to becoming an older boy with considerably more. The practice rides down the Lane, marked this passage. The predictable crash into the shed at the end of the Lane was the greatest entertainment for the older kids and their payoff for giving up their time to teach us. It was all a little sadistic.

I jumped on my brother Barry's blue bike and off I went with a big kid pushing and calling encouragement. There was no time now to let fear take over, but as I heard the tires crunching over the gravel, my terror increased. I could skid out at any time, be thrown off and have a screaming hot graze down the side of my leg.

Half way down I felt the bike take a lunge forward from an extra hard shove and I suddenly realised that I was on my own. A little depression on the foot brake meant a skid. Too much brake meant a wipeout, but it did help to cut the terrifying speed. Then, before I knew it, the wall loomed up before me. The bike and wall collided and I was thrown off somewhere in between. A quick check for grazes and cuts and then a long push back up to the top again for the next attempt. Butterflies, moths and frogs were careening out of control in my stomach but I had to try again. Perhaps this time I could learn to stop before crashing into the shed. I looked to the top end of The Lane and winced as I saw several of the older kids laughing at my attempt. My face went red but I was determined to do better this next time.

"Nice ride little Davies....... What's that blood on your leg?"

"You shouldn't be so hard on the wall mate!"

"Guess you won't be needing to borrow my bike anytime soon," my brother Barry called out, adding to my embarrassment. "Probably nothing left of it after you've finished anyway."

As soon as I reached the top of The Lane and pointed the bike downward again, my brother Barry grabbed the seat from behind and yelled, "hang on Kevin or you'll be all over the gravel!"

Barry pushed as hard as he could and I felt the speed build even more. He had told me before that I needed to get more speed so I could stay upright and this time he was going to make sure I did. But his good intention to help me was not my concern right now. I just wanted to stay upright and on the seat. I was scared out of my pants. He seemed to push me for a long time until about 30 metres from the end when he let go. I have never moved so fast on a bike in my life. I suddenly forgot everything I had learned. I froze with fear, couldn't coordinate my foot on the brake pedal and, instead of jamming it down backwards to slow myself, I let the pedals turn forward. The wall came up before I knew it. I hit it side-on and was jerked off the bike onto the nastiest patch of gravel my young skin had ever encountered. Yeeouchh!!

As I picked myself up, I saw blood seeping through a large patch of dirt on the side of my leg; the other leg this time. When I started to investigate the extent of my wounds I saw that my big toe had a chunk of skin missing and blood oozed out from under the nail; one of the hazards of never wearing shoes. My arm ached and as I pushed the bike back up The Lane I started to cry. "That's it," I sobbed to myself, "I'm not getting on the bloody thing again! I don't want to ride. It's too hard." By the time I joined the kids at the starting point once more, I had convinced myself that learning to ride was over for me that day, I was sore and I was scared. Some big kid comforted me and asked softly, "hey Davies, do you want to try again? You almost got it that time. You're pretty good."

I missed the smirks on some of the other faces standing behind me, which was just as well because that would have made me really stubborn not to try again. When moments such as these arrived for me, as they do in the process of learning anything new, I usually went quiet, withdrew and turned away from the challenge convincing myself that another attempt later, after calming down, would do the trick. This time was no different and in fact was made worse by the damage I was doing to my body. But slowly all the comforting, encouragement and flattery broke through a crack in my fear. I knew that I wanted desperately to learn to ride like the big kids and I knew that if I left it now it would only take longer. This thought took hold and a little courage found its way into my heart. I took a deep breath, looked up at the faces now grinning at me and said through my tears, "Yeah, I'll try." "But don't push me so hard. I don't want to go so fast."

"Sure thing, Kev," said Barry. "Here, hop on mate and I'll take care of you. We'll do a good job this time, you'll see."

How many times I rode down The Lane, I don't remember. But I do recall that by the time we finished I was sore, I was grazed, my face was tear-streaked, but I was no longer afraid. The last two rides down, I rode by myself and braked successfully, stopping just before I hit the wall. My stomach was settled and I felt that I had just jumped over a huge hurdle. I could get on and off a bike and I could ride all on my own and stop safely as well. Oh I was hurting alright, but I was happy that in the face of my fear and in front of the other kids, I had mastered this challenge. I was now a real bike rider. Yeah! Life felt so good at that moment. The taunting from the older kids had stopped. I even heard a few cheers of encouragement from them. My brother Barry came over and punched me lightly on the arm.

"Beauty mate, you beaut!" he said. "You've got it Kev. You can ride now. That last one was your best."

I grinned inside and felt warm and confident. I had done it and already I felt more accepted in the group. I felt that someone had just pinned a big medal of honour on my chest and my pride lasted well into the evening. Now if I could just convince Barry to loan me his bike so I could ride and get better at it.

When bike riding was over for the Saturday, a group of us made our way through the hedge from The Lane to sit in the sun on the front lawn. I was picking gravel out of my cuts and grazes and wiping the blood away on the sleeve of my shirt. Warren, Party and Carl were doing the same. Bobby, who had already learned to ride a bike before he came to the Home, sat back with a grin on his face.

"What are you grinning at Parata?" asked Warren.

"Nothin' much mate," said Bobby, "but you kids look like you've just had a tough game of footy. Look at Kev with that big graze down his leg and skin hangin' off his toe. And look at Carl all beaten up and bloody. E tama, sure glad I learned to ride on grass.

"Where did you learn to ride, Parata?" asked Carl.

"On the Marae, mate," said Bobby. "My Koro taught me."

"Did you have a good bike?"

"Nah, it was an old junker, but it still went. My Koro kept good tires on it and they were always pumped."

"Did many of you kids have bikes up there?"

"E tama, Carl Newman, you think we're rich or something? My Mum and Dad had no money to buy a bike and neither did my Koro. We collected old rusty ones from the junkyard and fixed 'em. Koro was great at that."

We sat thinking about this and enjoying the warm sun on our backs. I was relieved now that the bike riding in the Lane was over. Some of it was fun but mostly it was hard work.

"How did you actually get to come to the Home anyway Parata?" asked Carl.

"E hoa Carl, that's a long story. I could say it's none of your business and you're a nosey bugger, but seeing as you told me your story I guess I'll tell you mine."

He paused to look at us for a second or two. Right then, if I could have read Bobby's mind, I would say he was still deciding whether or not to let us into his private world. We all had personal stuff to share and we did, but there were secrets too and I knew at that moment that he was deciding which ones he would tell us.

"I used to live up near Warkworth," he began, "but a few things happened to change all that."

Bobby was a Maori kid originally from the Northland area, of Nga Puhi descent. "When I was a few months old, my parents, who were pretty young teenagers, gave me to my Mother's parents, you know, my grandparents."

"How come they did that?" asked Carl, "didn't they want you any more?

"Not like that, mate," said Bobby. "My Mum started early in life having kids and she already had my older brother and sister to look after."

"So? Lots of families have more than two kids, so why not your Mum?"

"Not much money in those days, mate," said Bobby. "My Dad only worked part-time 'cos it was all the work he could get. He didn't have a whole lot of money coming in. Havin' another kid around was more than they could handle."

"I bet it was," said Carl " 'specially knowin' how much you can eat at one sitting."

Carl said this with a grin but when he saw us glaring at him he became serious again. There were no spoken rules about story telling but there was an understanding that all of us had our personal histories and they were exclusively ours to be respected by all. Life stories were serious stuff.

"What did your Mum and Dad do, Bobby?" I asked.

"When my parents found that they couldn't manage all us kids, that's when they decided to send me to my grandparents."

"Jeez that must've been tough."

"Nah, lots of kids in other families on the marae were brought up by their grandparents or an aunt or uncle. My Grandparents wanted to have me anyway 'cos they liked having kids around. Besides, I got to see lots of my Mum and Dad and also my cousins at my Aunty and Uncle's place. It wasn't like I was sent away, I just moved into a different house. Everybody else lived close by so I visited all the time. That's what it's like on the Marae. We're sort of separate but we're all together at the same time."

"Did your Mum and Dad still love you?" asked Carl. "Did they still want to have you 'round?"

"E tama Carl, it wasn't as bad as your situation mate. There was no hitting or yelling or fighting. Jeez, nobody was even angry. My Grandparents just stepped in and told my Mum that I could stay with them. They were doing it to help out."

Bobby went on, "I grew up with my brother and sister and my cousins. We played together all the time. Hell, we had meals together in different houses and I often slept over. That was just the way it was."

This wasn't so bad, I thought. *Nobody was rejected, nobody got drunk and angry and beat anybody up and nobody sent Bobby away. He might have been poor but he was happy. Lotsa people loved him.*

"Sounds like a good home, Bobby," said Warren, "so how come you ended up here at 109?"

"Yeah well, I'm not finished mate," said Bobby, "that's the good stuff, the bad stuff's to come."

He looked away and became serious all of a sudden, which was not like Parata. There was no smile on his face now.

"I had just had my sixth birthday when a bad thing happened," he said.

"What? What happened?"

"There was a fire in my Aunty and Uncle's house late at night. Both of them were suffocated by smoke and died, and so did my older cousin. The younger one ended up in hospital with really bad burns to both legs."

"Jeez! How did that happen?"

"Dunno exactly," he said, "but it was late at night and nobody had a chance to get out before it spread. I was staying at home with my grandparents when it happened. When I got up that morning my Nana and Koro were sitting at the table crying."

"Jeez Bobby," I said, "how did you deal with that?"

"Not good mate," he said, "I still think about it lots. I loved my Aunty and Uncle and my cousin. They were kind to me."

"So what happened?"

"Everybody on the Marae was out of it. People were sad. Aunty and Uncle were really popular with everybody. My Grandparents didn't know what to do 'cos my Aunty was their eldest daughter and she was special to them. They were really sad most of the time after the fire."

"Did you stay there Bobby?" I asked.

"For a while, but then I couldn't 'cos my Grandparents got sick. They were so sad about Aunty and Uncle and my cousins that they just seemed to get older and lose all their energy. They even talked to my Mum and Dad about them taking me back but their house was full."

"So what happened then?"

"Well as far as I know they talked to the Tribal Council on the Marae about finding some other arrangement for me, some other place to live."

"Oh yeah?" said Carl, "seems like they were just trying to get rid of you."

"E tama, Newman, it wasn't like that at all. They both love me and would have kept me there if they could. But they were getting older and after the accident they didn't seem to be able to look after me as well as before. It was like some big part of them had been killed in the fire with all the others."

I thought about what it would be like for me if something like that happened to Mum and Barry and me and it made me shudder.

"So then what happened Bobby?" I asked.

"I dunno exactly, but one day two people from the Council came and told Koro that they had found a place for me."

"Was it here Bobby?"

"Yeah, right here at 109 Mt Smart Road," he said. "Pretty quickly after that all the arrangements were made and I was on my way down here to Onehunga."

"Goodbye Bobby," said Nana tearfully. "I'm going to miss my favourite mokopuna. Remember that I love you my boy, especially when you get lonely."

"She gave me a big hug and my Koro gave me an even bigger one. I can still feel it now. And he said some things to me that I remember."

"What'd he say Bobby?" I asked.

"He said, 'we're gonna miss our favourite mokopuna, son. You think of us all up here 'cos that's gonna help you when things don't seem so good down there. Remember your family and remember that you have one even though you're living away from us. One day you'll come back. We'll come down to see you and you can come back to visit anytime. Remember that.'

"My Koro looked at me with those strong eyes of his and spoke to me like he did many times before." 'Tough situations in life, my boy, are often better dealt with if you can step outside of yourself and watch the events unfolding from a distance as if you're a spectator watching another person. Just like a movie, Bobby, or watching a game of footy. You're in the crowd and you're watching yourself acting. That way, my boy, you can see all the sides of life; the funny stuff as well as the serious stuff. That way you can laugh as well as cry sometimes. That'll help you through. You'll see. And always remember that we are here and we love you. You know what that feels like and you need to learn how to bring that feeling back from time to time; to make it real so you know it's true. That will help you cope with the lonely times in life, you'll see.'

"And did you leave after that?" asked Warren.

"Yeah, after saying goodbye to my Mum and Dad. That was hard too," he said. "I don't want to talk about that part much. But I knew then that it was what I had to do, so that made it a bit easier. But now that I'm away from all of them, I miss them a lot."

After Bobby's story we sat quietly thinking about him and his family. As usual nobody had anything to say. I didn't think that I would have coped with the same situation as well he had. He seemed to have an inner strength that I felt I lacked. I admired his way of laughing at life. But I guess I never really paid much attention to the times when he might have felt lonely or sad. I could laugh at life too but not in the same way as Bobby. To him, dealing with serious and happier moments were equally important parts of his life. I found this difficult to do, like the time when I got into trouble after being caught stealing a packet of Craven A cigarettes from a Tin Tax Corner store so we could smoke in the trees before going to Waikaraka Park on Wednesday night. Bobby laughed it off with a casual, "e hoa Kev, Guess I'll have to get the smokes next time and hope they don't catch this Maori," whereas I worried that my mother would think badly of me and how stupid I felt getting caught. I could laugh at it a lot much later, but at the time it seemed to weigh heavily on me.

Bobby seemed to come out of his early childhood experiences with some really strong lessons to fall back on. He knew that not far away, up on the Marae, there were lots of people who loved him and thought about him. He knew, even as a young kid, that he would always be wanted and welcomed by any of the people there. That's a big thing to know. Unlike me, he never seemed to avoid the sad times. He just seemed to be able to turn life on its head and laugh. That was his way of dealing with it. Easy for some I guess.

"Stop pickin' at your scabs, Kev," said Warren, "they'll never dry up that way. And Carl, your leg mate, what a mess. Better get that cleaned up. And why don't you wipe that blood off your nose. It looks like someone hit you with a cricket bat."

We laughed and were suddenly snapped out of our thoughts about Bobby. He'd finished his story and we were all a bit groggy from sitting in the sun when the lunch bell rang.

"Time to go mates," said Bobby. "We'll find out from Fernsy if we're allowed to go to the flicks this arvo."

"If we're allowed, are you gonna go Kev?" asked Warren.

"Yep," I replied," "wouldn't miss it."

"Me too," said Party.

"And how about you Carl Newman?" asked Bobby, "or do you think you'll have to stay home to get your leg all bandaged?"

I laughed at Bobby's use of Carl's full name. How did he know that to use it at times like this endeared him to Carl as a good and caring friend? Bobby was the only one who could pull this off. He really liked other kids and occasionally this was his way of showing affection. When one or the other of us said "Carl Newman" it usually came out as an admonishment, a little bit like when your Mum used your whole name instead of just your first. In that moment you knew she meant business.

"Yeah, well, it's a bit sore," said Carl.

"Tell you what, mate," said Bobby, "I'll ask Ms Pomeroi if she'll bandage your leg and look after you while we go off to the flicks at the State. What's the picture anyway Warren?"

" 'Count Of Monte Cristo' and my brother said it's good."

"E Tama that's too bad for you Carl. You're gonna miss out on all that sword fighting and stuff," said Bobby. "But you know what I'll do for you mate? I'll wrap your leg with an old bandage I've got that I don't use any more. It's in my locker. Then you can come with us."

"Jeez Parata. You think I'm crazy? I'm not touching that dirty old rag of yours. I'll get Pommy to bandage it for me instead."

"And while you're at it Newman," grinned Bobby, "ask her to tuck you into bed in the sick bay while we go off to the flicks."

Our stomachs were growling but we were laughing as we went to wash our hands for lunch. Ham sandwiches and home-made tomato soup! Mmm-mmm.

Guy Fawkes Day

Over years I can remember
how we celebrated Guy Fawkes Day
We'd spend all week gathering wood and junk
and anything that burned on a fire.
People turned up with truck-loads of logs.
Kids came by with branches they'd found.
We searched the hedge 'round our paddock
and gathered up dry scraps of gorse.

Then every day the week before,
on our way in the morning to school,
we'd stop in the paddock and look at the pile
and imagine how high it would grow.
And then at night we'd check again
to see what was dumped that day.
We'd pick up the wood that had fallen down
and throw it back up on the top.

There was always talk of fireworks and rockets,
and things which would light up the sky.
Each one of us boys knew the bag we'd get
would be full of the loudest noise and,
our excitement would brighten the dark.
But rockets in bottles were the best,
'cos they went to the moon and back
and fell down to earth with a whooosh.

As the day approached we repeated the rhyme
we said it over and over:
"Remember, Remember, the fifth of November",
it helped us get through the week.
This day was a big event for us;
this was as big as it got in the Home.
Almost as big as the bonfire itself,
the legend just grew in our minds.

And during that week, with permission of course,
we lay our Guy down in a barrow.
We'd spent the week making him out of straw
stuffed in old sacks and bags that we found.

We put him in pants, tied his shirt round his waist,
put his socks and shoes on his feet.
A hat on his head and gloves on his hands,
he was ready to wheel about town.

Off we went, a group of us kids
intent on collecting some money.
We walked up and down Onehunga's main street
asking people for pennies or more.
We collected the money, we had none ourselves,
then we gave it to Fernsy to spend.
All the time we walked around and around
we chanted this verse out loud:

"Remember! Remember!
The fifth of November
Old Guy Fawkes sits on our fire.
Hang him on a sharp stake,
Poke him in the eye,
Who'll give a penny for our dead-dog guy?
If not a penny, a halfpenny'll do.
If not a halfpenny, God bless you!"

On the night of the fifth, excitement was high,
with cakes, tea and sandwiches too.
After placing our Guy on the top of the pile
and before even the first match was struck,
we gratefully accepted our generous bags:
Catherine Wheels, Roman Candles and boom!
There were scary bangers, annoying 'Tom Thumbs'
which cracked 'round our feet and our legs.
But the best part was when the fire burned high
and it lapped round old Guy Fawkes head.
We saw his feet burn, his coat catch on fire,
and just when the flames were roaring bright
and the sparks shooting high in the sky,
we saw him slip down from the top of the pile,
slide into the middle and disappear
and at that point we let out a cheer:

"Guy Fawkes, Guy Fawkes burning bright!"
No more blowing up parliament tonight!
No more fire crackers, no more fun,
No more bonfires to warm our bums.
Guy Fawkes, Guy Fawkes, is gone this year,
Guy Fawkes is burned up, let's all cheer.
So Remember, Remember, the fifth of November
when Guy Fawkes was burned to an ember.

Maskell Street

Mum came to me one day after breakfast and said, "Kev dear, I'm going over to Nana and Grampa's house on Saturday and I'd like you to come with me."

I replied with a barrage of excited questions.

"Is Barry coming with us? Are we staying there all day? Will we stay overnight?" and, "Oh yeah Mum, when are we leaving?"

"Not until Saturday morning dear," she said, "we still have all this week to go yet. And of course Barry will be with us. He wouldn't pass up a chance to ride on the tram and the bus."

"D'ya think I'll be able to see John, Mum?, I asked.

"I'm sure your cousin will love to see you, Kev."

"Do you think Grandpa will have his ducks out?" I asked, "And what about the tree- tomatoes, do you think they'll be ripe?" And do you think Grandpa will take Nana shopping down to St Helliers so I can go down with them? Will Grandpa play footy with me on the lawn Mum? And - "

"Whoa, Kev, I'm sure you'll get to do all those things and I'm sure that Grandpa would love to play footy with you and Barry."

My Mum, Joyce Davies

Saturday morning rolled around and, as early as she could, Mum bundled Barry and me out the door to walk to Tin Tax Corner to catch the tram to Auckland where we would connect with the St Helliers' bus before walking the short distance to Maskell Street and my Nana and Grandpa's house.

"Number 55, we're here," I said, "number 55 Maskell Street. Do you think Nana and Grandpa are home Mum?"

"Oh, they will be home alright Kev, they're expecting us," she answered.

As the three of us walked through the front gate, I slid the palm of my hand over the brass number '55' on the gate post. I looked up to see Nana open the front door and begin to walk down the front steps toward us.

"Oh it's so good to see you, Joyce," said Nana, "and you too Barry and Kevin. I haven't seen all of you for ages it seems. Look how big you boys have grown."

"Tell Nana how old you are now Kev," said Mum.

"I'm six Nana," I said shyly. "I'm six and I'll be seven next year."

"Yes you will dear," said my grandmother, "now come here and give your Nana a big kiss and a hug. Oh that's nice," she said as I hugged her tightly. "You always give such nice hugs and kisses, Kev. Now what about you Barry, how old are you?"

"I'm nine and a half Nana," said Barry.

"And look how big you have grown since I saw you last. My, my, what do they feed you boys in that home?" Nana asked. "So, c'mon Barry, a kiss and a hug for your Nana? No? A bit shy are you? Not even a hug for your Nana? Oh well, here's a hug from me to you." Barry squirmed out of Nana's grasp. As usual, he didn't want to be cuddled. Nana was no exception.

"Grandpa, Grandpa," I yelled as I caught sight of my grandfather coming around the side of the house and called out to him, "Grandpa, I want to see the ducks."

"Hello Joyce, it's good to see you," said Grandpa, postponing my demand while he greeted Mum, "and little Kevin here seems

full of his usual energy. You want to see my ducks eh, Kev? C'mon
then, give your Grandpa a hug and then we'll go and see. I think
there's even some new ducklings. C'mon Barry. I know you'll
want to feed the ducks.

"Quack, quack, quack," I called as we approached the pen
where Grandpa kept the ducks housed. "Quack, quack, quack,
ducks. They look pretty muddy today, Grandpa."

"They love to get into the water and slop it all over the
ground Kev. If the shallow pond I made them was deeper, they'd
be swimming."

Like all old people, my Nana and Grandpa seemed ancient
to me. As long as I can remember, Grandpa always wore grey
striped suit pants held up by a pair of suspenders neatly in place
over his shoulders. His striped shirt was the type that he could
attach a stud collar to and sat snug around his neck. Sometimes
he would even be wearing a tie. Never did I see him in shorts and
a casual shirt except once at the bach in the summer. Nana was
always in a pleasant floral dress sometimes with a cardigan if it
was cool. Occasionally she wore a hat but mostly reserved that
for Sundays and church visits. Her neat grey hair was always tied
up in a tidy bun on the back of her head. It suited her. I never
thought of them as a relaxed, casual couple. In their dress at least
they always seemed to me to be one step away from leaving soon
for church.

Watching the ducks waddling around in their shallow pond
soon had me thinking of camp and the beach and swimming
out to the pole. I guess it was that Grandpa had mentioned the

ducks wanting to swim that brought on my excitement to tell him about my own experience.

"I can swim Grandpa," I said proudly. "I learned up at camp this year."

"What about you Barry?" asked Grandpa, "I bet you can swim. A big fella like you!"

Barry grinned at this.

"Now Barry," Grandpa went on, "can you remember the name of our big brown duck over there with the coloured feathers,"

"That's Henry, Grandpa," said Barry, "I'd know him anywhere with all those colours."

"Good boy Barry. You remembered. But do you remember what happens when ducks fly upside down?" asked Grandpa with a sparkle in his eye.

"What happens Grandpa?" I asked.

"Oh, I forgot that one Grandpa," said Barry. "What happens to them?"

"They quack up!" said Grandpa with a grin. "Get it?"

"I get it," said Barry, "you mean 'crack up' don't you Grandpa? And they're upside down."

"Oh you're such a smart fella Barry. What about you Kev? Do you get it?"

"I don't get it Grandpa," I said.

Barry was grinning his big grin and Grandpa chuckled out loud. "Oh you boys are funny. It's good to have you here. You make Grandpa feel young again. Barry, you feed the ducks from this tin. You know what to do. Then we'll go and see if we can find any ripe tree-tomatoes."

"I know the tree Grandpa," I said. "It's big and bushy and has all those red fruit hanging on it that look like eggs. You know, the ones Nana makes her pudding with and we eat it with custard. Yumm Grandpa, it's my favourite."

"That's it alright Kev. You sure don't forget much do you?"

We walked around to the front of the house after the feeding and looked for our favourite tree. There it was, exactly as I remembered it, with dozens of the distinctive red fruit about egg size, dangling down at the end of their stems. Like most New Zealand kids I was unable to separate the image of the fruit with the taste and smell of eating it raw or cooked.

"There's lots of tree tomatoes Grandpa," said Barry. "I can see a ripe one."

"Do you boys know that tree-tomatoes are really called tamarillos?" he said as he passed one to each of us.

We split the skin as we'd been taught and ate the yellowy-orange flesh from inside. It was a delicious taste.

"I could eat these all day," said Barry. "Seeds and all!"

In his shed Grandpa found the small rugby ball, which to me looked like a giant tree tomato, and took us on the back lawn to play. He loved playing with his grandsons proudly teaching us a few tricks he knew from his own playing days. He was a good teacher although I had trouble remembering exactly what he had taught us the last time we had visited. Barry didn't seem to have this problem. He showed Grandpa all the footy skills he had practised on the paddock during the week. Then he'd turn to me and say, "you remember how to kick the footy, Kev. I showed you how to do it last week. Remember? Why don't you show Grandpa."

We visited Maskell Street every two months or so and I always looked forward to it. Grandpa did everything that grandfathers' reputations are built on; playing footy with us, gardening, building projects, going places, talking to us and teaching us things. I loved the occasional holiday we took with my grandparents driving us in their car all the way to Wellington after school was out in December so we could spend a part of the summer at the family bach around at Red Rocks. Grandpa had all of us cousins helping him make a tool-box once and after the box was finished I looked at it proudly as if I had built it myself. He loved to get us kids all involved, which made us feel important. Nobody felt left out when Grandpa was around, except once, when my cousin Grahame got bawled out for misplacing one of Grandpa's tools. He accused Grahame, took him aside and gave him an angry lecture on being careless. We all knew this was unfair but didn't say anything. Grahame was hurt and upset and we were all left wondering about this outburst from Grandpa.

I remember a time at Maskell Street when I was a little older, perhaps seven or eight. I was playing rugby-league for a team made up of Home kids that had been organised by someone in the community. I was eager to tell Grandpa all about it.

"I'm in a footy team Grandpa," I said proudly. "We play every Saturday morning."

"What position do you play Kev?" he asked.

"I'm in the backs and I get to run a lot," I said. "There's seven in our team and we wear blue jerseys. It's fun. And we've won all our games. The coach says we are good players and we have a good team. We usually play at Waikaraka Park."

"Do you have lineouts and scrums Kev?" asked Grandpa, "you know, like in a real footy team?"

Homekids League Footy Team

I liked Grandpa asking questions like this because it showed he was interested in me playing rugby. The game was an important part of his life. I could tell this when he taught me new things. I felt proud telling him how much I loved to be out there running around with all the other kids. He had even been a rep-player himself. His brother Teddy, my uncle, had become one of New Zealand's greatest All Blacks. Rugby was in the Roberts' blood, and hopefully mine.

"No," I said, "I just 'play' the ball when I'm tackled, Grandpa. You know, give it a little kick and then pass it off to Warren or Colin."

"Oh, you must be playing rugby-league Kev," said Grandpa.

"Yeah, that's right Grandpa," I said, "it's a rugby-league team."

Right then something changed. Grandpa became serious. The smile left his face. I felt some uncertainty rising somewhere between us.

"It might be lots of fun Kevin but you shouldn't be playing league. That's not a good game to play," he said.

"Yes it is, Grandpa," I said, "it's lots of fun and the coach even bought us a Tip-Top ice-cream after our last game."

"No Kevin, league isn't a good game and I don't want you to play it," said Grandpa now looking at me with his most serious face like the time he caught Barry and me taking tamarillos from the tree before they were ripe. He wasn't being friendly any more. He looked like he wanted to teach me something but not about footy or building things or ducks.

"We don't play that 13-aside game in our family, Kevin. The Roberts have never played league."

I was kind of confused at this. It didn't occur to me that there was even a difference between rugby and rugby-league. All I was doing was playing footy and having lots of fun doing it. At my young age I had certainly never spent a second thinking there might be something wrong with the game I was playing. "Why not Grandpa?" I asked

"Because the people who play league are not nice people and I don't want you mixing around with them."

"Why aren't they good people?" I asked. "Do they do bad things?"

"That's right," said Grandpa, "they swear and curse. They take the Lord's name in vain, and drink beer and fight. Most of them are Maoris and we don't mix with them."

He was almost angry now as he said this. I felt caught in a conversation that I didn't want to have.

"You're a bit young to understand, Kevin," he went on, "but we don't mix with the type of people who play league, you know, Maoris and Islanders and others who live in those communities. They're not our type. Our people are in our church and they are nice people and I want you to mix with them. Why don't you just stick to playing rugby."

"But Grandpa," I explained, "Bobby Parata is my friend and he's a Maori and he's good."

"I know you might think they are Kevin, but they're not really nice people deep down. They're a rough crowd Kevin. And most importantly they are not Christians like we are."

He went on at length about this and I found myself withdrawing. It completely threw me and I eventually stopped talking. I couldn't think of any thing else to say. Anyway, Grandpa was not talking about footy any more. He had now switched to the church, to God and Jesus and how people who played league were not fit to be around. Eventually he sensed how uncomfortable I had become. I stood quietly staring at him, not having a clue what to say in my defense.

"Well, just remember Kevin," he said, "you should stop playing for that rugby-league team and play rugby-footy instead. Rugby's much more fun anyway."

On the way home in the bus with Mum, I told her about it. "Grandpa doesn't like me playing in my league team, Mum," I said, "he thinks I should stop and play rugby instead. He said that people who play league are not good people. Why did he say that Mum?"

"Kev, your Grandpa is right even though you don't like it. It's mostly the rough people who play league and we don't mix with them. The people we mix with are in our church and those people are not. They're different than us and we should keep to our own. That's what Grandpa is telling you."

"Yeah Mum, that's what he said too but I like to play footy for my team. It's fun and the coach is nice and he thinks I'm a good player. I've scored a try in every game so far."

"You should listen to Grandpa, Kev, he knows best about these things."

"Warren plays, Bobby too, Party, and so does Colin, so why shouldn't I?" I pushed, although I knew I was fighting a losing battle.

I looked out the bus window and thought about all this. None of it seemed right to me. It just didn't make any sense.

Over the next few days, I thought about what had been said to me. It bothered me, so I decided to talk to my friend Warren about it.

"My Grandpa thinks I shouldn't play for our league team, Warren. He thinks only Maoris and Islanders play league and he says they're not good people. What do you think mate?"

"You better play on Saturday, Kev," said Warren, " 'cos the coach won't like it if you let him down. You'll be letting the team down too," he added.

"I don't think Maoris and Islanders are bad people, Warren. And I don't think League is a bad game. It's a good game and it's lots of fun." I said.

"That's why we're in the team, mate," he grinned.

"Yeah, I know, but I wish my Grandpa hadn't said all that stuff and I wish Mum hadn't backed him up."

"Forget what they said, Kev. They don't know any Maoris or Islanders anyway except for your Mum. She knows Bobby Parata and he's a great bloke. You know how much she likes him. And she knows Miss Pomeroi and she's a Maori and your Mum's gotta like her. Don't forget Kev, Bobby's a really good mate to us and he helps us play better 'cos he's played league before, when he was younger. And he's got those bloody long legs of his, mate, and his big knobbly knees. Must hurt like hell to tackle him eh? Lucky we play with him and not against him." He paused, looking around. "Bobby's family all played league and that's why he's so good at it. My brother used to play league when he was younger and he was a good player. He said it's just as good a game as rugby."

"Yeah," I said thinking about all this. "Hey..... ah..... Warren, who are we playing on Saturday anyway?"

"Don't know yet, Kev, but I think we get to wear those new jerseys with the V-stripes around the collar, mate. Just like a real league team."

Our coach turned up every week to drive us to the game in his truck. One day a week he also came to the Home after school to show our team some new tricks and spend time helping us learn the differences between rugby-league and rugby. We knew he was a good coach and a nice man. Our team was made up of all my mates and we just loved it. Somehow he made us all feel like heroes especially if we had run with the ball in the game or made a break or put in a nice clean tackle. He always found something good to say to each one of us. Besides, we won all our games and that said something.

"You Home-kids sure know how to play as a team and run fast and tackle hard," said the coach one day. "I think you can win the comp this year. Whad'ya say boys?"

Next weekend when it came time for our team to play I couldn't wait for the game to begin. I decided not to talk about it to my Grandfather any more and also not say much to Mum either. She didn't come to stop me when the coach arrived in his old truck to drive us to Waikaraka park for our game that day. I figured that even though Mum was concerned about all this, she wasn't going to stop me having so much fun. So off I went feeling a whole lot more comfortable knowing that while Mum agreed with Grandpa, she still wanted me to play for my team. That was my thinking anyway.

I never saw Mum as a person with racist attitude. I mean, I never thought of her not liking other people just because of who they were. She was a person who seemed to like everybody. Years later, when we lived in Wellington, I caught her once in a while saying things I had heard others in my family say about Maoris or Islanders. I was alarmed but not to the same extent that I was at my Aunts and Uncles. In the Home it never occurred to me that she might feel differently about Maoris or others. It was obvious that she loved Bobby and treated him as if he was part of her family. I looked on Bobby like a brother and it seemed to me that Mum treated him like a son. She seemed to get along well with Pommy who was Maori. A few others in the Home like the Lees and a couple of other Maori boys she seemed close to, and loved them the same as all other kids. But I realize now that just because I didn't see a double standard, one did not exist.

When I was older I remember a conversation I had with family outside of church one Sunday morning. One of my Aunts had seen me about town on Friday night that week with my girlfriend. She queried me with a smile on her face in front of a group of my relatives, including my mother and grandmother.

"Oh Kev, who was that I saw you with on Friday night down on Lambton Quay?"

"That was my girlfriend, Aunty," I said.

"That wasn't your girlfriend, Kev," she said, "you wouldn't be going with one of them."

"What do you mean, one of them?"

"You know what I mean. She's a Maori or Islander or something isn't she? She's one of those."

"Yeah. She could be from Bali for all I care. What does it matter who she is or where she comes from?" I asked.

"Oh it matters alright Kevin," my Grandmother piped in. "There are plenty of nice Christian girls in the church, why don't you go with one of them?"

I looked at my relatives staring back at me from their circle. Mostly they were grinning, probably at my obvious discomfort. In deference to my grandmother and resisting the urge to say something nasty, I walked away and headed home by myself absolutely fuming at what I had heard. I went over and over in my head the conversation that had taken place and was infuriated at the blatantly ignorant attitude of my family. *If this is what Christians do and say,* I thought, *I want no part of it.* I was angry but, as usual, stuffed it down and pushed it aside.

That incident became a point of contention for me in my relationship with my family and had a significant influence in turning me away from the church, home and even my family. I talked more about this with my mother again later.

"Mum, I just don't get it why you and the others in our family are so down on Maoris and other people of other races."

"Well, Kev, we're not so much down on them but they're not the same as us," she defended, not sounding all that convincing.

"They're different and we just don't mix with them. I mean, they're people too I know, but we don't have to mix with them. I don't want to anyway."

"Are you saying something like, if you were down in Newtown waiting for the bus and you were late getting to work, or church, and you decided to catch a taxi and the one waiting at the stand was being driven by a Maori or East Indian driver or somebody with a dark skin, that you would not get in that cab, but wait until one driven by a pakeha came along?"

"That's right Kev, I wouldn't get in those cabs. That's how I feel. Probably nobody in our family would."

"But Mum," I said shocked to my core, "that's a racist attitude. Don't you see that?"

"No it's not dear," she said, "it's just how I feel. All our family feel that way. And lots of other people do too. We don't want to mix with those people at all. They're not our kind. Don't get me wrong. There's some lovely people among them I'm sure and I know that there are even many Christians as well. But they are still not our kind. It's best if we keep to ourselves and they do the same."

"Well, I don't feel that way at all, so I must be different from all of you," I said, angry and hurt that my family held these attitudes. I realized strongly at that moment, that I was alone. The differences in my upbringing compared to that of my cousins and other family members hit me then and stayed with me for a long time after.

The up-side of those conversations was, that it seemed to help me determine my own path in the world and to forge my own beliefs and values. This was difficult but all the same I felt myself drifting away. In the overall scheme of things though, it wasn't that bad. I learned to stand on my own two feet and to explore my own beliefs and not ones that were imposed from outside, or from my family. For me, Christianity was not a role model I was attracted to. I had learned early to see through many of it's teachings. There was a lot of phoniness going on. Somehow, some of the good parts had stuck, like loving others and wanting to do good things for other people. But I think that was because Mum was that way herself and I just copied the qualities I liked. I was becoming more aware of the ones I didn't like as well, like the double standards held by my Grandpa toward Maoris and Islanders. I knew clearly that some family members had adopted his attitudes and I wanted no part of those. I felt strongly a determination to find my own path, which unconsciously I had probably been treading all my young life.

I learned to question what I was told and what I heard, and this was a good thing. Most of the stuff I had been told over the years concerning religion, life, and rules to live by, just made no lasting sense to me. My family, it seemed, could only view life from their chosen religious position. If Jesus said it, if it was in the Bible, then it must be true and definitely the approved way to live. In fact, any other way was unnacceptable and the way of the sinner and the damned.

Not long after my Aunt had made her made her point at church about my girlfriend and stirred up my emotions on this issue, I found myself alone at Lions Rock after spending a day spear-fishing around Cook Strait at our bach. I often took myself off around Red Rocks way to spend the day snorkelling and spearfishing. I was content in the wild setting of coast and sea and perfectly comfortable by myself. I would spend a morning fishing, having made a big fire earlier over smooth rocks and, later when I came out of the water I cooked the fish on the rocks and under sand, hangi style. These were fulfilling days for me in the hot sun by the sea, eating fresh fish.

There on this particular day by Lions Rock, facing a roaring sea, the wind in my face and the crashing waves in front of me, I yelled out a few things that had become important at the time. The previous week thoughts of my earlier life in the Home, my family life in Wellington, school, church, the pressures I felt around religion and the direction of my life had been rattling around in my mind weighing in on me. Faced with the wild sea in a wild place, an outward display of personal angst seemed entirely appropriate. I felt an urge to release pent up energy, a sort of purging of personal demons.

"God and Jesus!" I bellowed. "I'm thinking that I don't need either of you in my life! Yeah! I'm even questioning your existence! I feel like I need to be in charge of myself and not wait until you two show me the direction I should go!"

I paused and took in a large breath keeping my balance on the rock in the face of the waves and the wind. I had my snorkel in my hand and I waved it about vigorously. This was a wild place and it called for wild words.

"I'll be taking care of everything thank-you very much," I yelled. "I don't believe either of you two, if you even exist, are of any use to me at all!"

I paused and took in a breath. I was prepared to say some pretty irreverant things but in my uncertainty I stopped short of outright denial of the existence of God. Lions Rock could withstand this huge force of nature but what if I was suddenly the target of His impatience and anger? This was not the time for any finalities. They would come later.

I decided to change tack for a minute.

"And the same goes for all you people who seem so concerned about what I'm doing in my life," I went on screaming into the wind. "I'm the one in charge. I'll be the one directing my life. Not any of you!"

I paused and thought about what I wanted to end off with.

"So...God and the rest of you...back off and leave me alone! I'll take care of my business, my way!"

I stuffed my spear-fishing gear into my backpack, left Lions Rock and trudged around the beach in the headwind to where I had stored my bike. I felt confident and satisfied about all the things I had just yelled out. Not realising it at the time, the moment at Lion's Rock in its spontaneity, would stand as an important turning point for me. I had just stepped up a rung or two in my personal growth. They hadn't been the easiest of things to say given the background of my family and my desire to stay on-side and avoid conflict with everybody I knew in my life. At that moment though, I felt I could live with this confrontation.

Although as a teenager I learned to re-define my own values on my own terms, as a child I still travelled often to Maskell Street but was never as comfortable with my Grandfather as when I was very young. Living a very separate life from the rest of my family as I did, created a natural distance between us and situations such as talk about what game I should play, created more. Years later, as a teen living with my Grandmother and Mother in Wellington, after my Grandfather had died, I tried to recapture the familiarity we once shared. It felt as if some sort of wedge had been driven in between myself, my Grandmother and my Aunts and Uncles.

The wedge, I think, was myself. I had changed while they remained constant in their familial ties and their belief and faith in religion and their God.

I even found that some distance between myself and my Mother had crept in. I was entering adolescence which in itself is a most difficult time of life. I sensed I felt significantly different about certain matters than she did, and this knowledge set us apart. It caused the creation of a climate of guilt for me about matters that should have been disclosed to my Mother. I became increasingly aware that Mum, Nana and my family might disapprove of whatever it was I chose to do in my life based on the teachings of their faith. My branching off into the secular world put me at odds with them all on numerous occasions.

It was the beginning of my conscious withdrawal and the perception that it was better for me to rely on my own judgement. Subconsciously this withdrawal led to being more closed than open and secretive rather than honest in my dealings with adults. I found that having no father to turn to as a natural mediator, arbitrator, or sounding-board, was a deficit. I was well into adulthood, living independently, before I figured out how to break through some of these barriers and to make more satisfying choices for the improvement of my character and subsequently, my life.

Little Lord Fauntleroy

"How-now-brown-cow. How-now-brown-cow. How now ....."

I was right in the middle of my weekly elocution lesson and all I could think of was when it was going to be over.

"How-now-brown-cow. How-now-brown.........."

"Yes alright. Kevin, let's go onto.....ah....The Rain......"

"The ryne in Spyne falls mynely on the plyne. The ryne in Spyne falls mynely on the plyne. The......."

"The *RAYNE*, Kevin, *RAYNE*, not *RYNE*," she said. "Remember please! It is The *RAYNE* in *SPAYNE* falls *MAYNELY* on the *PLAYNE*. Do you understand?"

"Yes," I said.

"Yes who?" asked Mrs Quinn.

"Yes Mrs Quinn," I said. "The ryne in Spyne falls mynely on the plyne. Th.."

"Yes, I'm sure. Now Kevin, try harder this time my boy. The *RAYNE*........"

Each Wednesday after school I trammed it all the way from Tin Tax Corner to Greenwoods Corner to get to my elocution lessons with Mrs Adelle Quinn, BESC. I didn't tell any of my friends about this because I was a bit sensitive to what reactions they might have. Any 9 or 10 year old boy would have felt the same.

For reasons best understood by herself, Mum had decided that I should learn to speak properly, which for her meant "just like Grandpa dear, just like Grandpa. He has a wonderful speaking voice. When he preaches, it sounds so beautiful. I want you to speak like him and not like these roughies around Onehunga."

"Oh, you mean like the roughies who play league and not rugby Mum?" I grinned.

"Yes exactly, dear," she said, "not like those people at all. I want you to speak like educated people speak."

"Is Barry taking lessons too Mum, so he can learn to speak properly?" I asked.

"No dear, just you," she said.

A few months earlier when I had paid a visit up in her room on a Saturday morning, Mum showed me her Thomas Gainsborough 'Blue Boy' print on her wall by the door.

"I think it's such a lovely painting Kev. He looks like a very nice boy, well mannered and cultured. It must have been so nice to live in that age. I would have loved to live then. I would have been a little girl in a big house with beautiful things all around and everybody would be so well educated and speak properly. Don't you think the 'Blue Boy' is lovely Kev?"

Well, standing there in my khaki shirt unbuttoned to the waist, my khaki shorts with a shiny smear of cow-dung down one side, a grass stain on the other, I looked at Gainsborough's Blue Boy and caught something odd in the look on the boy's face.

Definitely Not A Blue Boy

"He looks like a sissy, Mum," I said, "and I can tell that he doesn't really want to be dressed that way. He'd rather be in a pair of shorts and play footy like me."

"Oh Kev, how can you say that? He is so beautiful."

Another time, on an evening I think, I sat on her seat by the window overlooking the courtyard as she busied about tidying her room.

"Here's a book I think you should read Kev. I read this when I was a little girl. Grandpa bought it for me. It's very old now, so be careful with it."

"Is it *Tarzan* Mum?" I asked, "or *Adventures With William*? I like those stories."

"Oh Kev, don't be silly, it's not *Tarzan*. Why would I read that? No dear, it's called *Little Lord Fauntleroy* and it's written by Francis Hodgson Burnett. It's all about a little boy who has to return to his family home in England after living in America. He lives with his grandfather who is not nice to him at all. Nothing like your Grandpa, dear. The boy's name is Cedric and he's such a lovely little boy who is so patient with his Grandfather in spite of all the nasty things that happen. Anyway Kev, why don't you read the book and see what you think."

"Does Cedric play footy Mum?" I added. "Does he like to slide down places like One Tree Hill? What about camp? Does he go to camp like we do? Can he swim like I can?"

Mum was a bit impatient with me. "Read the book Kev, then you'll see."

The first thing I did was flip the pages and look at all the sketches that had been drawn. They weren't very good. They showed the main character Cedric in various poses: with his grumpy old grandfather; with the big dog who looked half asleep; with a silly, frilly little girl with a head of curls and a big dress with puffy sleeves; in the garden (for God's sake) next to the maid with glasses who had her arm around his shoulders. The book was so old the pictures were all black and white and sketched by hand. At least Tarzan and William books had coloured pictures, painted by a real artist. I had a Tarzan picture which I kept in my drawing booklet. I took it out now and again to try to copy it exactly. It wasn't easy getting the shape of the face and the body right. I worked at it to make it look real. I was trying to teach myself how to use shading like real artists did.

Poor Cedric, who was really Little Lord Fauntleroy, had to wear clothes I had only ever seen girls wearing in the pictures at the State Theatre; silly white shirts with lace collars and lace down the front, satin shorts with ribbons on the legs, socks - which the girls at the State called stockings and made us boys snigger - up to the knees and shoes that looked like they had never moved faster than two black snails; black and shiny with buckles all over. Needless to say, I was not in the least interested in fashion, being as young as I was, but all the same there was no chance that I would allow myself to be dressed like Cedric. I tried to picture him in our paddock at the cowshed, feeding the chooks in the evening, or running away from the bull when it chased you away from the cows. For the life of me I just couldn't see Cedric trying to tackle Bobby Parata round his big knobbly knees in a game of footy on Saturday morning in our paddock. The thought of him sliding through a big soft cow-pie was too much. The mess!

Forget about swinging in the trees or joining in an acorn battle with Carl, Warren, Party and me. Cedric was too much of a sissy. He was a bit like those people who arrived in New Zealand from England and went to the beach at Mission Bay or St Helliers in their suits and ties. Even their kids wore the same and sat in the hot sun playing in the sand. And forget about going to camp; Cedric wouldn't last two seconds. He wouldn't even be able to get down the long path between the flax bushes to the beach and the oyster reefs. What the heck would he wear swimming? And would poor old Cedric be able to swim out to the pole and dive off? I doubt it. I just couldn't see Cedric doing any of this stuff we did in a normal day. Not in a hundred years!

I read the book... well... parts of it. Cedric, who was actually quite a nice kid, had to go to live with his grumpy old Grandfather. It took a while, but because Cedric wasn't afraid to talk to his Grandpa and suggest being positive rather than negative, grandfather began to change. Half way through the book he had warmed up to his grandson and by the end of the book he had learned to love him. The bonus was that Grandpa became a reasonable old man who people liked and Cedric gained an inheritance.

But it was all so silly to me. Nobody lived like that in my world, calling everybody "Sir" or "Madam" and having fancy cups of tea in the living room with grumpy old grandfather and old ladies who couldn't hear a thing. The most exciting thing that Cedric ever did was to go into the kitchen and sneak a piece of cake off the plate left there by the maid. No, Little Lord Fauntleroy and his life in the big house with his grandfather was not a story that pulled me in or left me any feelings of excitement.

Now, Tarzan, or The Phantom, or William? Those were stories I could relate to.

"So, what did you think of the book Kev?" asked Mum.

"It's alright I guess," I said, not quite being honest.

"Oh, I would have loved to live in those days," said Mum again. "I could have lived when Cedric was around. It would be lovely to wear all those frilly clothes with fine lace collars, fringes and ribbons."

"Mmmmm...... not for me, Mum. I think I like it better here at the Home."

"Oh, but Kev, you would look very handsome in such nice clothes. That big white collar would set off your curls. You would look so beautiful. Sometimes I wish you had a little sister so I could dress her up in beautiful dresses and ribbons."

I drifted over to the door looking for a way out of this conversation. I didn't like it when Mum talked this way looking at me like I was some little doll she liked to play with. I didn't like her dressing me up and slicking my hair with water and fluffing up my curls. I much preferred to be bare-foot in my cotton shorts and khaki shirt mucking about in our huts, riding bikes down the Lane or going off to the matinee at the State on a Saturday with a group of the kids from the Home.

Oh Kev, You Could Be Just Like Cedric

In Mum's quest to present me as well cultured, I continued taking elocution lessons with Mrs Quinn for several weeks but I was not enjoying my time there reciting verses and sounding out every word just like the 'educated' people did.

"It sounds as if they have a marble or a plum in their mouths," I said one time.

Bobby or Party or Warren didn't speak like that and I didn't want to either. I didn't want to speak like Carl though, he had an annoying whine in his voice. I kept going to lessons because I didn't want to hurt Mum's feelings. She wanted me to take these lessons so much and had gone to some trouble to get Mrs Quinn to squeeze me in. So I kept on going... for a while. But the day the word got out and some of the Home kids found out that I was taking elocution lessons, was the day I decided to make a change.

"Where do you go after school on Wednesdays anyway Kev?" asked Warren one day.

"Up to Greenwoods Corner on the tram," I replied.

"What for?" asked Party. "Do you have to see a doctor or someone like that?"

"Yeah, it's the doctor eh, Kev?" said Bobby. "Gotta get your leg fixed after that hard tackle I laid on you last game eh?"

"No, I have to see Mrs Quinn." I couldn't lie. "I go there every Wednesday to take elocution lessons."

"Eh hoa mate, electrocution lessons?" said Bobby Parata. "What for mate? Just stick your finger in a light socket. You can get electrocuted for free and you don't even have to take a tram to get there. I'll even show you how."

"El-o-cu-tion Bobby," I said, "not electrocution you goon. I'm having lessons to learn how to speak properly. My Mum wants me to do it."

"What d'ya do Kev?" asked Party.

"You know, say poetry and verses over and over and Mrs Quinn corrects me and tells me how to say it the proper way."

"What the heck does your Mum want you to learn to speak like that for?" asked Warren. "Next thing we know Kev'll be sounding like someone in the royal family."

"Say something for us Kev," said Party. "Say the one you said last Wednesday."

"Yeah mate, come on," coaxed Bobby. "Let's all hear it."

"Oh yeah, you think I'm a fool? You blokes'll just laugh at me," I said.

"No we won't," said Warren. Promise not to eh, Bobby? Party?"

"Ok," I said, "here goes: She-sells-sea-shells-on-the-sea-shore. That's how it goes and I'm not saying it again. And I'm not saying any more either."

"Aww come on mate, just one more."

"Ok, one more and that's it," I said. "The RAYNE in SPAYNE falls MAYNELY on the PLAYNE. There, I've said it."

"Eh tama, mate, you sound like that bloke on the radio just before the Wednesday night hit-parade comes on: 'Good ahfternoon laydies and gehntlemen and it's such a lovely ahfternoon for......' You sound just like him."

We laughed. Bobby was so funny when he got going. Warren and Party had turned away from me and I could tell that they were holding down a big laugh. Bobby looked at them, burst out giggling and pretty soon all three were roaring.

Bobby took a big breath and said, "I bet you that Mrs Quinn gets you to say 'How Now Brown Cow'. I had to say that once when some dingbat teacher in the primmers decided I couldn't speak properly so she made me say that over and over. She kept at it for about two weeks but it didn't work. Too much Maori in this fella, mates. Been talking Maori-pidgin-English for too long and can't change."

"How long will you have to keep going Kev?" asked Warren.

"Until my Mum says it's enough or Mrs Quinn tells Mum that I've learned to speak properly."

"Far as I'm concerned," said Party, "you speak properly now. I can understand you. Eh, Warren, what about you?"

"Yeah Kev, mate, you speak alright now. We all understand you."

"Dunno 'bout that, mate," said Bobby. "He was talking in his sleep last night and I couldn't understand what it was he said about his girlfriend or even what her name was. I think he needs more practice, mateys. Eeeee!"

Warren and Party couldn't hold back. They laughed so much that pretty soon I joined them. Bobby could be really funny even when you were trying to be angry at him.

Next Wednesday I arrived at Mrs Quinn's house and told her I was feeling sick and had to go home right away.

"Alright then Kevin, I'll see you next week. Perhaps by then you will be better."

However, next week I decided to miss the lesson altogether. Instead of getting off at Greenwoods Corner I stayed on the tram until Royal Oak and then got off. I filled in what I thought was about an hour and then caught the tram back to Onehunga and walked home. I did this on several more occasions during my Wednesday lesson times. I never talked to Mum unless she asked me how the lesson went and then all I said was, "it went well, Mum. I learned a new poem today," or, "oh, the lesson was cancelled today, Mum, 'cos Mrs Quinn was sick."

The following week on Wednesday, Mum met me at the door of the Home as I arrived back from Greenwoods Corner.

"How was the lesson today Kevin?" she asked.

"It was good Mum," I ventured carefully. I was nervous as she was right there waiting for me. This was not usual. And it was "Kevin" not "Kev", and that was not usual either.

"Was it as good as last week or the week before?" she asked.

My radar switched on. There was no smile on her face. This was not going to be easy.

"No Mum, it was about the same."

"Well, how would you know?" she asked me. "You apparently have not been attending the lessons for some time so how would you know?"

"What do you mean Mum?" I asked. I understood that at that moment any denial was going to be useless. I was positively the worst liar in the Home. When caught in these situations my face went red, and I lost my usual confidence in speech. Anybody questioning me would have no problem detecting I was not being straight. I knew she had me, no question. *Time to take my medicine,* I thought. I could feel the tension between us.

"All I know is that Mrs Quinn came to the Home earlier today to talk to me and told me that you have not shown up for lessons for four weeks now. You haven't been going and yet you've been telling me that you have. You've been lying to me, Kevin, and I don't like that. I'm very angry about this."

Her face had gone pale and as she leaned toward me, she had one hand on her hip while pointing at me with the other. I felt threatened. I just wanted this to be over so that we could go back to being friendly with Mum calling me 'Kev' instead of the more intimidating 'Kevin'.

"Yeah... well... Mum," I stammered. "I started missing the lessons 'cos I didn't like them any more and I didn't want to say anything 'cos I thought that you would make me keep on going."

"Did it not occur to you that I was paying for the lessons and by not going you have been wasting money that I have saved up so that you could improve your speech?" she paused. "Why didn't you say anything to me?"

Mum was looking at me with her most severe face.

"I was afraid that you'd be disappointed and would talk me into keeping on going. I don't like the lessons, Mum. I don't like learning how to speak like that. It feels so sissy to me."

"It's not sissy, Kevin. It's, it's ...." she searched for the right word "..... it's... refined... that's what it is. I don't like the way everybody speaks around here and I wanted you to be different."

That hurt. Everybody around here was like me.

"But Mum, I am different," I said gently. "I'm me, and I kinda like the way I speak. I think that I sound just like Party and Warren and Bobby Parata. I don't want to be like that little boy Cedric in the book you have. I don't want to talk like that and I don't want to dress like that. That's Little Lord Fauntleroy Mum, and I'm me, here in the Home. That's why I didn't want to take the lessons any more."

"Well Kevin, I'm very disappointed that you lied to me. And I'm disappointed that you don't like the elocution lessons. I was trying to do what I think is best for you and you have not been very nice about it. Why did you not just come and tell me that you didn't want to go anymore? Money doesn't grow on trees you know."

"I'm sorry for lying, Mum," I said. I didn't know what else to say. I felt stuck.

The tears began. I felt absolutely terrible like I had plotted all of this just to make my Mother feel bad. I had let her down in the worst way and she was letting me know.

"I suppose that it's no use making you go back to Mrs Quinn now, but you will have to do something to make up for the money you have wasted and for your dishonesty. I have to learn to trust you again Kevin, because right now you have damaged what we already we had."

I couldn't speak through the tension and the tears. These times when Mum let me know that I had failed her and wounded her with my behaviour were the very worst times for me.

"I want you to do some extra jobs, Kevin. When you have finished your regular job you are come to me and I'll tell you what else you'll do. You need to do this each day for a week. This is your punishment for being so dishonest. Mind you don't forget now. Do you hear me?"

"Yes Mum," I said meekly, "I'll be there."

With that, she turned away from me, leaving me standing, feeling terrible about everything that had happened.

Much later though, I let out a breath I had been holding in for a long time and relaxed myself.

It was really over.

I had known for a while now that my dishonesty would eventually catch up with me and it finally had. I felt a big sensation of relief. I had no more reason to hide all this away from the other kids. I didn't have to lie to Mum about it any more. But best of all I didn't have to go to elocution lessons with Mrs Quinn any more. It was over.

"No more electrocution, eh Kev? Eh hoa, that must feel good," said Bobby with all his teeth showing.

"E-l-o-c-u-t-i-o-n, Parata, you dingbat," I said. "And yeah mate, it does feel good now that I don't have to recite any more of those silly, soppy, sayings and sound like a sissy."

"E tama mate, you do sound different though. Whaddya think Warren?"

"Sound a bit like you've got an alley in your mouth Kev, mate," said Warren. "Why don't you just spit it out and then you can talk like the rest of us."

"Better still mate," said Bobby, "why don't I give you some of my electrocution lessons and then you'll be so shocked you'll spit that alley out quick and fast. Eh hoa, Kev, speaking like that Mrs Quinn wanted you to, it's not good for you."

Party grinned at me. 'S all right, Kev," he said in his usual quiet style. "You might talk funny but you're still our mate."

I was back. I felt like a load had just lifted off me.

"Come on mates," I said, "it looks like it's gonna rain soon so let's go and kick the footy in the paddock a bit, then we can watch Stretchy milk the cows before tea tonight."

The Copper Kettle

At the same time that Carl Newman got his arm caught in the wooden mangle, I was burning my hands on hot clothes boiling away in the copper kettle in the Laundry. This was a bit painful but not half as bad as Warren's job of hanging the clothes out to dry. That was one chore I hated. Having to carry heavy wet laundry out to the clothes-lines and peg them up with water running down my arms to my elbows and into my sleeves, was not something I wanted to do. Warren could have that! I did my job with burning hands in the two huge, shiny copper kettles we had for boiling the clothes in. I had to feed the fires underneath and bring the water to a boil. Ms Pomeroi put in just the right amount of washing powder and 'Reckitts Blue' which made the clothes bright and white and sometimes was rubbed onto our hands or legs by a staff member if one of us sustained a bee sting or two while playing outside. Then I stirred the clothes with the stick so that the water could get to all parts. After they boiled a while I had to take them all out again, put them through the ringer into a washtub full of cold water for rinsing. Next, they were put through the ringer again and dumped into baskets which Warren and one of the Lee boys took outside to hang on the lines. We had jobs to do all of the time but the laundry job was kept strictly for Saturday mornings because it needed more time and more boys. It was a busy one, but somebody had to do it.

Doing regular jobs and chores at the Home was just part of living there. Everybody was expected to pitch in, cooperate and not whine or complain. I hated some chores and tolerated others. My approach was to get the job done as quickly as I could so I could get on with other things, especially on a Saturday.

A job none of us minded at all involved tidying up the wood pile after the truck dumped a load in the space near the furnace room attached to back of the laundry. The wood was used to feed the fire that heated the boiler ensuring that there was always plenty of hot water for the laundry and for a bath on Saturday night. Once the dust settled and the truck left we scrambled into the yard and quickly put all the wood into piles of different lengths and sizes. When that was done and the senior kid in charge was satisfied, we grabbed the pieces we wanted for hut building. It was obvious that we worked harder at gathering wood than at any of the assigned chores. Getting to choose the best pieces for huts was our incentive and pretty soon there were piles here and there with some of us standing guard. As soon as we could, we'd start building.

Party, Bobby & Carl

Huts in various stages of construction, soon dotted the cow paddock. I loved hut-making time, especially with Warren, Bobby and Robin. We worked through Saturday morning when our jobs had been done. By mid-afternoon we had finished and still had time to build a sled to take up One Tree Hill for some fun. I had a hut design with two rooms and an entrance and the other kids were always asking me what they should do next like I was a master builder or something. And when the building part was done we managed to find old sacks somewhere to line the floors and material to hang over the walls. Nothing like having a cosy place to sit and read our comics in the light of an occasional sun-ray which found a crack in the wall to stream through.

Over the course of several months I was assigned to do all the jobs on the staff list. I loathed cleaning out the furnace room. Once in a while depending who was with me, we did get carried away painting our faces with soot so that we looked like one of the Indians in last Saturday's State serial. I liked to work in the veggie garden, carefully weeding the carrots and radishes and munching on a few which always seemed to dislodge themselves in our fingers. I avoided the silver-beet like crazy because if there was ever a food which repulsed me, it was that particular green. The cream-shed job I liked also because it was done quickly and into the bargain I was able to scoop two fingers of thick cream off the top of the bowl as I switched off the light on the way out the door.

Cleaning out the cowshed was one of the best jobs even though it was the muckiest of tasks. It had to be done daily and under the watchful eyes of Gordon Stretch or, Stretchy, as we referred to him if he was in a particularly cranky mood. He seemed older to me than even Jim Palmer or Frank Bickerton and those guys were ancient. Stretchy kept his distance from us young kids and I often wondered if we did things to make him angry at us because there were times when his red hair was redder than usual. He was a good bloke though, mostly friendly and kind to us.

Jim on the other hand was always friendly and smiling. He had taken on the role of extra staff-member it seemed and was often rounding us up for this job or that. Jim was great at organizing fun things to do. You could play jokes and tricks on Jim whereas that was out of the question with Stretchy because you were never sure what mood he might be in. On any given day

Stretchy was often milking the cows. With him there we knew that the clean-up job we had been assigned to had to be done well. If he was in his playful mood with a group of us younger boys in the shed flicking cow-dung at each other, he squirted the hose at our legs when we were not looking or were chasing the cows out for the evening. It was nothing but fun. Work was never going to be this good again for any of us.

"For goodness-sake Kevin Davies, use the stick to hold the clothes then you won't burn your hands," said Pommy back at the copper kettle in the laundry.

There was no time for dreaming about wood piles, hut building or cowsheds when you were assigned to the laundry. Concentration was needed and Pommy made sure we remained focused.

"I'll do that job, Kev," yelled Warren, "if you come and hang these clothes on the line."

"No thanks, Warren old pal," I said. "I think I'll just keep burning my hands."

"Tell you what Kev, I'll do the copper kettle job twice for ya if you just hang these clothes out once."

"Make it four times and I might consider it mate," I grinned.

"Jeez Kev, that's not…"

Just then Bobby burst into the laundry. "E tama Ms Pomeroi, come here quick, Carl's hurt himself. Badly too. His arm's pukeru."

We flew into the mangle-room to see an obviously upset Carl stuck in a jam by the largest mangle with his arm outstretched.

My first reaction was to reach out to Carl, to help. Probably not the wisest action under the circumstances.

"Better not touch him eh, Kev," said Bobby. "He's got his arm stuck in there. Might do more damage mate."

I wanted to help Carl because I felt how painful this must be for him. But I was afraid to touch him in case something went wrong. I knew we had to hurry.

Pretty soon a couple of the senior kids arrived, fiddled around with the gears on the mangle, and somehow released the two huge wooden rollers. Bobby supported Carl under his other arm. He screamed as he was moved.

"Broken arm I figure," said Jim Palmer. Jim, one of the oldest kids in the Home, was someone we all looked up to. He seemed to have an explanation for everything. I don't know if he really knew as much as I thought he did, but most of us paid attention when he was around.

"Poor bloke. Must hurt," said Jim. "Hang on Carl mate, we're here to help."

Quite a few tears and screams later, and a sling in place, Carl was helped over to a bench just outside the laundry room to rest and wait.

"How did it happen?" Jim asked Bobby.

"Me and Carl was putting the sheets through the mangles and he started skiting, saying he could put his hand in between the two rollers on the small mangle. He said he was tough and could stand a lot of pain. I said he was crazy if he did that. But he did it anyway."

"What do you mean he did it anyway?" asked Jim.

"He let his hand go in all the way with one of the sheets and then he just grinned at me and said, "See Parata, that's how tough I am! I told him to stop or he'd have a hand like my nose, flat and wide."

"What happened next?"

"I dunno exactly," said Bobby, "but I was turning the handle on the big mangle and Carl was supposed to be feeding the sheets in when I felt the mangle tighten. I looked up and Carl had half his arm stuck in between the rollers. I guess the small mangle was peanuts for him and he was keen to try his luck in the big one. E hoa Jim, that's when I ran for help. *You're a bloody fool, Carl Newman,'* is what I told him but he did it and I'm still not impressed. What's going to happen?"

"He'll have to go to the hospital to get his arm in a cast. I'm pretty sure that it's broken."

"Broken? Jeez! Tough job this, doing the laundry!" said Bobby. "If I knew he would've done that I would have told him to turn the handle while I fed the sheets in. But you know our boy Carl."

"What d'you think Ms Pomeroi?" asked Jim. Pommy was pretty good at keeping an eye out for us when we worked in the laundry. She knew there were many situations where any of us could get injured. Simply by not paying attention to the hot water, the fire in the copper and the big mangles, we could do some damage to ourselves. If it wasn't Pommy, there was always staff about in the laundry.

"The doctor will definitely have to get Carl to the hospital to take a look at it that's for sure," said Pommy. "Jim, I'm going to wait for the doctor, so will you organise some kids to help bring Carl over to the front room? Be very careful with him though."

This incident had put us all in a serious mood which seemed to make work go faster. Before I knew it, I was out of the laundry and had wandered around the back near the furnace room. I looked for a place by myself because at times like these I needed some space away from other kids, to calm myself, to breathe and bring my feet back to ground. The sun was warm as I sat in it and began quietly daydreaming. I often slipped into this mode as if it was my way of dealing with the stress of living in such a large and active family. I never felt it unusual to go to a favourite place where I knew I could be alone.

My mind flipped to my dream I often had. *In a place where nobody else goes and at a time when few other people are about, I begin to dig into the ground. I work furiously to get below the surface and pretty soon I have shaped out an entrance to what will be my underground house. The plans are clear as I excavate deeper. There will be two rooms: one for working, reading and living in, and one for sleeping. Above ground there is a walnut tree that will help feed me. It is also a great tree to climb for fun when I emerge from my house. Each time I dream, I'm either in my house or working on it. There are colourful rugs on the floor, furniture set about and paintings hanging on every wall. As I sit in my green armchair I notice how quiet it is. I'm never lonely or bored. My underground house is very comfortable. There's often music coming from my radio and steam from the kettle on my stove. I love to sit back with a cup of tea on a quiet afternoon, reading or daydreaming in my chair.*

In my underground house I am safe from all the challenges of the world. I work hard to keep it clean. Often, it feels like my home is inside of me sometimes as much as I am inside of it. I am reminded of it and taken back to my special place through the dream. It is where I go to gather my thoughts, to be away from people and feel my real self. My house is my place of solitude. Nobody has come to visit me but I feel fine about that because I really do want to keep it a secret and that's why I built it underground. When I want company, I go out and visit people or meet them somewhere away from my house.

In contrast to my daily routines at the Home, none of these demands exist in my dream home. Fernsy or Mum or Pommy are not chasing after me to be on time for this or that. I'm not banging into kids constantly whenever I turn a corner. I don't have to eat in the dining room with 30 other boys and I don't have to sleep in a dormitory with other noisy kids. I can retreat and be quiet; sit alone, reading my comic, sipping my cup of tea.

Bobby and Warren had now finished in the laundry and joined me in the sun.

"Where's Party?" asked Warren.

"Probably doggin' it from the veggie garden this morning," said Bobby. "Party don't like all that weeding. He has trouble telling the veggies from the weeds."

"I bet he wouldn't if he had to eat weeds," I said.

Just then Party turned the corner by the furnace and joined us.

"Thank God that's done," he said.

"Eat any radishes?" Bobby asked. "Or did you dig them out thinking they were weeds?"

"Radishes! Which ones are they?" he grinned.

We sat quietly now, staring ahead of us, not talking, not thinking. The warm sun streaming onto the back steps of the furnace room calmed us. Saturday chores sometimes had the effect of numbing the brain. It was easy to 'zone-out'. But soon Warren piped up and before long he was talking about the movies.

When there were no huts to keep us occupied, no firewood to put away and no more jobs to do, we were allowed the luxury of leaving the Home on a Saturday to visit one of the movie theatres in Onehunga, the State and the Roxy. The Roxy had the occasional movie that attracted our attention but mostly it was boring with nothing we wanted to see, or the theater staff decided they didn't want to tolerate hoards of boys acting up on a Saturday afternoon. The State however, where we went most often, welcomed us and showed a regular Saturday afternoon matinee often screening: Tom Mix, Roy Rogers, The Three Stooges, The

Marx Brothers and The Lone Ranger. The serials were particular favourites, Rin Tin Tin especially and so was Lassie. And what's more they had a cartoon to open the show.

Roy Rogers - how we loved Trigger his horse and sang along with Roy as he rode the trail, "Git along little doggie". There was The Lone Ranger, "Me Tonto, him Lone Ranger. Tonto help 'Kimo Sabe' catch bad guys. Tonto track them in desert!" - pulled us in to see what bad guys he would be capturing next. And Tom Mix, with his slick, tough ways, was always able to outwit the outlaws and defeat whole tribes of fierce and savage Indians. In those days along with Tom and Roy we figured it was ok to kill off as many 'Injuns' as possible, especially if they had just attacked an innocent wagon train or a settlers' ranch house, which they seemed to be doing all the time.

Hollywood movies were full of racial stereotyping and not-so subtle prejudice. This reflected their society according to them and they served up the images regularly to reinforce those divisions. America was a racially divided country then and compared to New Zealand, still is today. The 'melting pot' image they have of themselves is perhaps a false one in terms of the genuine integration of racial groups. Hollywood has always been a leader in depicting, but also exploiting, the racial divisions that really exist. Even though we relished a regular dose of these movies, their subtle messages never seemed to seep through to damage our community at the Home.

No doubt we fell into the Hollywood trap from time to time without thinking about it. Our own tribes of Iroquois and Seminole 'Injuns' back at the Home, in our play times, acted out from time to time on the front lawn attacking each other and unsuspecting white-folks. But, even though there were Maori kids and the Lee brothers among us, we didn't think in terms of what was just or unjust when it came to the movies. No problems seemed to arise later from watching this stuff. It was simply us Home Kids and whoever the hero of the week was, against all the savage Apaches, Commanches or the featured 'bad guys' in the latest serial. Home kids were always on the same side. The movies were pure entertainment and on the walk home after the show, we diffused the stereotypes we had seen by retelling the stories. The lack of any conscious dividing lines between us kids, contrasted with the obvious racial divisions perpetrated in the Hollywood fare of the week. Our sense of commaraderie and family helped to keep those kinds of divisions at bay.

It cost us 5 cents to get in to the State - sixpence in those days. That was a lot of money and often we didn't have it. So, unknown to the staff at The Home, we would get permission to go to the matinee, some of us without money, and sneak in by joining a group of people streaming past the ticket-man at the door. Sometimes, if we had money, we kept our sixpence back, sneaked in anyway and bought some Jaffas or an ice-cream at half-time. Some kids never had money to buy anything to eat in the pictures but we all shared what we had. A Jaffa, stuck into the top of the ice-cream changed the colour and added to the taste we savoured for as long as we could. Then, often in the middle of the weekly serial, or even as early as the opening cartoon, some kid would drop a Jaffa onto the floor. It would roll down the incline all the way to the front making a rattling noise as it did.

The whole theatre held its breath and kept silent as we waited for the smack into the wall at the end of the orange-chocolate ball's roll. It never failed. A small cheer went up every time this happened, just like it did every time Bugs Bunny signed off his cartoon with, "that's all folks!"

Warren's movie talk was still buzzing in my head even after I had walked down to the cowshed. Barely past the concrete apron of where the cows came in to be milked, I heard Bobby call out from the gate, "Hey Kev, Carl's back from the hospital. Let's go and see him."

Party and Warren were still hanging around the furnace room when I got there so the four of us trudged off to visit Carl in the sick-bay.

"Is he alright Bobby?" I asked.

"Dunno mate, haven't seen him yet."

My Mum, was in the sick-bay with Carl. He was looking pretty pale. Even so, the stack of three new-looking comics on the side table did not escape our attention.

"Come on boys, come in and say hello to your friend Carl."

"Hey Carl," I said, "you're back early. Are you ok?"

He was lying back, his head on the pillow and he mumbled something about "cast." He pulled his arm out from under the sheet and showed us the biggest cast we had ever seen. Carl's arm was covered in white plaster from his shoulder to his fingers.

"E hoa Carl they sure wrapped you up," said Bobby.

"Does it hurt?" asked Party.

"My brother had a cast like that but it was on his leg," said Warren.

"How long will you have it on for Carl?" I asked.

"Two months," he mumbled groggily.

"Two months! E hoa mate," said Bobby, reaching over the bed. "I guess you won't be needing these comics then. You'll be in too much pain to read."

Carl protested with a quiet whine but managed a grin as well.

"Two months? You're not going to have to do jobs for two months?" asked Bobby, "Jeez, you blokes, lets get out of here and back to the big mangle in the laundry. I've got a plan."

We turned to leave. It had already been a long day especially for Carl. But he pulled us back with a whimper. He pointed to his cast with his other hand which held a pen.

"Oh boys," said Mum. "he wants his friends to be the first to sign his brand new white cast. The nurse said it was alright to do. Come on then don't be shy. Who's going first?"

"Sure Carl, we can do that for you," said Bobby. "Kev, you go first."

I wrote, *"See you on the footy field in two months Carl."*

Warren wrote, *"Remember this: hanging clothes on the line is safer than using the mangle.....Carl!"*

Party grinned and asked, "How do I spell freezing shower," before he wrote, *"You lucky dog Carl. You don't have to take a freezing shower in the morning."*

"My turn now, mates," said Bobby as he grabbed the pen and printed in big letters down the length of Carl's cast just one word, *"SLACKER!"*

We laughed. Carl protested and Bobby pushed us all toward the door,

"Come on mates," he said. "let's get over to the mangle room and I'll show you how our boy Carl managed to work his way out of jobs for two months. Maybe you could try it Warren, then you wouldn't have to hang all those clothes on the line. Save you burning your fingers too Kev," he added.

Laughing and walking out of the sick bay, Bobby threw over his shoulder, "I guess I'll have to make your bed and help you wash in the morning Carl mate. Maybe even feed you porridge at breakfast. Us mangle operators and laundry workers gotta help each other out!"

Big Game in The Paddock

The ball bounced in front of me, hit me on the head and somehow landed in my arms. I ran along the goal line towards the right hand touch.

"Kick it Kevin, kick it!"

"Boot the bloody thing out, Davies. Where're you running to?"

I dropped the ball to my foot, kicked it with all my strength and watched as it sailed over the touch-line.

Not bad for an 8 year old, I thought.

"Thank Christ for that," yelled Winston Jones. "Finally it's out!"

"Shut up Winnie, " said Mick Toogood, "Leave Davies alone. He might be small but he's fast!"

I loved playing footy in the paddock with all the other kids , which we did regularly in the winter months. Winston 'Winnie' Jones was older than me and he was a tough nut. I was a bit afraid of him but didn't worry too much because he wasn't in my circle of friends. Micky Toogood was like his name, a good guy. He was older than Winnie and stuck up for us younger kids.

All it took to get a game going was for Frank Bickerton or one of the other big kids to walk around calling out "Footy game on the field in 10 minutes. Be there if you want to be in a team." I may have been one of the smallest kids at the time but I was one of the first to line up and wait for Frank and others to pick the teams and get the game started. We loved a rugby game which was no surprise, growing up in New Zealand as we did. At least once during the week after school in the season, we were out on the paddock playing. Sometimes, if not enough kids turned up for a full game, we spent the time kicking to each other, practicing passing and tackling. On Saturday mornings though, after our jobs were done, the numbers were always there for two teams to have a good game. It was a ritual we looked forward to regularly, our Winter Saturday game. Being at the Home was like being in a club, a great situation for young guys like myself to learn the basics of rugby and to constantly test one's courage and skill and to have tons of fun into the bargain.

When I was a bit smaller, about 7 going on 8, all the other kids seemed so big to me. Because I had grown to know them I wasn't afraid to get right into the game and tackle, or at least attempt my version of one. It was just like playing with brothers in a big family.

Mathew, Me & Barry

As I got older and my skills developed along with my muscles and strength, I could run, pass, kick and tackle with them all. Whenever there was a game on, I was there, competitive yes, but always looking for a good time full of fun. Winning at anything, especially footy, was never my primary concern. I loved to play and be part of the pushing and shoving and the "take that you bugger," and the "run, for God's sake, run!" and all the other comments thrown in for good measure and the praise from older kids and those better than me. Playing footy with the kids at 109 was as good as sledding down One Tree Hill or swinging like Tarzan in the trees at the front of the Home.

One Saturday, we had a plan to go up One Tree Hill for some sledding, but it was raining when we got up in the morning and it didn't look like easing off. At breakfast Frank announced that One Tree Hill was off and all those who wanted to play footy should be down in the paddock at 1 o'clock just after lunch.

"Only if you've finished your jobs though," he added.

Some of us were talking about going to the pictures but when footy was mentioned that plan was quickly shelved. Any chance to wear one of the jerseys that the Home kept for games was not to be missed. When we put on that jersey, as old and tattered as it usually was, you would have thought we had just been selected to the All Blacks. Pride was on every boy's face.

"Wear an old pair of footy shorts," Frank warned, it's gonna be muddy."

We split into teams and pulled on the jerseys, which had been dumped out of the two canvas bags they were kept in. I looked at Robin and grinned because we were wearing the blue and white hooped jerseys of our favourite team, Auckland. Barry kicked off and the game began. Gordon Stretch took the ball on the full...*heck, I'm glad I'm on Stretchy's team,* I thought...and ran hard into the opposition. He was a big kid with big muscles and fierce red hair. After a ferocious ruck the ball came out and was passed along our backline. I got it, ran a couple of yards and then passed onto Warren 'run like a hare' Francis, and yelled, "Go, mate, go!" He tried to swerve around Dave Porter but Dave had his number and decked him with a good tackle around the legs. Warren went down, the ball popped loose and landed 'thwack' right in the middle of a large moist cow-pie, recently dropped by Daisy or Millie or any of the cows that grazed in our paddock.

"Aww shit!" yelled half a dozen kids.

"I don't care," yelled Bobby Parata as he bent down and scooped up the ball that was now almost completely covered in cow dung. Bobby took off to half way and just as Robin Partridge was going to tackle him he dumped the ball onto Party's head. I'm pretty sure he just faked doing it, but because it was raining and the cow dung was particularly slimy, it just shot out of his hand and on to Party.

"Parata, you bugger!" yelled Gordon. Party was a favourite of Stretchy's and he felt a certain responsibility to defend him.

"Only a bit of cow dung, Party," said Bobby. "It's all clean grass anyway. Won't hurt. Just a bit of a stink, but nothing anyone would notice coming from you."

"Won't hurt eh, Parata?" said Party as he scooped a big blob off the side of his head and flung it right at Bobby's face. "Try this then!"

That was all it took. All of us younger kids ran to the nearest cow pie, scooped up a handful of dung, and started throwing it at one or another member of the opposing team. Cow dung was flying everywhere. The rain shower, which had settled soon after we started the game, had made the dung quite sloppy and some of it stuck where it landed. The best cow pies were the ones that had dried a bit on the top before the rain. When you picked them up you kept your hand clean but underneath it was slimy and wet. The game came to a standstill with the older kids trying to break us up, but by now we were too much into the battle. It was both horrible and fun. I was laughing as I copped one wet piece just below my eye. I threw a good one back at Jim, he ducked and it hit Les Allen right in his chest. Les, one of the older kids, was a bit hard to read at times, unlike Stretchy, Jim Palmer or Mathew Lowen. He was friendly enough but didn't suffer fools easily and when he copped the cow pie I threw, it was like 'the shit that broke the cow's bum'; sort of sent things over the top, if you know what I mean.

Well that did it!

"Ok you little twerps" yelled Les. "I've had it, fair and square and I'm not taking it any more. Davies, get over here!"

"Sorry Les, sorry," I said, "but I was aiming at Jim and he ducked."

Looking at Les I could hardly keep from laughing but he looked pretty fierce so I kept saying I was sorry. Jim of course had a large grin on his face. So did many of the other kids.

"Too bad for you, little Davies," said Les who now held me by my collar. He smeared the dung from his chest onto my cheek as I pulled away to lots of "awww's " from the other kids.

"That's enough you little buggers," said Stretchy. "If you want to keep throwing cow-pies go over by the cow sheds, there's plenty of big steamy ones there."

"Yeah, lets get on with the game," said Frank as we walked back to our own end of the field. "Barry, you kick off again at half way."

Barry placed the ball, looked downfield, stepped back a couple of paces and kicked a high ball to re-start the game. I was proud that my brother was always chosen to take the kick-offs in games. He often spent time on his own practicing. If Barry liked an activity and he wanted to increase his skill, he would invest time working on himself to improve. This was his solo time he loved as if he'd found that having others around was only distraction. So now, when it counted, Barry kicked a high accurate ball which gave his team a chance to get downfield and pressure the opposition.

Suddenly we were back in the thick of our game having got the inevitable cow-pie fight over and done with early. In all our games, if the score was too lopsided, one or more of the big kids changed sides to help the losers out a bit. This time it was Jim Palmer who I regarded as an adult because he was tall and had to shave. He crossed over to our side to a few cheers. Jim tore his way off the back of our scrum, and with the ball tucked under his arm he fended off a tackle from Bobby Parata, and charged down the short side of the field. Since he had changed to our team I kept fairly close to him because I thought it wouldn't be long before he got the ball and did something tricky and I wanted to be in the right place when he did.

So there I was, on the outside of Jim, straining to keep up, watching him fly past man after man in the opposition. He side-stepped Alister and had only Hongi to beat. I could see that he was going to score. Jim ran straight at Hongi, and yelled, "hey Kevin, come on, here it comes," as he flipped me the ball. I was at top speed, level with Jim. I ran onto the ball and charged for the line up ahead. My little legs hit the ground faster than they ever had before and they needed to because looming up behind me was Hongi Wihaapi who could run as fast as a wild pig and tackle as well as any All Black. He was fearless and he was about to level me.

One Tree Hill

"You better scoot, Davies," he yelled, "cause I'm gonna flatten you!"

But the line was close now and I scooted as fast as I could, diving to score just as Hongi hit me. We rolled over and slid a few feet and as we did I forced the ball down. Hongi lay on top of me with his full weight bearing down. Behind us a loud cheer erupted.

"He got it. That's a try! You little beauty, Davies. Score's now 13 - 11 to us. Come on boys, we can beat those buggers!"

I got up out of Hongi's tackle, brushed off some dirt and a smear of cow-dung, and walked proudly back to my team at halfway.

"Good stuff Kev, you showed 'em how it's done!" said Warren.

"Nice going little fella," said Jim Palmer as he walked past and ruffled my hair. "I like being on your team, mate. Best bit of support play I've ever seen."

"Watch out Barry, your little brother's getting to be faster than you!" yelled another kid.

As I turned to watch the other team kick off I felt proud of scoring. The compliments rang in my ear and a grin came over my face. From up the field my brother Barry gave me a 'thumbs-up' signal. Even Hongi was grinning at me. I would dream about this try for days afterwards.

It had been over an hour now since Frank had whistled the start of this footy game and even as the ball was being retrieved by Henry Lee after being booted out, Frank said, "that's it kids. One hour's up. That's the end of this one." Even though my try had put our team ahead at the time, we finished the game three points behind. With a sinking feeling, we watched as Barry casually landed a long range penalty kick from a sharp angle that put his team in the lead.

"Nice one Barry," said Frank Bickerton, "and right on time too. Where'd you learn to kick like that?"

Barry loved footy as much as I did, or any of the other kids for that matter. He had great skills and could run fast like I could only wish for. I always imagined that he would become an All Black. When he went to Otahuhu College he played in the same team as Mackie Herewini who was already developing a reputation as a young bloke with a future in the game. Later, when I was older, Mac was selected for the All Blacks and became a star. He could run and kick better than anyone and he was so fast and tricky that opposition players often didn't know what he would do next. I loved watching him play because he seemed like a master to me, so confident and fluid. He could do anything on the field with the ball in hand. Often, when I watched, I would remind myself that Barry was a team mate of Mac's. Sometimes I told others about this and felt immensely proud.

One time I went to Kilbirnie Park in Wellington to watch Barry play. He was easily the best back on the field running fast and smooth and always breaking a gap or two. He set up a couple of tries and scored one himself. Then he kicked the goals. His tackling was sure and hard. Not once did his opposite number get through because Barry was up on him early and flattened him with a good tackle. I thought he was brilliant and told him so after the game.

"You're a good player brother," I said. "Keep playing like that and you'll make the reps."

"Don't know about that mate," he said. "I'm not good enough for that level. Don't really care either. Playing for this team is good enough for me."

I couldn't believe he would sell himself short like this. After watching Barry, I could see that he was a better all around player than I could hope to be. What impressed me most though, was his ability to beat a man when he had the ball. I wished I had that kind of confidence. Barry was a good player to watch because when the ball came to him, there was always something on.

He never let praise get to him, shrugging it off and grinning. Rugby was just a game to him, to enjoy and have fun at. He was able to put it in its proper place and not let it take over too much space or intrude into his personal time. It was a game no more important than his job or his social activities. Even though I was sure he could become a good rep player, I felt good that he had this self assuredness about keeping the game where he could manage it.

The game now over, we walked off the field to the sideline where the canvas bags were. There was a lot of kidding among us. The game had been hard but it had been fun. Some kids who resented a particularly aggressive tackle laid on them, or even a large cow pie blob thrown when they were'nt looking, had to get over their resentment and leave their grudges behind on the field.

In this way we all learned about life I guess. There was a time and a place for everything and some things you didn't like were better left behind so that they didn't get in the way later. Life and friendships would go on and we knew this more and more as we grew older.

I took my jersey off, walked off the field and put it into the bag with the other dirty ones. I felt good about myself. By the time I reached the gate I had forgotten the score but not the action and the fun. For sure I would dream like I had before and like lots of New Zealand kids did, imagining myself scoring a try for the All Blacks and hearing the crowd cheering loudly. The Saturday footy game was a highlight of the week during the winter season and for 30 boys was the best activity to work up an appetite for dinner. More importantly it drew us further together as a group, the old and young kids, and helped to encourage the respect we had for each other.

The Front Room

I was sitting in the old comfortable chair over by the windows reading the latest Phantom comic and enjoying the early morning sun warm against my back. The windows were up and Henry Lee was on the wide ledge while his younger brother Norman was kneeling on a bench beside the table leaning on his elbow, with his head firmly into his own comic. Several other kids were scattered throughout the Front Room reading, writing, some doing last week's homework, and others at their lockers shuffling through the collections of personal treasures. Bobby Parata peered in from the dining room and walked toward the windows.

"Cut it out, Parata," barked Carl.

"E Hoa, what did I do?" said Bobby innocently.

"Keep your bloody big feet to yourself, Parata," whined Carl. "you're always kicking me or treading on my feet. Leave me alone will ya?"

We all looked up. There was Carl going on about something again. It was only Wednesday last week that we had walked into the Front Room after dinner listening to Carl bawling away and accusing someone of having broken into his camp box and taking his latest Blackhawk comic.

"You took it Parata, I know you did," he had wailed.

"Why would I take your comic, Carl," smiled Bobby, "when I know you always write your name in big red letters all over the cover so everybody will know it's yours? You think I'm that stupid?"

"Well one of you lot took it, I know. It's not here and-"

"Ah, shut up Newman, you're always complaining about something," snarled Les Allen with some authority. "Take a look at the size of the lock on your camp box. Do you really think anybody's gonna break into that?"

"Well it was here." Carl droned on while one by one we ignored him and went back to our own stuff.

Camp boxes were an important part of life in the Home, and Carl wasn't the only one to have his heavily protected by a big shiny chrome lock that some family member had bought for him. Each of us took some care keeping our boxes locked so that the contents would be safely out of sight and out of mind, if you know what I mean. With all the usual 'camp' stuff inside as well as personal treasure, you couldn't be too careful. The camp box was a kind of symbol, a large talisman, which served to remind us of all the fun and excitement that lay ahead in the year. Years before I got there somebody had made a box and started a tradition of collecting comics, chewy things and shiny stuff to store away so that they could be had up at Camp during the Christmas holidays. Sometimes generous relatives brought along sweets on visiting days that were often stored away. Pieces of string, lead weights to be used as sinkers for the fishing line and a prized pocket knife received as a birthday gift that year all found their way into the box. Boys are notorious for hoarding away found-objects, which often become personal treasures especially when someone remarks, "what the heck are you keeping that junk for? You'll never use that!"

The greatest value of the camp box was that it really did remind us that the fun times at camp were up ahead at the end of the year. When times sometimes got tough at school or in some other personal way, there was always the box sitting there when you opened your locker to remind you that the very best time of your life was coming. With that awareness we were all helped to get through the challenges.

At Christmas time, the Home shut down and the Home kids spent a glorious six weeks up at our Mahurangi Heads Camp. Camp boxes were built during the year, some sturdier than others, some hold-overs from past years and some brand new. When I was just a really young kid I grabbed whatever box I could find and put stuff in it and didn't care that it wasn't locked. But when I was about 8 I wanted a new box, so I did what most kids did and built my own. I used solid pine wood and had a half-hinged top with a shiny hasp screwed on so I could attach my lock to it. I painted it dark brown and brushed my name on the top in the bright yellow paint that Mathew Lowen had given me. On days when I lifted my box out onto the table I could see the yellow letters of my name from way up the end of the Front Room. And hanging from the hasp was my new shiny brass 'Acme' lock, which Mum had bought me for my last birthday.

Camp boxes were a source of pride and excitement and the treasures within were sacred. We never had much in the way of personal property and that's why the boxes took on such importance in our minds. In some cases they contained all that a kid owned. During the year they gradually became full of precious things. There was a respect for the boxes and what they stood for. I never thought much about anybody breaking into mine. I only cared about what I had in there, constantly going over all the things in my mind in anticipation of going to camp at Christmas time. My double-bubble from my Aunt and Uncle in America was in there. The occasional Mackintosh's toffee bar sat flat on the bottom. Comics, especially my favourite 'The Phantom', a new pencil, a drawing pad, chewing gum, a shiny new pocket knife with a wooden handle, which I imagined was from my Father, were in there too. Two books that my Mother had given me, 'Wind in the Willows' and 'William Joins The Football Club', lay on the top where I could see them. My magic rock I had found the last time we walked to Scott's Beach to dig pipis, was sitting snug in one corner right next to the bird I had carved from an old piece of kahikatea I had picked up on the path down to the beach at camp last year.

Best of all though, stuffed away in the back of the box, was my fishing line with brand new string that my friend Warren had got from his brother one weekend when he was out visiting him. I had it wrapped around a stick that I had carved especially and I had proudly wound it in the style that my Uncle Max had taught me the last time I had seen him in Wellington.

"That's how all the real fishermen do it, Kev," he'd said.

I planned to get some hooks and a sinker from somewhere later in the year to make it into a real line ready to catch sprats and maybe a legendary snapper once we were settled in at camp. I could hardly wait to get there.

In reality though, the Camp at Mahurangi was a fairly scrubby place with a rocky shore and quite an unattractive outlook. But in our minds it was an idyllic seaside resort offering all the excitement of the best holiday place any kid could go to. All we needed were the basics like good food, sunshine, a bunk to sleep in, and a good fishing line. Apart from those and whatever we had stored in our boxes during the year, there was no need for anything else other than the comradeship and good company found among a group of boys all intent of having a holiday of fun. Camp was legendary among all the kids at the Home.

The Front Room Opened Onto Trees, Lawn & Garden

The sun in the Front Room was becoming warmer now and I was well into my comic. The Phantom had just finished rounding up the last of the crooks who had stolen the treasure out of the jungle temple, so I rolled my comic up and returned it to my locker. I joined Henry on the window ledge in the sun. He had a chunk of plasticine and was fashioning from it, little dishes, bowls and boxes into which he was putting flies that he had caught on the window and then laying over a small plasticine lid to keep them captive. Sometimes, instead of a whole lid he

159

would simply lay a thin strip over the fly so it was trapped and couldn't escape. The ones he had finished he put aside in the sun before making the next one.

"What the heck are you up to Henry?" I asked.

"I am trapping flies Kevin, and putting them in prison," explained Henry. He had a very precise way of speaking.

"Prison? What the heck for?" I asked.

"Oh, you just watch Kevin," he said without looking at me.

I turned my eyes to his little prisons and after a while I understood, although not entirely approving. I didn't like needlessly killing insects, crabs, or any animals including 'dirty' flies. But my fascination with what Henry was doing prompted me not to say anything. The sun on the plasticine was hot enough to melt it slowly. Already in the first bowl I could see that the lid had buckled and caved in trapping the fly inside in a bed of liquid, making it impossible for it to get away although it was struggling fiercely. Pretty soon it's wings stopped beating and its legs stopped wriggling as the molten plasticine spread over its tiny body. The dish next to it had the same thing happening and the fly in this one already had its head covered and was not moving.

"I get it Henry, you want to kill these flies. I guess you don't like flies eh?"

"I hate flies Kevin. They are dirty and they carry disease. Flies deserve to die."

"There's hundreds of flies Henry, probably thousands, so I don't think you're going to get rid of many," I observed.

"Oh yes I will. I have killed dozens already this morning and I am determined to keep going for a while yet."

I touched some of the hot plasticine and it stuck to my finger.

"That's hot stuff Henry," I said.

"I figured out that it has to be hot enough to melt and today is a good day for that," he said. "The temperature is just right, and here on this window-sill it is hotter than anywhere else. Probably 30 degrees this early. That is hot!"

For a moment I hesitated and then I said, "Don't you think it's a bit cruel Henry, killing flies in melting plasticine? They don't have a chance, and it must hurt like crazy."

"Oh, that is the whole idea Kevin," said Henry. "Flies are dirty. They carry diseases. They need to be wiped out. And I have decided to help in their extermination!"

Over on the big table, Henry's younger brother Norman Lee, had taken his stamp album out and was flipping pages over and talking excitedly about his collection. Simon Gear and Dave Porter had their heads crowded in. Carl, Warren, Bobby and a few other kids were on the outside of the group. I loved stamps and Norman had a great collection. How a kid so small as Norman could have a collection this good was a mystery to me.

"This is the one-penny Queen of England," he explained in the same precise language as his brother, "and this is the one-penny emu from Australia. On this page is my Mauritius collection that I got for my birthday last year from Uncle Chou."

"Chew-mew-who's-chew?" blurted Carl.

"Shut up, Carl. Hey Norman, where's Mauritius?" I asked.

"Oh, Mauritius is a group of Islands off the east coast of Africa, Kevin. They are way out in the Indian Ocean, a long way from Madagascar."

"Madagascar? What kinda car is that?" joked Party who had just joined us.

"Why do they have such great stamps Norm?" I asked.

"Well, Uncle Chou told me that to make some money for their country they decided to print attractive stamps like this so that lots of people would buy them. Collectors are always looking. There are many more countries in the world printing fancy stamps now so they can make money too. Hungary is one. You should see theirs. I have some." He flipped to a double page of huge stamps with brightly coloured painted flowers and with 'Myagar' printed on them in large letters. But the strange thing, which brought out lots of "oohs" and "ahhs", was that the stamps were all different shapes. Not the usual squares or rectangles, but long thin rectangles, circles, triangles and even one in the shape of an 'H'.

"Jeez, these are great," I said, "look at the size of them! But I still like the ones from Mauritius though, Norm," I reached out to flip back to that page. "Look at that turtle, and that shark, they look like they're coming right out at you."

"That is called 3-dimensional drawing, Kevin," explained Norman.

"How does he know all this stuff?" whispered Party.

"You know he's a brain-box. Both the Lees are!" whispered Warren right back.

We craned over Norman's shoulder to get a better look.

"They look real," said Warren, "wish I could draw like that. Hey Kev, you can draw like that."

"Not as good," I said.

I thought about my drawing and especially the panther I was working on. I kept my drawing pad under my bed and took it out now and again to work on whatever was occupying my attention. I didn't want kids seeing what I was drawing until it was finished. I didn't know it was called 3-dimensional, but I had done a bit of shading. I knew that shading let you pull the image off the page. If you did it right it sort of popped out at you. At least that's what my teacher had told me and after practising, I was beginning to get it.

"Hey. Partridge, Francis, come here you kids. Davies, never mind getting your drawing pad, come over here," called Mathew Lowen from the windows. "I bet you can't beat me at car spotting."

"Bet we can Mathew," I said as we hurried over. "You're getting older and you can't see so well any more."

"Cheeky bugger," said Mathew, but softly, so I knew he didn't mean it in a nasty way. I liked Mathew. He was nice to me like he was nice to all of us younger kids. He sometimes even played with us or gave us things that he had found. When the wood arrived each month, Mathew would be out in the paddock helping us build our huts. A few of the older kids did too, once in a while, but not many. Mathew seemed to like creating new things and I learned a lot from him. He was like a second big brother to me. He was well liked by the older kids too. And oh, he was a great footy player. He could run fast and swerve and tackle anyone, and then after the game he always came up to us small kids and told us that we were really good players which made us feel good.

"Alright geniuses, what's this car?" he said, bringing me back.

"Humber," I blurted.

"Vauxhall," said Party.

"You're all wrong," said Mathew, "It's a Hillman Minx, last year's model, 1949."

And he was right, as usual.

Whenever we played 'car-spotting' from the Front Room windows, Mathew beat everybody at recognizing the type of car that went by. From the windows to the road it was about 50 metres, the road being partially blocked by a hedge. But if you were quick, and Mathew was, you could see the car for a second or two as it drove past the front gate, which was always open. Somebody would yell "car" as one was spotted way over to the left coming down Mt Smart Road. All eyes were on it as it neared the open gate and then, "Plymouth, Austin, Vauxhall, Packard," was yelled out by one kid or another over the top of other voices. But if Mathew was in the game he would say something like, "you're all wrong, that was an Austin A-40," and then he would go on to teach us how he knew this. All cars had distinctive shapes, markings and stylings, with chrome pieces here and there. Mathew knew all of these recognisable signs at a glance and could tell in a second the make, model and year of the car.

We loved to play this game and especially with Mathew because we always learned new things. Some kids really wanted to know about cars but others like myself only gathered for the game because Mathew was good fun. The only other kid who possibly knew cars better than Mathew was my brother Barry. He could tell at a quick glance the make and model of every vehicle going by including motorcycles. I was always astonished at his knowledge and how fast he was. I'm sure Barry had even taught Mathew. We sometimes argued with Mathew, mainly because that in itself was fun, but we didn't question Barry. We learned early on that when it came to cars, Barry really knew his stuff.

"Motorcycle!" yelled Carl.

Then a few seconds later Warren blurted out, "BSA 250!"

"Wrongo," said Mathew, "it's a Velocette 150, 1947 model, import. Look at the box on the far side by the rider's leg, that's where the gear-shift is." Don't you short kids know anything?"

After dinner on Wednesdays, but only in the winter months, I hurried through my dishes-duty and made sure I was back in the Front Room for the start of the 7 o'clock '1ZB Hit Parade.' For half an hour the disc-jockey worked his way through the ten hits from the week before until he announced, "and now, what you've all been waiting for, the #1 Hit Of This Week as picked by fans like you all around New Zealand.........."

"Oh Yeah, I bet #1's gonna be 'Rock Around The Clock' again," said Bobby Parata. "Guess who sings it Davies?"

"That's easy Bobby...... You!" I answered.

"E tama mate, I know I'm good...but, no, come on, really, who?" he asked again.

"Bobby Bill Haley," called Warren.

"and the.........?"

"Comets!" we all yelled at once.

"One, two, three o'clock, four o'clock rock. Five, six, seven o'clock, eight............"

It didn't take much to get us all singing this favourite, and as the top-spot neared we sang it out in anticipation of Bill Haley being crowned King again for the tenth week in a row.

I loved Wednesday nights listening to the Hit Parade. We were allowed to stay up and have a half hour of spontaneous craziness together. Only Pommy from the staff sat in with us and now and again we checked to see if she was tapping her feet or swaying with the rhythm which she usually was. Later, at bedtime, it took us all a while to settle down, especially Warren Francis who was a bit of a ham actor and had a good voice. He kept breaking out in "gonna rock around the clock tonight" making us all laugh and giggle and bringing in Pommy who threatened to stuff socks in our mouths if we didn't settle down and get to sleep.

"I wouldn't mind so much if some of you could hold a tune," she laughed. "Now, in case you've forgotten, Kevin Davies, Warren Francis, and you too Robin Partridge...and Bobby Parata, it's a school day tomorrow!" she said as she switched off the light.

Once every four months or so on a Saturday night we all crowded into the Front Room to watch a movie. Nobody missed this event and seats would go early after dinner was over. We were always in a festive mood after spending a day up One Tree Hill, or playing footy for Te Papapa Club, or just hanging out with the pigeons in the coops down in the paddock letting them fly out and watching them return home again. Some kids would have spent the day with relatives and were now glad to be somewhere that felt more relaxed and familiar than their often emotional family visits. A kind person from one benevolent group or another brought along a projector and a movie; anything from a Pirate Saga, to a Hopalong Cassidy Western, which had thirty kids whooping, "hi-ho Trigger," or hollering "heave-ho-me-hearties", for over an hour or so.

I had rushed in early on this occasion, partly because I had no after dinner jobs to do, but mostly because the movie of the night was 'Captains Courageous'. Whether on purpose or by accident they chose to show us this movie once a year so some of us had seen it a few times. I knew most of the script by heart and we all anticipated the action with rising cheers or forlorn moans. There was the Captain of his mighty ship sailing over the bounding-main, trading, fighting off pirates and seeing that his men stayed healthy and alive in the face of great odds. His men loved him, as they should, because he was a great Captain, and we all loved him for the same reason.

As the story moved on, there he was trying to save his vessel from crashing disastrously onto the sharp and jagged rocks, fighting the horrendous storm and being heroic in terrible conditions. I was drawn into the action and soon found myself on deck with the brave Captain watching in horror as he began to lose the fight for survival, even yelling "no, no, not the rocks!" as the waves swung the boat precariously close to a sharp and jagged outcropping. The Front Room fell silent. I looked around. Some kids had their faces covered. I saw Les Allen and Barry sitting stoically at the back taking the action in bravely as only older kids could. At that point the music changed to a sombre tone and once more my attention was riveted back on the Captain, my Captain.

In order to stay at the helm of the ship like all courageous Captains must do in a storm, he had lashed himself to the wheel stanchion with one end of the rope and to the main mast with the other. As the storm took over and the rocks struck the hull with a hideous ripping sound, men were hurled to their death or crushed under the weight of falling timber. A huge wave swept over the deck of the ship and snapped the main mast as if it was a matchstick, sweeping it, and all before it, off the side of the ship. I watched the tightening of the safety harness the Captain had tied around his waist. Startled moans went up around me as I drew in my breath in anticipation of the rope slicing into my Captain's body. It tightened with the incredible tension, and finally began its terrifying cut.

Cries went up all around me. Tears came into my eyes. I couldn't bear to watch the terrible death of my hero. Our Captain for the past hour or so, had just died in the most horrific way as he was trying to save his ship and his men right here in the Front Room. What horror! What tragedy! What sadness! It didn't matter how many times I had seen this same scene, my reactions were always the same. Captain Courageous was my hero and he was remembered by all of us for his incredible loyalty to his men and for his staggering bravery even when death took him savagely.

The music rose, the credits flashed on the screen, someone turned the lights on and pairs of hands went up to eyes. Heads everywhere turned aside.

"Davies, you were bawling! You were crying in the pictures. We could see you mate," said Bobby Parata with a grin.

There was no hiding it and I didn't even try to as I wiped away my tears of sadness, which came every time.

"Yeah, well Bobby, it's a sad story and he's a great captain," I said. "He's the sort of brave man I think my Dad was probably like," I added. I wanted to talk more about my father right then but it wasn't the right time.

"Alright then boys," said my mother, put all the chairs back before you go off to bed." As we left to go up to our dorms, I said quietly to Warren, "Mathew was crying too."

Billy Big Balls

Our paddock was two acres of grassed field where we grazed about a dozen cows at any time. In the middle there was a cowshed, painted dark red and big enough to milk five or six animals at once. A local farmer had sold the cows to the Home and the deal was that each year he also be allowed to run some sheep in the paddock which was good for him and good for us in that it kept the grass down and made our footy field good for running on even if we did have to dodge clumps of sheep shit. There was a chute on one side of the shed used by the farmer for loading his sheep onto the truck when he took them away. Off to the left side was a big cement trough filled with water for the cows to drink. As we became older the senior kids taught us how to milk cows properly by holding our whole hand around the teat and squeezing and pulling at the same time. Milking was sort of serious business at the Home especially as this was how we got all our milk and cream.

"Hey, if you want to know if the milk is pasteurized little Davies," said Gordon Stretch one day, "just come over here, mate."

I walked toward Stretchy who was sitting on his milking stool and bent down to take a look. The next minute a stream of milk shot across my face and out of the gate. It felt thick and warm.

"Oh yeah, Kev, it's parsteurized alright!" confirmed Gord.

I looked at him blankly.

"You know, Kev, past-eur-ized? Past-your-eyes!" he said with a grin.

I loved the cows. Even though I wasn't the age to be officially allowed to be on milking duty, I did learn to milk and if Stretchy or Matt Lowen were in the shed they let me have my turn. I even hung around later to help them carry up the heavy buckets of milk to the cream shed where it was poured into large oval stainless steel containers and allowed to sit covered overnight so that the cream would separate and lie thick on the top. When it was ready to be scooped off, it was ladled into bowls and served to us fresh each morning on top of our steaming hot porridge at breakfast time. With brown sugar to top it off, the warm porridge mixed with the fresh thick cream was simply delicious.

After that it was back to the cowshed to let the animals out, hose it down and sweep it clean of cow dung and dirt. At any milking time, the cow shed railings held several of us young kids waiting to see if the senior kids would let us in to try our hand on the stool. Sometimes if Stretchy was in a hurry because he had to go to footy practice or do his homework and couldn't let us milk, he would squirt streams from the cow's teat right toward us and into our open mouths. The taste of the warm milk right out of the cow was the best.

"You kids look just like young birds getting fed by their mothers," he'd say.

The day the bull arrived I ran from where we were building our latest hut in the paddock, jumped the fence and hung out near the gate. Some kids even sat on the gate but I kept a distance back preferring to be safe rather than sorry. The farmer who brought the bull in once a year had driven his truck through the bottom gate and was attempting to get him down the ramp and out onto the paddock.

"Come on Billy, get 'er movin'," said the Farmer.

"Yeah, come on Billy Boy, get your balls moving down that ramp," some kids called.

"Don't worry boys," said the farmer, "he knows what he's here for and once he gets a whiff of those cows he'll be down that ramp as fast as you can shout "Billy Big Balls!"

Finally, when Billy proved the farmer right and came bolting down the ramp, there was a huge noise. I felt afraid that the ramp would collapse, Billy would crash onto the ground, go completely crazy and charge at all of us crowded at the fence and spear me with one of his fearsome horns.

"There he is fellas," said the farmer, "he's down now and pretty soon he'll be rarin' to go. Mind you don't get in his way," he added winking at us.

Over the next few days I went to the fence to check on Billy and see what he was up to. The cows of course, had not taken one look in his direction and continued their daily munching of grass as if there was no danger posed by this three ton bundle of muscle and steam. I was scared of his huge bulk and couldn't figure out why the cows weren't just as afraid. After school on the Wednesday of Billy's first week in the cow paddock, I was there wondering what the heck his visit was all about when Colin and Carl joined me.

"Has he done any cows yet?" asked Colin.

"He hasn't chased any since I've been here," I replied.

"Come on Billy Big Balls," yelled Carl. "The cows are over there, why don'tcha go over and jump on one?"

"He'll get to them when he's ready," said Colin.

"Ready, for what?" I asked.

"Haven't you seen a bull jump a cow Kev?" asked Colin.

"I have," said Carl, "I've seen lots. I've seen bulls with weiner's so big........."

"Sure Carl, sure," said Colin. "Watch Billy for a while Kev, especially when he gets nearer the cows, we'll see some action."

"Ok," I said, unsure of what he meant but not letting on too much that I didn't have a clue what they were talking about. I sure wasn't going to show my ignorance of these matters in front of someone like Carl.

Well, I sort of knew what was going on but didn't admit it to myself or any one else. I admired Colin, with his air of confidence about farm animals and the daily goings on in the paddock. He seemed to know a lot, which probably came from having grown up on a farm before his Mom died and his Uncle placed him in the orphanage. Up to this point, even though my

Mum and I had spent a year on a farm in North Auckland before we were accepted into the Home, my knowledge of farm life in general had been pretty limited. Then again, it's entirely possible I was diverted away from dramatic intimate events like these because someone, - my mother perhaps - thought that I needed protection from such raw animal displays of intimacy. Perhaps it wasn't the Christian thing to do. Certainly no one in my family had ever talked to me about natural stuff like this. I felt a bit embarrassed that I didn't know what the other kids seemed to know. I liked to be part of all of the constant buzz around the Home so this time I pretended I knew what was going on.

A few days later putting the finishing touches on our hut, Carl and Colin stopped off to help me with some old sacks to line the floor. A yell from the fence made us look up. Billy was near the cowshed and had his forelegs up on a cow's back. The cow moved away and I thought, *I would too if that big brute Billy was jumping all over me.* But Billy was not so easily put off. He just moved closer to the cow and raised himself again up and over her rear end.

"This is it, Kev, this is it," said Colin. "Watch this!"

I was glued to the spot, my eyes on Billy and the cow, oblivious to everything else around me.

"Yeah, yeah, there it is," chuckled Carl. "Look at the size of that -"

"Shut up Newman," someone said.

I looked to see 'there was what' and when I did it suddenly dawned on me. Billy Big Balls was sporting the largest penis I had ever seen and I had taken many showers with many kids by this time. It had somehow appeared and was now ramrod straight from Billy's gut. The cow was fixed firmly to the spot under Billy's massive body and I watched as he bounced forward on his hind legs and then pounded his body a few times against the cow's rear before sliding down to the ground again.

"He's done it, he's done it," said Carl over-excitedly.

"Uh huh," said Colin.

"I guess so," I added, a little unsure of what I had seen, but not too slow now at putting all the pieces together. The whole incident had taken a few minutes and now both the cow and Billy were back ignoring each other and onto the more interesting activity of eating, it seemed. I came to understand a lot from this one incident. After watching Billy and the cows and listening to Colin's explanation, it seemed as though I had just witnessed the most natural event in the world. I felt that I had crossed over from being a little kid to someone who knew lots of stuff about life, certainly some of the secret stuff. I noticed that there were some other kids who were just as ignorant as I was and they were also taking in the show with a quiet pleasure written on their faces.

"Well," said Colin. "Looks like we'll be having some calves in the spring. It'll be fun seeing those little buggers prancing around. Have you ever fed milk to a calf Kev? Now that's a treat!"

"No yet," I said, "but I can't wait!"

A few of us were kicking a rugby ball down on the footy field the following day. An errant boot from someone drove the ball high and far and it landed with a smack scattering a great flock of squawking seagulls from the area around the water trough near the cowshed.

"Cover your heads you kids," called Gordon Stretch, "those gulls are ready to do some heavy damage."

It wasn't so much the gull-poo he was referring to either, we had all been dive-bombed by a bird or two and had on occasion felt the vicious peck of a gull's beak, so we knew what he was talking about.

Once in a while when we had some time to ourselves and the weather was sunny, some of us would head off down to the cowshed with the intention of catching a seagull. I was a bit afraid of this, especially after the time when I was the one who ended up with a long scratch on my arm from a particularly aggressive bird. Why we did this is a bit of a mystery but if you can imagine young boys feeling the excitement of a mix of fear and adventure, then I think you're on the right track.

One of us would have a wooden box ready and I was usually the one asked to locate the long string rolled onto a stick like a fishing line from underneath the pigeon coops. We would set the box with it's open top facing down on an angle, propped up on the stick so that when the stick was removed the box landed on the ground bottom up and trapped whatever was under it. On the ground under the box we scattered some bread scraps that Pommy had given us from the kitchen and then unrolled the string all the way into the cowshed where we hid and waited for our unsuspecting prey. Pretty soon a few seagulls appeared overhead ready to land on the trough for a drink of water. Before long one of them spotted the bread under the box and like good gulls always do, hopped down and walked under thinking about nothing but food.

"Now!" I yelled.

Henry Lee who loved this part of the game, yanked hard on the string. The stick jerked out, the box slammed down and the trapped gull began squawking. I led the charge to the bird.

"I'm not taking it out, Henry, you do it," I said.

"Not me, I'm too scared," said Henry.

Carl was with us and as usual he showed his fearless side which we knew was linked closely to his dimwitted side. He slid his arm under the box to feel for the gull. Not once did he keep an eye on the gull through the sides. We knew what was coming.

"Yeeeoowww," yelled Carl. "That hurt."

"You dope, Carl," said Party. You've gotta get it by the back so it can't peck you."

"Yeah well, you try if you're that smart Partridge."

Party grinned, slid his hand in carefully from the side and quickly flipped the box up while jamming his hand down firmly on the bird's back at the same time.

"No problem Carl, I can do it," he said.

The seagull's eyes were red, its head moved from side to side and it was squirming to get its legs free from under its body. One large red leg popped out and distracted Party for an instant so that he released some pressure off the bird's back. That was when the gull struck, pecking three times on Party's small pale arm.

"Owwww!" he yelled.

"Oh yeah, now I see Partridge, you sure can do it!" gloated Carl.

The bird now struggled free, flapped its wings furiously at us and squawked away to safety.

We were soon back in the shed hiding and waiting for the next flock to appear. Sure enough, the birds would fly over, land on the trough, and 'Mr or Mrs Hungry' would take the bread bait and fall smack into our trap. After a few catches we had all mastered the art of grabbing a gull and holding it tightly so it couldn't escape. Meanwhile, one of us at a time, would see how brave we were by putting our hands close enough to the bird's beak allowing it to lay on a good peck or two. After a while we lost our fear of the gulls and watched them when released as they flapped and screeched their way skyward and out of our clutches.

A wind had come up and there was an Auckland chill in the air, so after the gulls had flown off to safety, I sauntered over to the furnace room to hang about with kids already there trying puffs from an acorn-pipe that somebody had fashioned, stuffed full of newspaper and lit. From the furnace door I could see several kids over at the pigeon coops. Years ago some of the senior kids had started to keep pigeons. These were not the motley kind you see flying about on city streets, but healthy birds that are kept for racing. A row of pigeon coops had been built on the paddock-side of the fence to the hen house lawn and there were always kids there on a daily basis.

"My bird's really fast today, Kevin," said Owen Major. Owen loved his pigeons and could usually be found hanging out around the coops

"Have you timed it 'O' ?" I asked., "I bet Les has got his watch."

"Yeah, it did the whole circuit in less than 50 seconds," said Owen.

Now that was fast, I thought, as I went to my coop I shared with Warren and Robin. We kept three birds and saw that they had plenty of food and water. We looked after ours really carefully. If other kids saw at any time that birds were not being cared for they would complain to an older kid who would warn you and then if you didn't smarten up, you were kicked out of your coop and your bird given to someone else. This discipline worked and all of our birds were well cared for and stayed healthy. Competition for a place in a coop was friendly but fierce.

I named my pigeon Red Feather but mostly called him Bluey, the nickname given to all red-haired kids in New Zealand. He was a beauty with deep red plumage all over, broken up by white streaks sweeping back along the wing and tail feathers. And fast! Bluey could fly faster than the wind, or at least that's what I thought. Sometimes we let them out singly but mostly we let them go together so we could watch them race the big circuit and then head for home. When they came in to land we all stood back a bit. They would only land if there wasn't a crowd around. I put my hand in and Bluey jumped onto the back of it. I pulled it out and held his back gently with my other hand. He was then secure in the pigeon grip we had all had to learn before we were allowed to have a bird.

"Three, two, one, go!" called Les Allen, "Let 'em go."

"Go Bluey," I said as I threw him into the air. "Fly fast Blue, fly fast."

"They're high today," said Barry to no-one in particular, but I listened because when it came to pigeons my brother knew what he was talking about. He had a way with these birds that was kind of magic. All the birds he had cared for were fast. He handled them easily and was gentle with them. They responded by being the fastest back to the coops. If your pigeon could beat one of Barry's, you had an exceptional bird. I had never beaten him, but I kept on trying.

"They're coming back. Hope you've got your clock working Les."

"48, 49, 50, 51, 52, ..."called Les, and as our birds landed we noted the time. Bluey landed at 55 seconds, well after Barry's bird and even after Colin's Blacky, who was known for being slow. I resolved right there that I would take really good care of Red Feather over the next week. Something must have been bothering him to only get a time around 55 seconds.

I stayed with the pigeons for a while longer and raced Bluey several more times. I loved watching the birds fly out, turn in a big arc and then head for home. I felt a sort of kinship with them as they sped toward the comfort of their coops. They didn't like to be gone for very long and when they landed on the small platform, they turned in a full circle before entering their door, hopping onto their favourite perch and looking proudly out. It was only a small cage but it was their home and they seemed content with what they had. I had a feeling that Bluey liked being part of the racing and that he looked forward to me visiting him every day.

Sometimes on a Saturday, certain senior kids were selected to race their birds in the local community pigeon races. They had portable coops made to carry them all the way to Waikaraka Park where they let the birds go and timed them in a special way to see who was fastest. I wanted to be one of those kids. I often dreamed of me and Bluey being known as the champion pigeon racing team for the Onehunga area. I knew that to get as good as that, I would have to beat Barry in a race first and I couldn't see that happening any time soon.

Way down near the bottom of our paddock we could see Billy Big Balls rearing up on one of the cows. Moving away from the pigeon coops we stopped to look and this time I grinned as I watched with full knowledge of what was going on.

"He's still at it eh Kev," said Colin.

"Yeah mate," I said. " I guess he won't rest until he's mounted all the cows. I wonder how he tells 'em apart?"

"Oh, he knows alright," grinned Colin. "Our friend Billy knows each cow personally and he keeps count too."

"What if he miscounts and visits a cow twice?" I asked.

"Well I guess that cow will have twins, eh Kev? Or even sometimes triplets."

"There's the dinner bell," said Bobby. "I was waiting for that 'cos my puku has been growling for the last half-hour."

"Yeah, trust you to hear it before anyone else Parata. You'd eat a horse if you could," said Carl.

"E Hoa, mate," replied Bobby taking off in the direction of his dinner. "Better than eating a couple of pigeons. But tonight I think we're havin' Mrs Davies Irish stew and she cooks it even better than my Gandma did."

"That's my kinda kai, Parata," laughed Party.

"Come to think of it though matey's, perhaps you better lock your birds up real tight tonight cos' this Maori gets hungry about midnight and I can't guarantee your bird will be safe. I particularly like red birds."

"Oh yeah Bobby? I'm gonna get you first!" I said as we raced away.

"You'll never catch this Maori - too fast for you Kev – mmmm mm - I can taste that Bluey right now. Nice with a bit of toast and Marmite!"

Upstairs

I climbed the stairs up to your room. They were narrow and dark like all stairs were in the 1940's. But they went up and I went up to visit you.

I was a young boy then, afraid and coping as best as I could with my new life. When I got to the top I sometimes would forget what I had climbed up there for and become distracted by all the boxes on the left of the landing. The boxes held all your possessions that you had carried with you from Wellington when you had to move because my Father, your Husband, decided he didn't love you any more, moved out and took everything with him.

Do you remember one time I found a pair of cup-things and asked you what they were and you said, "put them back Kev," and didn't want to talk about them? I thought they were for a hat and I don't actually recall when it was I found out that they were used to pad your bra, to give you a bigger bust. I like the idea that you were worrying about your appearance then.

You would have been around thirty. It's nice to know that you wanted to look good in spite of all that you had been through.

You always liked to wear colourful and fashionable dresses with smart shoes to match. Accessories, like the jewellery you chose carefully for yourself, were often left lying around your room and sometimes I picked them up to look closer at them or even play with them a little. In those days you topped each outfit off with an attractive hat adorned with the feathers and jewellery. I'm sure that you looked forward to your fortnightly pay at the Home so that you could take the tram to the city and spend an afternoon shopping for new delights...Karangahape Road and Queen Street were your favourites I remember.

For the first time in years you could shop and carefully spend without having to explain to 'Jack' where the money went. You must have felt independent in those moments back in your room going through the day's purchases and trying on a piece or two. Looking at yourself in the mirror and seeing how beautiful and smart you looked, surely brought back some deserved pride and happiness out of the disappointments in your past.

When I turned at the top of the stairs your door was right there and I knocked on it like you asked me to. There was your bed up against the wall as I went in, and your dressing table next to it with its big round mirror. Behind the door when I closed it, I caught a glimpse of myself in your full-length mirror before I walked over to the window that looked out on the courtyard between the dormitories and the covered area. There was a padded seat built into the space below the window and you had sewn some floral material on it and made an attractive cover. I loved to sit there when I visited you.

Was it then Mum, that you read to me from that book you had been saving?

Or was it then that you swept me up in your arms and smothered me with kisses?

When was it exactly that you chased me around your room, and threw me on your bed and tickled me 'til I giggled and laughed out loud?

And did you then quieten me down and hold me gently and lay together with me all drowsy and warm, feeling the love?

And then, when the dinner bell rang, did you pat my bum and say quietly,

"Go on, Kev. It's dinner time. Off you go now."

And on some mornings did I climb your stairs to find you gone? At those times do you know if I went into your room and played with the toys you kept for me in a box under your bed? I cannot remember what exactly was in the box or, whether it really even existed. Perhaps I imagine it.

Or, perhaps on some evenings when I visited you after tea and before bedtime in the dormitory, you snuggled with me and said,

"Oh, Kev, why don't you sleep with me in my bed tonight? I'd like that very much!"

Perhaps, or did I imagine that too?

Your room was there.

The stairs were there.

But were you there?.....Mum?

Did you call me up to visit?

Or, like me, were you afraid that other boys in the Home might tease me and call me 'mummy's boy' if they knew that I was visiting you too much?

Were you afraid of that Mum?

Did it make you hesitate?

Did you find yourself waiting for your 'days off' to spend time with me, like when we went to visit Nana and Grandpa at Maskell Street together?

I have trouble recalling my visits to your room Mum. I have no lasting picture of us sharing mother and son love. You talked to me seriously about issues from time to time, but there is a blank when I try to retrieve images of you chasing me, tickling me, telling me funny stories and giving me a mother's hugs and kisses.

Perhaps I have just forgotten. Perhaps I can only imagine.

Perhaps you were there after all.

I hope you were Mum, and I hope you did.

And what about you over all those years at Mt Smart Road? Did you ever feel free enough to gather me up in your arms and tell me you loved me to pieces?

Did I ever feel free enough to run to you when I hurt myself, when I cried or just needed your warmth and your love?

I hope I did.

And what about my brother Barry?

Did he visit you like I think I did?

Did you call him to your room?

Did you play with him?

Read to him? Tickle him?

Hold him and tell him that you loved him?

Did you do that Mum?

I hope you did.

It is difficult to recall many 'bad' times at the Home Mum, but one has stuck with me and is worth remembering. In the staff lounge where we sometimes gathered to sing songs around the piano, I sat on a stool one day by the window looking out. You had been away on a holiday and I was waiting for you to return. In you came with your hat and coat on and rushed over to hug and kiss me.

You asked, "Did you miss me Kev?"

And I replied, "Yeah Mum, but not too much 'cos Pommy looked after me really well. We had lots of fun together. She....."

You went quiet and looked at me in that moment and I didn't realise from my small boy place that you were feeling hurt and rejected. And you couldn't know that what I had meant by my answer was that you needn't have worried about me while you were away because I was being well-cared-for. I never wanted you to worry because you had, too much, already.

Eventually you said, "Well Kev, I guess you think Miss Pomeroi's more fun than me. I've only been gone for 3 weeks and it sounds like you've already forgotten about your mother."

You began to cry, picked up your bag and left me with the remark, "Why don't you go back to Miss Pomeroi then, if you think she's better than me?"

I look back down all those years now Mum and I can feel my shock and hurt. I was a small boy standing and holding onto a growing feeling that I had just caused some irreparable damage between you and myself, but I didn't understand what.

I only knew that hurt remained with me.

I didn't understand then that you were carrying a huge amount of it as well.

Was it then, Mum, that I felt the hurt inside, just like you probably did?

Was that when the understanding began that I could hurt you by doing things you didn't like?

Was that when the guilt started to accumulate which made me feel uncomfortable?

Was that when I decided that I would never knowingly hurt you again?

Was that the moment you showed your neediness to me?

Has it lasted with you Mum as long as it has lasted with me?

The Garden Party

109 Mt Smart Road was a beautiful property. Looking out from the front room windows lawn stretched all the way to the entrance at the main gate. Privacy was ensured by the large hedge that ran the width of the property. Behind the hedge the lawn was home to a variety of native and exotic trees. Some trees were huge, tall enough for brave boys to want to climb, leafy enough to get lost in, and with trunks too round for two young boys to link hands and expect to touch. There was the big soft, multi-branched Puriri, which also lends it's name to the huge moth which often frightened us on warm nights when it flew blindly in through open windows. A tall Rimu and a red flowering Rata possessed the center part of the lawn. There were also a couple of Karaka trees whose berries we sometimes mistook for acorns off the huge oaks when we collected them as ammunition for the annual skirmish. And in the far corner near the stile we climbed over to take the short cut to Mt Smart Road, grew a large bushy Kowhai tree with gorgeous yellow bell-shaped flowers attracting every Tui, their nectar-collecting tongues flicking out of their long sharp beaks, on their way to the trees on the slopes of One

Tree Hill. Spread here and there were native punga, attractive tree ferns and flowering shrubs. Once the lawn had been freshly mowed, perhaps on a Saturday morning after a light rain shower, the grass raked up and the dead-wood and leaves removed, the front lawn with its small flower gardens really was very beautiful. It was a tranquil setting, occasionally interrupted by the shouts of young boys intent on games of adventure or indulging in a seasonal outbreak of the 'Acorn Wars.' _

Once a year, in late November the Home hosted a Garden Party on the spacious front lawn. After announcing the date to us in the dining room, Fernsy would concern herself with nothing else than preparations for the event. We learned early on that this was Fernsy's personal project. It was what she dreamed about. She became more lively than we had ever seen her when she was planning the Garden Party. Deciding for us what we would dress up in this particular year was only one of her tasks.

On the day in question, she appeared in the latest summer dress with shoes to match which she purchased on a shopping spree to Kirkaldies on Queen Street. She managed always to crown each outfit with a magnificent hat, the envy of all the women present, created by some artistic milliner in the city.

Oh how Fernsy loved the Garden Party. Her beloved great dane Donnie in tow, she would walk the whole area pretending to marshall us boys in our proper stations but not fooling us for a minute that her real intentions were to parade herself around and to simply show off. It was Fernsy's chance to reap as much admiration from the assembled guests as she could and she did this with style, grace and charm. After all, she was the Matron of the Home and in charge of thirty boisterous boys of various ages and energies, a position to be admired but not envied. The Garden Party was always a huge success and, as well as the invited relatives, dignitaries and church folk, it attracted many from the neighbourhood curious to see what went on with all those boys in that place behind all those trees. Even the occasional local politician took a back seat to Fernsy and the event itself. She made sure that invitations were sent out weeks in advance and in some cases followed up with a reminder. This was a fundraising event for the Presbyterian Society and Fernsy never lost sight of that.

Of course the Society itself was grateful for the promotion because as a side effect, they reaped any financial rewards which came their way through donations to a charitable cause. Events like the garden party helped to attract those able to give in large amounts. In those days affluent church members saw it as an honourable duty to support causes that benefitted the poor in society. The string of Presbyterian orphanages throughout the Auckland area housed many children of the poor and needy and benefitted greatly by the generosity of these donors. They might have seemed stuffy old men and ladies to us but their hearts were in the right place when they dipped into their pockets to make sure that the homes had the financial base to operate adequately.

All of us boys in the Home looked forward to the event, in part because of all the attention our costumes would attract, but also because we knew we would get a chance to sample some of the delicious cakes, cream sponges and ham sandwiches set out on the tables for all. Among these delights sat attractive plates of lamingtons, the pink and the chocolate kind; brandy snaps and cream puffs, gone in a second once you inhaled them into your mouth; heavenly melting-moments small enough to stuff in whole and savour the wonderful sweet creaminess; plates of buttered gems with that favoured gingery aroma sitting attractively next to devonshire scones with strawberry jam and cream on each half; pikelets with gooseberry jam topped with cream; afghans, meringues and every boys' favourite: the staple sausage roll. Trifle with extra custard was offerred as if what was there already was not enough. And, to top it all off, lashings of whipped cream sat alone white and inviting in bowls here and there ready to be spooned generously onto each boy's plate. There was even an ice-cream treat late in the afternoon and jugs of cordial set aside on a table among the cups and glasses.

But the center-piece on the table, as at every New Zealand garden party, was the wonderful pavlova sitting resplendent on a huge plate decorated with all kinds of fruit and berries, a hint of the summer to come. The traditional pavlova was the lodestar; the beacon of the food table. Guests saw it and relaxed, happy now that the white sparkling merengue cake was in its place of splendour. It was the most excellent navigation-aid through a table of abundance and once seen one knew that all would be well.

The 'pav', as it is affectionately known in every New Zealand household, is simply constructed with well beaten egg whites and sugar, spread to make a circular shape as large as the presentation plate itself. Depending on the whim of the chef several layers are added to the initial base. When made well some of the merengue mixture remains soft inside and, if made especially well, some of it becomes delightfully chewy. Once the final tier is spread in place and the merengue has set, whipped cream is added along with fruit. Pavs establish a personal distinction with the decorative additions of bright green kiwi fruit, deep red strawberries and other selections. As every New Zealand child knows and every adult remembers, pavs are often not all they appear. The final test is in the taste no matter how attractive they look in the setting. Reputations are at stake whenever a pav is presented.

As expected, the energy level of every boy present was driven to heights unimagined by the inhalation of these delicious sugary sweets. Boys lay in their beds that night long after 'lights out' with eyes wide open tossing and turning and trying to get to sleep. Some even felt a little sick as they drifted off dreaming of the piles of goodies they had seen and eaten and some would tell stories about this for days after the event. Spoiled though we seemed to be at the Garden Party, we were well aware that it was the church women who had worked long hours to supply the fete with enough food to feed an army. We knew where our good fortune lay and we were grateful for their generosity.

Every garden party had a theme and we all dressed accordingly. I don't remember who suggested it, but in the year I turned 8 the theme for the garden party was 'The Wild West' and as soon as Fernsy announced it, cowboy talk was all you could get out of any kid.

The Cowboys Serenade The Guests

"Hey pardner, you gonna be at the garden party?"

"I'm just an old cowhand on the Rio Grande,"

"Hi ho Silver," and..... "Git along little doggie," were frequent calls as boys passed each other going about their business. A little corny but borrowed straight from the Saturday matinee at the State.

On the Saturday a week before the event, it was warm and we should have been getting ready to go up One Tree Hill for some sledding, but we were all in the Front Room getting fitted into our cowboy costumes.

"Stand up straight for goodness sake Kevin," said Pommy. "How on earth am I supposed to measure your leg if you keep moving about like that."

"What colour pants will I have Ms Pomeroi?" I asked.

"Eh Hoa Little Kevin, I don't know. Probably be made from those sacks over there. That's how real cowboys made their pants and you fellas want to be real cowboys don't you?"

"Will I have coloured tassles down the sides like Tom Mix has?" I asked.

"Sure will," said Pommy, "I'll sew 'em myself. E tama, these boys," she sighed.

Garden parties were not really Pommy's cup of tea but out of a sense of duty and loyalty to Fernsy, she involved herself energetically in the preparations. We knew that if you wanted something altered with your costume, Pommy was the one to see. If you wanted black shoes she would find a pair. If your hat was too big she would adjust the size so it didn't slip down over your eyes every time you reached for your six-guns. Nothing seemed too much trouble for Pommy around Garden Party time but the truth was that she found that time passed more quickly for her if she occupied herself with helping us kids get our costumes in order. At least this was better than wishing that she was somewhere else. Where Fernsy saw this as her chance to mingle with dignitaries and to be the star of the show, Pommy seemed strangely out of place among all the finery, pomp and ceremony. Mingling with church ladies and being among such fanciness was not part of Pommy's background. She was more at home on a back porch with good hot cuppa talking with family and friends. We were fortunate that she chose not to shy away from her responsibility to have us kids fitted into our costumes and looking good.

On a good day at the Home you could play tricks on Pommy and she would just laugh. You knew that sometime later she would get you back with a trick of her own which we understood was her expression of love and we loved her in return. Not many days went by that she didn't slip us something extra from the kitchen or pause as she was walking to the laundry or the cream-shed and ask how we were doing or whether or not we were still upset over some accident or mishap that had recently occurred. Pommy had a way of reaching every kid in the Home so that we all saw her as a sort of surrogate mother, certainly a person we could go to for comfort, sympathy and even a warm hug. So, it wasn't any accident that on this morning when we had to be outfitted in our costumes for the up-coming Garden Party, we turned to Pommie for help. She was the best.

On the big day we crowded into the Front Room dressed in white shirts, red neckerchiefs, pants with wide legs and chaps embellished with colourful tassles all the way to our 'cowboy boots.' When each kid was outfitted accordingly, Pommy handed out hats to fit at all angles and marked our names on them. The excitement and nervous tension we felt about the event later in the morning was almost too much for us to handle. For a couple of weeks leading up to this moment we had pestered the Saturday staff to let us go to Onehunga to see the western serial on at the State. We played Cowboys and Indians in the paddock or on the front lawn among the trees and we rode the range on our broncos all over One Tree Hill. By the time the Garden Party rolled around we were walking the walk and talking the talk. The Lone Ranger and Tonto had nothing on us.

With a final cinch of my belt on my pants I looked about me to see cowboys everywhere. *This was as good as the movies,* I thought. I could see myself in the other kids: all western shirt with a Tom Mix neckerchief, pants with coloured tassles and a great hat to top it off. I was fairly bursting with excitement. Then, before the guests arrived and we were finished dressing and milling about, Fernsy unveiled the best feature and biggest surprise. She had spent much time in the preceding weeks making a large costume and on this sunny Saturday morning she took us all outside on the front lawn to see what she had been up to. Two older kids, previously chosen and well practised, took their places inside the costume and with a whinny or two it was transformed into a horse walking toward us. It was a fabulous horse with a smooth, shiny, black felt body and a white mane. Its eyes and mouth were shaped by white felt also and when the horse began to trot toward us, it threw back its head, snorted and whinnied and shook its flowing mane. We loved it on sight and immediately lined up to climb into the saddle. Fernsy, the clever creator, stood to one side beaming proudly. She was looking forward to the admiration she was soon to receive from the guests who would be arriving soon, while we were only focussed on 'riding the range' with this beautiful horse in front of us.

Hi Ho Silver!

One by one us younger kids mounted up, grabbing hold of the reins with their shiny silver buckles and designs hanging down from the bridle and we yelled "Hi Ho Silver", and "Giddyup Trigger!" To us, with images on our minds from the last western we had seen, the horse moved like a real horse, all over the lawn. But each time we dug in our spurs and said "gee- up Silver," a voice from the front whispered back to us, "if you dig your heels in again, Davies, or Francis or Partridge, we're gonna hose you down at the cowshed later. Now cut it out!"

The guests had arrived, mingled and sat politely through a couple of speeches, Fernsy collected all of us cowpokes into a group with our horse in the front so that Guests with their box-brownies could snap off photos and throw all kinds of compliments at us. Then with our straw cowboy hats set at rakish angles we launched into our rehearsed songs of "Home On The

Range", 'I'm A Lone Cowpoke', and 'Red River Valley.' In polite adult style, the visitors applauded our choir and called for more. By this time Fernsy was literally beaming from the realisation that her hard work getting us to practice the songs had paid off.

After the concert it was decided that I should get up on the horse in true cowboy fashion and lead the group of cowpokes past all the visitors, raising our hats in a western salute of "Howdy Folks" and "Yeeehaaa!" Just as we completed the 'ceremonial ride', by some pre-arranged signal I'm sure, the horse bucked and threw me off chaps and all, where I landed on my bum in front of three horrified Presbyterian ladies. That was the point when Fernsy and the staff stepped forward and invited everybody to the afternoon tea tables.

"Remember your manners boys, visitors first," she commanded.

I dusted myself off and headed straight for the pavlova. But it wasn't 'our' manners that Fernsy needed to be concerned about. While the guests settled in around the table set especially for them, Donnie, Fernsy's huge Great Dane, approached our table set several metres away beside a flowering Jacaranda. While we were busy doing the horse show and, to his delight, no adults or kids were around to 'shoo' him away, Donny began sniffing out the plates at the centre of the kids table. We watched in horror as he stuck his huge nose between the sausage rolls and the pavlova and opted for the meaty stuff. Walking forward we watched as two rolls were inhaled by the massive hound and then in spite of our warning cries of, "get the heck out of the food Donnie," he launched his chops fully into our savoury favourites, the ham sandwiches.

Well that was enough for us. We yelled together, "here Donnie, here Donnie, come on boy, get away from the food!" Donnie being the size of a small horse was not put off by these feeble attempts at distraction and completely ignored us until some kid grabbed him by the collar and yanked hard, dragging that 'dog-immitating-a-pony' to a safer place. Donnie's huge tongue slurped up all the tasty morsels left around his jowls and promptly headed back to the table.

Meanwhile the adults continued their polite conversations sipping dainty cups of tea and holding plates of their favourite cakes. None of them had even noticed the commotion going on by the Jacaranda and if they did they probably put it all down to boys being boys with the usual horseplay thrown in for good measure. For them, a dog around boys at a garden party event, was normal, so they were not wise to what was actually going on. For this, Fernsy was grateful.

Donny however, must surely have been thinking that this was his chance to get a reward for all the rides he had given to cowboys earlier that morning when Fernsy had let him out of his kennel. The big great dane easily broke the grasp of the kid holding him back and headed to the table for more food. Two creampuffs were devoured in seconds before he turned to the plate of sausage rolls again and dragged the whole lot off the table and onto the ground. No half measures for this hound. We cringed because sausage rolls were another favourite of ours. By this time many boys were yelling and calling but Donnie ignored them all. This was too good to be true. His huge wet nose turned next to the plate of fruit tarts and suddenly all the shouting ceased. Donnie checked and listened, took a big sniff and, fearing nothing and no-one, grabbed the whole plate in his massive jaws and ran off to the trees.

"Let him go, let him go," said Jim Porter, "he's got the fly cemeteries and you know how much we hate those things."

It was true. Every party we had ever been to, there was always a plate of small fruit tarts that all the adults loved but which all the kids hated because the small raisins in the tarts reminded us of dead flies. No kid with any pride at all would touch a fly cemetery. So, when Donnie fled with that plate of tarts we fell quiet, thus encouraging him in his impeccable taste of garden party cuisine.

"Good work boys," said Fernsy sternly but trying to hide a smile at the same time. She had watched us deal with Donny while standing at the guests' table hoping that no-one else would notice. And now appearing at our table obviously relieved, she said, "Bad boy Donnie. Now you just go and sit over there under that tree. I'll deal with you later. Go on! Get! You Bad boy!"

As soon as Donnie heard Fernsy's scolding voice he hung his head and tail and slunk away like a small fox terrier over to the tree.

With Donnie now out of the way, we approached our table ready, willing and able to eat. The adults at their table seemingly unperturbed by all this frantic action going on nearby, were sipping their last cups of tea and brushing sugary powder off suits and dresses. We launched into our food that Donny had chosen to ignore and stacked our plates up high. Oh, it was all so very wonderful. Boys and cakes go well together in any setting and the few surviving old photographs glued into some of the guests' albums would later show smiling kids up to their noses in cream puffs and merengue.

When the last crumb of the pavlova was gone we turned to the sweet cordial to wash everything down and put us all in sugar-heaven. Finally, the prospect of an afternoon ice-cream treat served later by the staff, would make this whole garden party experience for us kids, a legendary pleasure to savour for weeks to come.

The New Zealand Bubblegum Factory

By the time the New Zealand Bubblegum Factory opened up for business on Manukau Road in Onehunga, I had already been chewing the stuff for a couple of years. My Aunt and Uncle spent a bit of time in the U.S. on their missionary business and occasionally bought back some Double-Bubble for the kids and they sometimes sent a small package to my brother and I at the Boys Home. I loved those little blocks of pink gum with their waxy packaging and the tiny comic inside. If I had enough to give to friends, I shared a few pieces, but mostly I stored them in my camp box for when we went to camp in the summer holidays. Once I had chewed through the perfumy flavour, the gum softened enough to be able to blow bubbles. I didn't seem to have a problem with this from the start, although I did have times in the very early novice-stage of scraping gum off my face from failed attempts. I wasn't expert by American standards perhaps, but I was skilled enough to be able to impress my Kiwi mates.

One Tree Hill

Adventures and events at the Home were sometimes big-time such as racing the Tip Top Special, the annual Garden Party, sledding down One Tree Hill and going up to camp at Mahurangi Heads. But there were small adventures too, some which became triumphs and remain now as fond memories. Small events like this one were often so exciting and 'bubbly', that they have stuck in my mind as tiny treasures.

I had turned 11, finally left Onehunga Primary and was now in Form 1 at Manukau Intermediate. On school days we walked up the long hill to Manukau. This took us past shops at Tin Tacks Corner and a distance away from the main Onehunga shopping area. Bobby and Party and me were half way up the hill one morning on our way to school when a man in a suit popped out of a doorway and said to us, "Hey you kids, have you ever chewed bubblegum?"

"Yeah, I have," I said.

"Nah," said Bobby.

"Not me," said Party.

"Well, I'll tell you what. Why don't you kids come back here after school today and I'll give you some gum to chew," said the man.

"E Hoa," said Bobby Parata, "we don't have any money Mister. We can't buy it from you."

"That's ok son. I'll give it to you free. Won't cost you a penny," said the Bubblegum man.

"We'll be here," smiled Party, "and right on time too!"

"You can count on that, Mister," chimed Bobby.

Classes dragged by for the three of us that day. We met at morning break-time sipping our free government milk in half-pint bottles.

"Gee, can't wait 'til after school," said Bobby. "You told anybody yet Kev?"

"Not me. I'm not telling anybody," I replied. "This is our secret, eh Party?"

"You bet matey!" whispered Party. "I'm gonna chew myself sick on that free bubblegum 'cos we may only get it once."

"I wonder what that bloke is going to do," I said. "Do you think he'll just give us free bubblegum and then say "see you kids later,"?"

"Yeah, 'course mate," grinned Bobby. "We'll get a whole load from him and stash it in our camp boxes and not give any to anybody else. We'll have free gum for years."

The last fifteen minutes of the day were chronic as we waited for the bell. Announcements were read out by the teacher in the classroom before dismissal. I listened carefully to hear if one of us was called to the Headmaster's Office as sometimes happened to a number of us Home Kids. But this time we had kept ourselves out of trouble and as soon as the bell rang, I burst out of the door and met the other kids by the gate to Manukau Road. We didn't walk, we ran down the hill and arrived puffing at the red door of the now famous NZ Bubblegum Company, shiny in its fresh coat of paint. It was the newest business on the block. Inside, the man was waiting.

"I knew you kids would get here fast," he said. "As soon as you can get your wind back, I've got something to tell you."

The three of us shuffled forward and showed him we were eager to start.

"My name is Mr Charters and I'm the manager of this company. We are in business to sell bubblegum, fellas, but first of all I'd like to get your opinion about our gum. You know, chew a bit and see what you think of it."

"You mean you're going to give us gum free just to see whether we like it or not?" asked Bobby Parata. "You don't have to do that, Mister. I like it already 'cos it's free!"

Party was grinning through his excitement, trying to say something but nothing was coming out.

"That's it young fella," replied the man. "I'll give you boys some gum to chew here and watch you try to blow bubbles."

"E tama," laughed Bobby, "this is gonna be fun. Free? I can't believe it!"

"Ok now lads, here's your first piece of gum each," said Mr Charters. "I want you to chew it slowly and when you're ready try blowing some bubbles. That's all you have to do."

"I'm ready," I said, popping a piece into my mouth. I had high hopes for being successful even though I had never said a word to either Bobby or Party about having had some previous experience bubble blowing.

We sat chewing and looking at each other. This chewing and grinning at the same time seemed not to be a problem for any of us. Pretty soon I watched Bobby tense up as he tried to get a bubble going. His brown cheeks puffed out, he crossed his dark eyes and looked down his flat nose. What he saw made him laugh. At the end of his nose a small pink bubble emerged and grew larger with each careful puff. This was the difficult part and suddenly Bobby lost control of his breath and the gum flew out between his lips and on to the floor. Even though I was preparing my own gum, I couldn't help laughing. He stood there with eyes wide open looking down at it.

"E hoa, mate," said Bobby, "I tried to blow a bubble but all it did was land at my feet."

"Watch this," mumbled Party who was lost in his own effort. He blew hard and a small piece of gum shot out between his pursed lips.

"Aww heck," he moaned, "I can't get it."

I didn't say anything. I just knew I could do it. A nicely rounded bubble formed itself outside my mouth and the more I blew air into it, the bigger it got. I stopped before it burst over my face because I had felt the result of that disaster many times before.

"Oh yeah, Kev's got one," said Party, "now watch me."

"I'm not watchin' you Party," said Bobby Parata, "I've got my own bubbles to worry about."

Mr Charters came over to me and asked me some questions about how I did that, "you know, blow a bubble like that sonny? How did you do it so easy?"

"Well, you chew, then you flatten the gum out over your front teeth like this," I explained. "Then you blow air through the gum and push it forward with your tongue until a bubble forms outside. Then you just go for it."

"Amazing," smiled Mr Charters. "Amazing! It actually works. This boy can do it."

"Hey Bobby's got one," Party blurted out.

"So have you," I laughed.

In the space of a very short time all three of us had figured out how to blow bubbles with the gum and Mr Charters was beaming.

"Here, here's some more gum boys," he said excitedly, "keep blowing for a while."

We did and it was no problem. We kept chewing and blowing and chuckling and laughing in between bubbles. In the meantime Mr Charters went to the back of his building and returned with two other men.

"Take a look at these kids and what they can do," he said. "This stuff really works and works well. Blow a few bubbles for these blokes, kids."

All three of us were becoming pretty good at this bubble thing. Our bubbles were emerging larger and stronger so it was no problem to show off.

"Jeez, you kids are great," said one of the men. "Where did you learn to do that?"

"It's in my family," I said. "All my cousins are good at it."

"Eh tama," grinned Bobby, "doncha know that us Maoris have been doin' this for years, even before the Pakeha arrived in the country? We used to chew the gut of the moa. Bubbles as big as your head."

"This is my first time," said Party quietly but proudly.

When we eventually left the NZ Bubblegum Factory later that afternoon, we left with free gum bulging in our shirt and pants pockets, each of us holding a paper bag full of the stuff and big grins on our faces.

"Now, can all three of you be here at the same time tomorrow?" said Mr Charters as we exited the door. "I'd like you to do the same thing again and this time I'll have another manager of the factory here to watch and also some more of my staff."

"Ok," we said together. "We'll be here right after school again Mister, just like today."

"I'll drag Warren along as well," I said and then adding with a grin, "You're sure you can make it Bobby?

"Make it? You bet Kev. If they're givin' away gum, I'll be here every day."

Party laughed, "Yeah, Bobby, you're always looking for free food. People would think you never got anything to eat!"

"The secret's in the 'free', Party mate," said Bobby, " 'cos if it's free it's kai te pai for me!"

Tip Top Special

Each year the Onehunga Business Community organised a Soap Box Derby. Kids from the community, their fathers and older brothers probably helping, spent hours building cars that ran on a free wheel system and would only move downhill. On Soap Box Derby Day in November, a big ramp was set up in Onehunga at the top of the hill beginning at the Presbyterian Church and going down past all the shops and the State Theatre. Cars raced off two at a time and rolled to victory, or defeat, at the bottom of the hill. After the first year of the event some generous soul from the Tip Top Company decided that it would be a good idea if the Home kids were involved as well. So we became the inheritors of the 'Tip Top Special' derby car, painted bright white with blue flashing from the grill in front down toward the back of the body. A large number '4' was emblazoned on the rear behind the seat. Of course, from the start, we loved it and adopted it as our own Soap Box car.

The Tip Top Special

All through October, a month before the event, the Tip Top Special could be seen going through its trials down The Lane, the driveway at the Home. Under the guidance of the older kids, young kids like myself, smaller and lighter, were selected to drive the Special. The senior kids would not be caught dead in a toy like this, being bigger and heavier and able to slow a soap box car down. They were the mechanical experts, inheritors of a vast knowledge of the intricate workings of any car, with motor or without. They formed the mechanical support team, a sort of pit-crew like all the grand-prix racers had. A driver was considered an insignificant but necessary part of the race preparations and one of us younger kids would count ourselves lucky to be chosen.

After a series of races against Les Allen's clock, one of us was chosen to drive in the big event of the year. Les was the serious

211

one among the older kids. I saw him as the 'brain'. He was always studying at night in the Balcony, getting his homework done for school the next day. Barry told me once that Les would get a good job because he did well at school and worked hard. He was the mechanic among us; the guy who knew about motors and how things worked. Later in life, Les joined the Air Force and learned how to fly. Much later he became a pilot of the big 747's flying from New Zealand to all parts of the world.

"OK, yeah, well then," announced Les, "it looks like Little Davies has the fastest time after several trial races, so he's appointed the Tip Top driver for this year."

"Hey, good for you, Kev," smiled Mick Reynolds.

"Thanks Mick," I said, noting some disappointment in his eyes because I knew that he had wanted so much to be the driver again this year. It felt good to be chosen but I just kept it to myself.

"Kapai Kev," said Bobby Parata. "When you need to practice just call on Parata Ltd., the best car mechanic in Onehunga. We'll help out and see that Davies wins the race this year, won't we Party?"

"Yessir, Bobby P Ltd," grinned Party. "Maybe Kev'll give us some Tip Top ice-cream if we do a good job."

"Tip Top ice-cream eh? E tama, gotta love that stuff!"

On 'Race Day', from the top of the ramp on the road next to the church, the hill down past the State and Sinclaire's Bakery looked pretty steep to me. I quickly scanned the crowd to see if I could see Ellen Sinclaire who was my girlfriend at Onehunga Primary. When I couldn't, I put my mind back to the race at hand. I would see her again at school on Monday and we could talk about the race then. Ellen and I were good friends and occasionally left the school at lunchtime to walk around the corner to her family bakery where Mrs Sinclaire would sometimes treat me to a fresh pie or a cream bun. I think she liked me being Ellen's friend, but she was also the kind of person who liked kids anyway. Ellen and I were late back to class one day and for punishment we had to clear the convolvulus out of the hedge around the school's footy field. This wasn't so much a punishment for us because we were working together and to this day I perversely consider convolvulus to be an attractive flower and not the insidious weedy-creeper that it really is.

"Now, remember what I told you Mate," whispered Bobby in my ear. "Keep the steering wheel steady, keep your head low, and drive a straight line. That's how all us Maoris learned to drive and that's why we're the best in the Grand Prix. My Grandfather drove the first car in Eketahuna don't you know."

"Eketahuna? What was he doing there?" I asked.

"Spending some time with the local constabulary - driving of course - driving them crazy!"

" OK, Bobby," I grinned, "I'm ready."

I looked at the car next to me, a chrome and wood special with very sleek styling. The kid driving it was someone I knew from our school and was always good at everything he did. He looked at me and didn't smile or say a word.

"Good racing," I said.

Was that a "ssssssss" I heard in reply?

"Ready... set... go!" yelled the starter.

The Special seemed to take forever to move and by the time I got to the bottom of the ramp I could feel nervousness building up inside. 'Mr Sleek' was ahead of me but I kept remembering to keep low just like Bobby had told me.

"Go, Kevin, Go!" I heard, and knew it was Ellen out there cheering from the crowd.

By the time the State Theatre, home of Tom Mix and Hopalong Cassidy pictures, rolled into view, I had caught the chrome and wood car and my front wheels were level with his rear ones. We whizzed past Burkett's Biscuit Bar flying at breakneck speed, and it was there that I pulled about a yard ahead. The wind whipped my curls apart and made my eyes water. It was thrilling to be behind the wheel of the Tip Top Special going so fast. My stomach tightened as I saw the finish line come up and I knew I had won this heat. This was my third race so far and I had won them all in fine style. I pulled the brake hard to bring the Special to a halt. Les Allen and my brother Barry crowded round to help me out.

"That was a great ride, Kev," said Barry, "your best one so far. That kid never stood a chance against you. Never know matey, might win the final yet!"

He gave me a pat on the back and ruffled my hair a bit. We looked at each other and smiled. I always felt a little closer to Barry at such moments. Events like this gave him the opportunity to treat me more as a friend, and not just his cheeky young brother who never seemed to do anything in a manner that satisfied him. I wonder if the leaving of our Dad earlier in our lives had caused him to take on a certain seriousness about life and to watch out that I was growing up to be responsible. There were times when he felt it necessary to clip my ears or to bawl me out for being careless with money or property. Nothing serious, but rather a reminder that I should watch what I was doing. But it was these times, like the Soap Box Derby, that he was able to show that he liked me and to offer some emotional support as well. It meant a lot. I felt warm and grinned at him. "Thanks Barry," I said.

We pushed the car back up the street to the assembly point at the back of the ramp. It was a warm afternoon. I felt like something cool to drink or even an ice-cream and wouldn't you know it, at that precise moment Bobby, Party and Warren walked toward me with big ice-creams in their hands.

"You lucky dogs," I said. "Where did you get those, cos I know you've got no money."

"Home Kids are allowed one free ice-cream," said Warren. "We got them at the tent. It's a Soap Box treat for us."

"Oh, but so sorry mate, you can't have one yet 'cos you're in the final and food'll just slow you down," explained Bobby with his usual wry smile. "Tell you what though, I'll get it for you and hold it 'til you're done."

"Oh yeah, mate," I said, knowing what Bobby was planning, "it'll all have melted by then."

"E tama mate, I don't think so," said Bobby with his teeth showing out of his wide smile.

"Parata," laughed Party, "it's not gonna get a chance to melt 'cos you'll have eaten it, you big hungry Maori. We know all your tricks!"

"The final for 9 and 10 year olds is next," announced the man on the microphone. "Kevin Davies in the Tip Top Special #4, and Alan Hill in the Kirkaldie Speedster, please get your cars to the top of the ramp. The race starts in five minutes."

Party, Bobby and Warren, now finished their ice-creams, helped push the car up to the starting line again. I climbed into the seat, grabbed the steering wheel tightly and jammed my legs onto the footrest blocks. I was nervous already and sitting there at the start, looking down the hill, I felt the butterflies gathering in my stomach.

It was always like this whenever I was involved in some competition that came down to just me against another kid. Whether it was the 100 yards dash at the summer sports day we held each year in the top field at the Home, in a running race at the Policemen's Picnic on Motuihi Island, or on Wednesday nights at Waikaraka Park athletics, it was always the same. I never felt nervous when I went to play footy because the result didn't depend entirely on me. And I never felt nervous when I took part in any of the competitions we had up at Camp, like the pipi-roast at Scott's Beach or the paper chase over to Martin's Bay. But the butterflies came flying in whenever it was just me on the line. It was like this as well, but even worse, whenever I had to do a test or an exam at school or run a race. I never did learn to control this anxiousness or to deal with it effectively. It dawned on me many years later that I wasn't a really competitive person. I was always intent on the enjoyment factor in sports or games. And I never overcame my fear of failing at tests and exams either. I'd do anything to get out of those extremely anxious moments to the extent that when it came time for me to sit my School Cert at high school for the second time after failing the year before, I developed a bad case of shingles and was given an aggregate pass based on my marks during the year. No matter how much I wished it wasn't so, the butterflies always visited me whenever it was one on one. They were rampant now. I felt sick in my stomach.

"OK Kev, mate, just remember to be ahead of that bloke in the other car at the finish line and then you'll win. I know you will," whispered Party in my ear. "And no looking out for your girlfriend Ellen either. She's in the crowd out there somewhere."

"I've got a feeling you'll do it mate," said Bobby. "Just remember what I told you and go like he – whoa - better not say 'h-e-l-l.' We're right outside the Presbyterian Church and you know what'll happen if I say that."

"You can do it Davies," someone yelled.

"The race is yours, Kev," said Warren. We grinned at each other and I gave him the thumbs-up sign.

"Ready – Set - Go!" called the starter. The 'Kirkaldie Speedster' and the 'Tip Top Special' rolled slowly down the ramp, onto the street and off down the hill toward the finish line. At this early point in the race the Speedster was just ahead of me and seemed to be pulling away. I hit a smooth spot in the street and drew level. My knuckles were white. I was still holding my breath I had sucked in at the start and I could feel the tightness in my stomach. The State Theatre flashed by and I knew we had half the hill to go. I flattened out and squinted a look at the Speedster and thought, "he's too high in the car. I can catch up and pass him."

Half way, and not far ahead of me, I saw what I thought was a large blob of red coloured ice-cream that somebody must have dropped. Before I could react I went through it and skidded, always my worst fear. The car swerved over towards the Speedster, my wheel almost touching Alan's. With a quick reaction I tried to straighten the Special back on course. The trouble was that I had wrenched the steering wheel too hard. My action had the opposite effect and the car went into a spin. I heard a gasp go up from the crowd.

"Turn your wheel the other way!" someone yelled from the crowd.

"Straighten 'er out mate, you can still beat him," said another.

But the Special now seemed totally out of control and went the full circle. By the time I had the car back on course, the Speedster was a full length ahead. I laid my head down flat, gripped hard and set off to the finish line. It was not over yet and knowing that the Tip Top Special was the faster car, I was determined to catch Alan. I could hear the thin tires on the road and feel every bump through them. Now I was almost touching his tail.... now

I was level with his back wheels - just a few yards more – and - we crossed just as the Special's nose drew level with the front wheels of the Speedster. We broke the finish line together, slammed our brakes down hard and both of us sat looking at each other unsure of who had won.

People were yelling and cheering, "It's a photo-finish, a photo-finish!"

"The judges have to decide," I heard someone say.

"Ah.... attention please ladies and gents," said the announcer. "The judges of the Onehunga Soap Box Derby have decided on the winner of this very close contest between The Kirkaldie Speedster and the Tip Top Special. What a thrilling race that was!......... Both boys are champion drivers but there can be only one winner, and...the winner is.......The Kirkaldie Speedster driven by Alan Hill, by just a dead bug on the radiator!.... now, that's close!"

I turned to the Speedster and gave a thumbs up to Alan whose Mum and Dad were approaching him as we smiled at each other. I felt pretty much the same as I would, had I won the race. I knew I had driven the Special as best I could. It didn't matter now that I had hit that ice-cream patch in the street. The judges had to pick someone. They had done their job. I could accept that.

"Too bad Kevin, you almost had him at the line," said Les before I had a chance to climb out of the driver's seat.

"Bad luck that you hit the ice-cream mate," said Barry, "'cos you would've won if it wasn't for that."

"Good drivin', Kev," called Bobby running with Party to the car.

"Yeah Kev, you almost won." said Party. "I thought you did."

"He did win but it was so close the judges had to decide," said Warren. "It's a photo-finish just like they have at the horse races at Ellerslie. My brother told me all about those."

"Shoulda had more driving lessons from Parata Ltd., Kev," said Bobby, "then you wouldn't have skidded on that ice-cream. I coulda helped you get outta that situation."

"Oh he did alright, didn't you Kev?" said Barry putting his hand on my shoulder. "Lotsa people would've skidded if they had hit that patch. I would've skidded too and I already know how to drive."

I looked up at Barry and caught his eye. With his hand on my shoulder and wearing his usual grin, I felt I had won even though I had lost.

"Besides," he went on, "the judges had to choose somebody and they did. You have to live with that."

I pulled myself out of the Tip Top Special one last time and said to Bobby, "Ok mate, where do I get my ice-cream now that I don't have any more races?"

"Well, I know where there's a big strawberry-ripple but it's probably all melted by now," said Bobby. "Or, you can just lick the rest of it off your front tire."

"Nahhh, I'll leave that for you Bobby," I laughed. "Your tongue's big enough and you don't like seeing food go to waste."

"Hey Kev, here's your ice-cream," said Warren returning to the group. "I got you a honeycomb special to go with your car. It's a Tip Top Special too!"

We watched Les and my brother Barry roll the car onto the back of a truck and tie it down. I took a big lick of my ice-cream and savoured my near win and all the excitement of the race. Life, at that particular moment, felt about as good as it could get.

"Come on mates, let's go," said Party.

The four of us walked up the hill in Onehunga, past the State, around the corner past the Presbyterian Church and off toward the Home.

"Gee...wish I had an ice-cream right now," said Bobby. "I sure would like to have a big honeycomb special."

"You shouldn't eat so fast Parata," I grinned. " But I tell you what Bobby, you can have what's left of the cone when I get down to it."

Sunday Was Church Day

Sundays, I never wanted to hurry, but it always seemed I had to. "Come on Kevin Davies," commanded Fernsy, "get those shoes shined and mind you don't get any of that polish on your nice clean clothes. Now hurry up boys, we are leaving in 15 minutes and all of you are to be ready and lined up out front."

I rubbed the Kiwi polish into the toes of my shoes and brushed as hard as I could not minding this part of the Sunday routine. I wanted to be sure that it all turned out right; not so much perfect, but at least right. So I dithered a lot making sure that I laid out my cleanly washed and pressed Sunday uniform flat on my bed so that it wouldn't get ruffled before I changed into it. Then I checked to see if I could notice my reflection in the shine of my shoes. My tie, light blue, I carefully placed next to the clothes on my bed and lastly my socks with the white hoops, I put on top of my shoes. I was now ready to change.

Homekids In Their Sunday Best

I know I was a bit of a slowpoke, but if they only knew how much I hated wearing shoes! They hurt my toes especially, and after walking in them for more than ten minutes my feet became unbearably hot. Most kids growing up in Auckland never wore shoes. Summer and winter in barefeet made them wide in the beam and leathery on the sole. You can imagine then how we felt when Sunday rolled around. I have sometimes thought that my irreverence toward the church, Christianity and religion as a whole, can be traced back to that Sunday morning church ritual and having to wear those shoes. I mean, I was not the one who decided that I wanted to go every week; it was always some adult who made this decision in the first place and it was a routine that I was forced to comply with. But in this case at that time, I had nothing against the church, God, or even Jesus. I just took my own sweet time.

I had nothing against Catholics either but as we walked up Epuni Street about three blocks away from the Onehunga Presbyterian Church one Sunday, we crossed the road and just as I stepped up on the curb I noticed a brown bottle in the gutter. I rolled it around with my foot and kicked it a bit.

"What sort of bottle is that Mum?" I asked my mother who happened to be walking beside me at the time.

"Oh that's a beer bottle dear," she said, "leave it alone because I don't want you getting dirty kicking that along."

I bent down and picked it up to look at it closer.

"Put it down Kev. It is all dirty," said Mum. "and besides, we don't have anything to do with beer."

"Who doesn't Mum?" I asked.

"We don't. Grandpa, Grandma, you, me , Barry. All of our family and our church. None of us like beer. We just don't touch it."

"Why not?" I asked innocently enough with a touch of naivety.

"Because we don't," said Mum. "It is not something God likes and so we keep away from stuff like that."

"But it's here, so somebody drinks it," I observed.

"The Catholics do," she said a little too quickly. "The Catholics are the ones who drink beer. Protestants don't do that sort of thing. It's dirty and we follow God's rules on this. But the Catholics don't and that's why they are in trouble with God."

"What kind of trouble Mum?" I asked.

"Oh lots of trouble," she answered. "You'll learn about that as you get older."

This was intriguing. I thought about it for a while afterwards. Catholics were obviously up to no good. I learned later that it was the Catholics who did everything bad like dancing, drinking, going to movies and to the races to gamble on the horses. Catholics played rugby league, played rugby on Sundays, the Lord's Day and worked on the Sabbath as well. What's more, Catholics had all those statues of Jesus, Mary, the angels and creatures covered in gold in their churches where they spent part of every Sunday standing up, kneeling down and crossing themselves rather strangely every time God was mentioned. They were on a different team alright and most definitely not the one my family were members of.

Occasional Sundays, Mum, Barry and myself would take the tram to The Baptist Tabernacle on Queen Street in Auckland City. Grandpa was the Pastor of the Elim Church which held it's services there. Lots of people would be inside and my brother Barry and I would sit in the uncomfortable chairs near my mother. The best part of the service for me was when we sang hymns and a lady played the piano. I loved the sound and was taken into the music as soon as she started playing. This helped me get through the boring part of the service, as did the thought of the cup of tea and all those great kiwi sandwiches at the end. As Mum often said, "there's nothing like a cuppa to pick-u-uppa when you're feeling down and blue," and after sitting through that whole Elim service I was more than ready for some pleasurable distraction.

Harry Valentine Roberts, my Grandpa, was one of those preachers who liked to move all over the place. He would catch my ear when he talked softly and then suddenly freak me out by shouting just like some of these present day televangelists. I fought to keep the giggles down and my laughing subdued. He had his very large Bible which he would hold sprawled open in one hand while he waved his other arm about and walked from side to side.

Grandpa Was A Preacher Man

Some Sundays I waited for his hand to slip and that Bible
to crash to the floor, but it never did. I wondered if he practised
these manoeuvres like Barry practised his goal kicking on the
field at the Home. Grandpa wore a dark suit which seemed well
cut to his slim body. He had a balding head with glasses on his
nose which he peered over the top of, at the congregation for
emphasis. H.V. was an athletic figure...all the Roberts were...and
a very attractive and handsome man. He was an easy man to like
and get along with, as long as you agreed with him.

There was no question that he had an air of authority because
when he preached at the Elim Church, when he spoke about
God and Jesus and the Bible, everybody believed everything he
said. There was no argument about him being right or wrong;
if H.V.Roberts said it, it must be so. He often repeated some of
his sentences over and over for emphasis, waved and waggled
his finger, raised his hand in the air, took his glasses off and put
them back on again. He was a very intense preacher and often
it was in his intensity that he lost me. I never understood much
of what he said in his sermons. Being a very visual learner, I
can recall the bible stories he retold in his usual lively fashion.
I have a legacy of images ranging from Adam biting into that
delicious but forbidden apple with a worm in it, Daniel in the
lion's den with his head stuck in that big cat's mouth, Moses and
his people walking through walls of Red Sea water, all the way to
the Last Supper with Judas pointing his grubby little finger at an
unsuspecting Jesus.

I was aware that my Mum and others in my family admired
my Grandpa for the Christian he was and they all tried to act the

same way and made sure that we all knew the correct path that God was showing us. I didn't like the correctness of it at all and I especially didn't like being told what I should believe in and what I should aspire to in my life so that my 'ticket to Heaven' would be guaranteed. That just didn't seem right in my book. I was embarrassed by their self-righteousness.

There was a time when my Grandfather hit the street corners of Auckland to, "spread the Word Of God, Kev, to spread the Word Of God," and at his encouragement and the assurance of Mum, I let myself be influenced to join him and several others on those evenings. I was amazed at how bold Grandpa was, preaching out loud there on the street corner with all the people walking by. I felt so self-conscious that I slunk into the background so I wouldn't be noticed by anybody I knew who might pass. After a few evenings at these 'saving the world for Jesus' street sessions, I called a halt to this pathetic attempt at evangelizing and stayed away like any sensible kid should.

Years later, when I was a teenager in a 'Youth For Christ' meeting in the Wellington Town Hall, listening to the American evangelist Billy Graham, I felt uncertain as I walked up to the front with my friends and cousins walking ahead of me, when Billy called for us to, "give your hearts to Jesus and be saved". Half way down the aisle I realised what I was doing and felt silly and so I went back to my seat. When my Mum and my family heard about this later they were upset. I had disappointed them and for a long time afterwards I felt guilty that I had spurned the call of God to a life of Christian dedication. But later I came to terms with my rejection and was kind of glad I didn't have to undo being "saved" by Jesus like my cousins and friends had been that night. As I watched them over the next few months, I was glad that I didn't have to act in that strangely pious way I saw them behaving. It all seemed so phony to me.

Boredom in church happened frequently. It was less of a problem at the Presbyterian Church with the Choir up front and the minister in his purple and black robes. There, I sat with all the kids from the Home, whereas at the Elim Church it was more difficult because there, I sat among adults. Distractions were in my mind frequently. I thought about my last footy game, the current drawing I was working on and the movie we had seen at the State Theatre not long ago. The music helped to break through the insufferable seriousness I felt in my Grandpa's church. Those folks in the Elim Church were not there to work through a service structured by traditional form and function like the Presbyterian Church; they were mainly concerned with saving souls and getting the word out. Evangelizing and proselytizing was their game and I was not up to that in any way at any time because there simply was no fun in it for me. After these Sundays at The Baptist Tabernacle, I was surprisingly pleased to get back to the Presbyterian church with it's rousing Weslyan hymns and the consistenly boring content of the Sunday sermon; for one Sunday anyway.

I never did feel like giving my heart to Jesus in the Elim Church, the Presbyterian Church (although they had the decency not to ask for such things) or any of the times someone in my family would solicit some response from me on this matter. I wasn't interested. What did it mean anyway? I liked the social side of things at church. It was there I found my enjoyment. I tried to live what I thought was a Christian life but I never took the step forward to cross over that line that others seemed bent on having me cross. I never followed my cousins and others down to the front at any Sunday evening service when the Pastor called for us, "to come and be saved by Jesus and to give your souls to him". I always felt at these times that this would be like giving my whole life away and I just was not prepared to do that. I had learned earlier on in my life to be very protective of my heart and my soul and I resisted any call or coercement, to give one aspect of these to anybody else, especially a being as remote as God.

Mum, I knew, thought the same as the rest of my family about all this, but she never seemed to preach directly at me like some of the others did. She was modest about it all and seemed quite comfortable being quiet in her beliefs. I felt that she fit more comfortably into the sedate Presbyterian Church rather than the flamboyant Elim congregation. She did remind me from time to time that I should love God because he loved me and that I should be good because Jesus loved only good people and they were the only ones who would go to heaven to live with him. But she never explained much about some of the strange stuff I saw happening in the Elim Church; stuff I wondered about then and later when I was older.

It always seemed to happen in the middle of a service at the Elim Church. The Pastor would be praying when somebody would stand up and start shouting out in some language I could never understand. When I first heard this I thought that these people were all missionaries and that they had learned the language of the particular country in which they had been living. But when I asked her, Mum explained that God was actually filling these people with his spirit and giving them a language to speak in. 'Speaking in tongues' it was called.

A person in the congregation would get up and say whatever it was God wanted them to say in his language of choice. In my teenage years at church, I used to listen for French, Latin or Maori, because I was a little familiar with the sounds of those languages, but I never did hear any of them. God seemed to always choose really obscure languages. Then, when the speaker was finished, another person stood up and gave what was assumed to be the translation in English so that the rest of us could all understand what God was trying say. I listened carefully to these translations to see if there was some really important message but I never heard one. All I heard was the same stuff I heard every Sunday in any church, Elim or Presbyterian.

Whenever these 'speakings' occurred, as they did most Sundays making them a significant phenomena of the Elim faith, I wondered if the same thing went on in any of the countries where these languages originated. Did someone in their churches get up and shout out God's message in English and another person give the translation in the language of that country so those people could make sense of it? I asked my Mother about this but she wasn't clear. I often wondered why she didn't get up and start 'speaking in tongues' or get up and give a translation.

I guessed it was because God only chose certain people for this job. And then I used to wonder why those particular people were chosen. Were they better Christians than folks like my Mum?

I was a skeptic from the beginning. I recognised dogma in the teachings of the church and how they wanted us to believe in everything that was in the Bible and all that they had come to believe as 'God's Truth'. Somehow I developed the courage to question and not just accept what was being said to me. My brother Barry had cut himself off completely from any church contact but it took me longer to reach that point. I felt that the family were keen to see that I adhered to the faith; that I should continue my education in the church. I felt this influence very strongly as a teenager, but inside I had other ideas. Sure, I attended church regularly over a number of years but I did so largely for social gratification and to satisfy my mother. As I matured I felt increasingly guilty about hurting her feelings and this was a powerful motivator to comply with Mum's wishes.

Years later, in my early twenties when education really kicked into my life, I would leave the church for good and reject the dogmatic doctrine of Christianity. So, in a sense my Mother was right to worry at the time when she warned me to be careful about what I read and what I listened to at college and university and in life at large. She was aware that the questioning of everything, including religion, came with the territory of those educational establishments. She saw this as a threat to basic faith and the first steps down the dangerous path to disbelief. The 'devil' it seems, was in the works for me. It occurred to me at the time that this was an admission of sorts, that the Church's belief in itself as the beacon of truth and light, was on very suspect and shaky ground.

And so it was that almost every Sunday morning around 10am the line of 30 boys and staff from the Home could be seen walking along in pairs, stretched out a full city block. The thick dark blue shirts we wore were prickly, the light blue tie, while contrasting well with the shirt, was tight and uncomfortable and the shoes on our normally bare feet were plain murder! It took us about half an hour to walk the distance unless an event occurred to cause a slowdown. This could be anything from the usual Sunday morning headaches or sleepiness, to a group of kids breaking off and watching that most religious of birds, the tui (also known as the Parson Bird because of the white feather tuft high on it's neck) in a hedge feeding off the small red trumpet-flowers full of sweet nectar.

Nobody ever went 'awol'. In fact we all arrived at the church resigned that for the next hour at least we would have to sit through the Reverend Turnbull's sermon. Just before 11am we were ushered inside to our pews to sing the opening hymn in our usual boisterous fashion and to listen to the Reverend's message. Nothing profound seems to have stuck with me in all those years of our Sunday routine. I do recall however, the impressive Harvest

Festival with so much food bursting out onto the church floor, a talking point by us kids on the walk home after the service. After the festival was over, the food was often sent to the Boys Home and we were always grateful for that show of kindness by the people of the Onehunga congregation.

The Presbyterian Church, like all other churches, had an open plate or soft felt collection-bag to hold whatever money people wanted to give as their Sunday offering. I sat waiting to put in my penny that had been given to me before leaving for church that morning. We grinned at each other up and down our pew. If the collector at the end of the pew had a bag, we resigned ourselves to simply dropping the penny in. But if the collection was done with a plate then the game was on. Some of us were quite skilled at flicking the bottom of the plate with one hand while pretending to put the penny in with the other. This deception was only possible if there was already money in the plate so that when we flicked the bottom there would be a small jingle of coins. The collectors never detected this because they actually never looked at the plate, always looking away as if they were a little embarrassed to be collecting money off people who had very little of it in the first place.

The rumour was that some of the older kids had the reputation of being good at putting in their penny and quickly lifting out a two-bob coin, or even a half-a-crown, without being seen. They said that if any of us younger kids tried that we would catch 'hell' later. At the time, keeping our penny back never seemed to be dishonest because we rationalised that we didn't actually put the penny in; we just pretended to. Neither did we offer the excuse that, "it's only a penny!" That large round copper coin with the kiwi on it was a treasure to us. In those days it was surprising what you could buy with it.

When Monday morning came around, the penny had usually burned the proverbial hole in our pockets and all through school we waited for the 3 o'clock bell which then saw us running through downtown Onehunga to Burkett's Biscuit Bar where they sold biscuits out of large square tins. The owner always had some that were emptied of complete whole biscuits and which contained only broken ones on the bottom. For one penny Mr Burkett would tip the contents of a tin into a brown paper bag and sell it to us. As we walked up the road toward the Home, we dipped our arms into the bag to get at the biscuits on the bottom. That's where the chocolate covered bits were and if we we were careful we would find a quarter or even a half of an oatmeal biscuit coated on one side with chocolate. We tasted every morsel; even the crumbs were savoured. We were in ecstasy faster than any religious committment would transport us, as we made our way up the road to Tin Tacks Corner and then home in time for afternoon jobs and the evening ahead.

Once out of church after Sunday service and formed into our two lines by Fernsy and the staff, we walked back toward the Home and the freedom of the rest of Sunday. While there were no pictures to go to at the State, no sledding up One Tree Hill and certainly no footy game on the paddock field, there were also no chores to do on Sunday either. *"Being a Christian had it's advantages,"* I sometimes thought.

By the time we had left Epuni Street and the church well behind, most of us had taken ties off, un-buttoned shirts and hung shoes over a shoulder by tying the laces together. Spirits were light and our voices louder now in conversation with each other. Already, a kind of freedom from the restriction of the morning was seeping in. My feet smiled each time they touched the pavement of the footpath and my neck relaxed once again having been spared the hangman's noose. Thoughts of a hot Sunday lunch with tasty corned beef, kumera, peas and apple crisp for dessert, evaporated any trace of the Reverend Turnbull's sermon and became the next best thing to Heaven in my life.

The Policemen's Picnic

At the foot of Queen Street at 8:30 am on Saturday morning the boat to Devonport would pull out and for a large group of sleepy boys that was an awfully early one to catch. On Friday night Fernsy chased us out of the dining room, the front room and off to bed. "Come on Kevin Davies, I told you before to get a move on. For a fast runner like you, you sure are slow around here. Hurry up you two over there, off to bed. I want all you boys up early ready to catch the Ferry at half past eight. If we miss it there'll be no Policemens Picnic for anyone!"

Inevitably, sleep was difficult that night. Warren Francis didn't help matters by taking this particular time to tell the story of the last movie he had seen. Dean Martin and Jerry Lewis were being their insanest selves in their latest flick, "Sailor Beware." Warren had gone with his older brother and now, when we knew we should be asleep, he chose to launch into the whole script in detail in typical Francis style. He spoke quietly and we posted the usual sentinel at the door to warn of staff in the area. You had to listen, it was so compelling and anyway how can anyone get to sleep when you're laughing so hard?

Pommy woke us at 6am Saturday morning, ran us down to the bath house and through the cold showers before we knew what hit us. Breakfast was light and fast and then it was back to the dorm to change into our khaki shorts and shirts, grab our swimming togs and race down to the courtyard where we all met. We complained like crazy, tried to take our time washing and dressing, and did all the regular boy-things just to get a rise out of the staff.

At these times, rushing to get ready for an event, I didn't seek out my mother for her help or approval. But once in a while I liked to have it especially when it came unexpectedly. I passed her this morning running back from the wash house.

"Morning Kev, but my, you look handsome this morning. Did you comb your hair?" she asked with a smile.

"Uh, oh yeah, Pommy did it Mum."

"Did she?" Mom exclaimed. "Could have been done better I think. Here, let me have a go at it."

She fussed and licked her fingers and tried to settle the curls down on my head, but as usual they wouldn't be controlled. Neither would I and pulled away. I hated anyone fussing with my hair even my mother, especially in front of the other kids. Anytime!

"It's alright Mum," I said. "It's going to get blown about on the truck anyway."

She looked a bit hurt as I walked away but it was one of those moments where, even though I knew my Mum wanted to fuss over me, probably because she never got much of a chance, I resisted. Most likely she wanted to hold me and feel my hair and just hug and stroke me. There must have been many times at the Home when she longed for those moments to present themselves so she could just remind every one that "see, we might be in an orphanage, but I'm his Mum and I love him." When these times occurred, like this time waiting to leave, she could hardly contain herself and her emotions. I fought against my urge just to let go, to encourage her hugs and caresses in that moment and to be the little needy boy around his mother. I wanted to feel that love as well. Both of us did and we must have lived through the years in the Home with an ache of an absence of much opportunity to respond naturally to each other's affection. Over the years this distance affected my vulnerability and made me wary of the normal closeness my mother desired both physically and emotionally. If it sounds a bit dysfunctional, it probably was and is.

I walked over to join Warren and Ross and a group of other kids.

"Hey Davies, are you running in the races this year at the picnic?" they asked.

"Yeah," I said. "How about you Warren?"

"He's running." said Ross. "You know Francis, never misses a race if he can help it."

"I know," I said, "and he's fast too, aren't you Warren, mate? A regular rabbit is our Francis, you kids. He's not called 'Rabbit Warren' for nothing."

Each year The Auckland Policemen's Association held a big picnic over on Motuihe Island for kids in all the homes and orphanages around the whole Auckland area. Not just boys either, girls were there as well although we never had much to do with them during the day. They seemed content with their own fun and we were most definitely into ours. There was some contact and some girlfriend-boyfriend stuff going on in the background, but I was too busy, and probably too young, to pay attention to any of that.

A big open bed truck with nice high sides pulled up at the bottom of The Lane and we all clambered on board. Thirty boys on the back sitting close together filled it to capacity. It was a bit uncomfortable but before we knew it we were driving along Karangahape Road and down Queen Street in the city centre.

"Bags the seat up front on the ferry," yelled Carl.

"Bags the one next to it," said Colin Graham.

"Bags the whole deck outside," laughed Party, "that's where I'm going."

"Bags the wheelhouse next to the Captain," said Bobby Parata

"Yeah Parata, the only steering you're gonna do is right up on the rocks at Devonport," said Carl.

"Eh hoa, Carl you know my Koro was the best at steering ships and I've inherited everything from him."

"Oh yeah, Bobby?" said Warren. "Was that ships or canoes mate?"

It didn't happen very often but I loved any trip on the harbour ferries or any boat when I got the chance. Sometimes the water chopped up a little but I never remember feeling seasick. That came later when I was a teenager rocking about in the tiny dinghy belonging to my Uncle Max way out on Cook Strait in Wellington where we occasionally went for summer holidays. On his famous 5am fishing trips I sometimes became so seasick that I finally quit going and took up snorkelling and spearfishing instead. It helped to be in the water and not on it.

My Mum though, she never got sick. She could stay out all day and fish and she just loved it. None of her sisters or her mother went anywhere near fish, unless they were in a pan or on a plate. But Mum was a woman of the sea, she could catch fish as well as anybody. In another life she would have been right at home on a commercial fishing boat. She might have been small but she was strong. And fish!? She never came back empty handed and hauled aboard many blue-cod half as big as herself. My Uncle Harry always said, "Hey Kev, you know that your Mum is the best fisher this side of Red Rocks don't you?" He was very proud of his older sister.

The truck pulled up outside the Ferry Building on the Quay just as people were boarding the ferry.

"Come on you kids or the ferry'll leave without you," called the man in the uniform. We ran up the gangplank, onto the deck and Colin and Carl headed right to the front grabbing the seats they had bagged.

"Mum, do you want to go outside?" I asked.

"Ok Kev, you pick a place."

A group of us settled on top of a large hatch cover outside sheltered by an air shaft coming out of the deck.

On The Ferry To Motuihe Island

"This is a good spot Kev," said Mum, "it's not so windy or cold."

Maaaack! maaaack!........two blasts on the ferry horn and we were off out into the Waitemata harbour and on our way over to Motuihe Island. The ferry made it's usual crossing to Davenport first and from there we excitedly boarded one of the two huge launches owned by the New Zealand Navy which took us the rest of the way over Hauraki Gulf to Motuihe. As we cleared the harbour I felt the wind in my face and hair and settled in for the excitement of this latest sea voyage. By now almost all the kids had joined us on the deck and the senior kids had set two large boxes down next to us as well. Fernsy, Mum and Frank Bickerton handed out sandwiches and before I bit into mine I checked it's innards. Wow, ham and relish! This was going to be the best trip ever.

It was a typical Auckland day, clouds about, some sun breaking through, a bit blustery, but fairly warm. As we cruised out into open sea the adults peeled off their jerseys and cardigans and we soon looked more like picnic people bobbing up every now and again to the ship's rail to check how quickly Motuihi was coming into view.

Motuihe Island is a small low-lying island with lovely sandy beaches in the Hauraki Gulf and was used by the New Zealand Navy for training purposes. In earlier times before white people had colonised the area Maori used it as fishing base. In the summer months particularly they would camp on the island and live off its fish and the shell fish that were plentiful. Who knows but even some of Bobby's ancestors might have been there. Motuihe had a good beach for swimming and a flat open field which the Police used as the area for the day's fun.

When we climbed off the Navy launch and made our way up the wharf to the picnic area we saw all the tents the police had set up where people could leave their stuff and where food was served. They even had a tent where they gave us free ice-creams in the afternoon and right next to it was a 'Lost and Found' and already there was one small teary-eyed girl under the canopy. Fernsy and Mum took charge and dragged us all over to the tent reserved for 'The Onehunga Kids' and we stored our gear and extra clothing there for the day. We ran off to the field where they were just announcing that the races would soon begin.

The next two hours were taken up with events like the 'egg and spoon race' and the 'three-legged race'. I fell face-first in the 'sack race'. There were skipping races for adults only and Mum came second in one of those. The obstacle race brought out lots of laughs especially when Bobby and Party couldn't find their way out from under the canvas sheet they had to crawl through. I loved the fun of it all; the noise, the crowd shouting, jostling and the kids yelling.

The last part of these events were the running races, the more serious events. I was nervous as usual when my race came up. Warren and I got through our heats and into the final and even though I tried my best I couldn't beat him. He always seemed to be a bit faster than me and I admired him for that. We competed with each other for sure, but we were best friends so it didn't matter much to me that Warren was obviously a faster and better athlete than I was. Party was quick too. I smile sometimes when I think about those races and wonder about my own competitiveness. Sure I wanted to win. Sure I wanted to beat Warren and Party. And sure I wanted my footy team to win all its games. But I lacked the true competitor's instinct to win in games and sports. It always seemed more important to me that I was taking part. Disappointment at losing didn't haunt me like it did other kids. At the finish line or at the end of the game, I was able to quickly put the event in perspective and concentrate on the pure enjoyment I felt at being there. If I did win I celebrated. When I lost I was able to admire the skill, speed and ability of the winner and for that matter all the other kids I was competing against.

Later, there were the senior kids races and Gordon Stretch seemed to win them all. He did well every year. Nobody could catch Stretchy but Jim Palmer won the long race around the whole picnic ground like he did every year. They had to run ten times around and Jim with his long bony legs seemed to tear out in front of everyone by the third or fourth lap. He was a natural distance runner because he had the physique and the endurance. I was sure glad they didn't have one of those races for our age group because I was never a distance runner.

"Ok you kids," said a big burly policeman with a friendly face, "it's time to head over to your tent for lunch. You remember where it is don't you?"

I ran to be sure to get some of those ham and egg salad sandwiches I had spied on the tables in the food tent and the plates of cakes they had set out. They were great and so was the ice-cream that the Police served us afterwards. It was a good feeling walking about the field, after our races, a tasty lunch in our tums and licking this wonderful treat. It wasn't often that we had any ice-cream.

"I've got honeycomb, what've you got Colin?" I asked.

"Raspberry ripple," he said. "What've you got Party?"

"Same as you," said Robin, "and you've got half of mine all over your face!"

There were a couple of hours in the afternoon when we were allowed to hang out or do some exploring before the boats left to return to Davenport to catch the ferry back to Auckland. Every year some of us followed a policeman on a walk around the island. The trail led over some farmland and down to the beach and, for much of the way, was pretty rocky. At the north end of Motuihe there was a high bluff with some huge Pohutukawa trees on top. The middle one had a rope attached to it and we knew what this was for. The older kids warned us each year not to say anything otherwise kids from other homes would find out about our secret. A few years earlier some kids had discovered that the Navy used this area as a rubbish dump. Their garbage wasn't old food or the usual smelly stuff. It was clothes and equipment that they didn't use any more and among this were their old Navy hats that the sailors had worn. This was our secret prize once we got to it. From the top looking down it wasn't possible to see all the clothes and hats dumped there. You had to know to get down below the overhang and forage.

Once across this bluff, our policeman guide said, "alright boys and girls, it's only two hundred yards back to the tents now and I'm running the last part. See if you can catch me."

Risky Business To Get A Sailors Hat

Most of the kids took off after him but a few of us stayed behind as we did every year. We scrambled quickly back up the top and rapelled down the bluff by the rope tied to the Pohutukawa tree. A couple of rope-burns later I was in the middle of a pile of old uniforms, boots and hats. Treasure Island for sure! Most of the clothes had been cut or torn but if we looked hard enough we were always able to find some hats in pretty good condition.

Of course the older kids found the best ones the quickest but I always seemed to have some luck.

"Got one," I yelled proudly. I had given my last year's hat to Bobby Parata but I planned to keep this one for myself.

"Hey Kevin keep it down will ya, they'll hear us," said Mathew Lowen.

The hats were put into somebody's pack following orders from the older kids. I climbed back up the rope and ran along the path to the field where we found everybody cleaning up and tidying the place. I joined an 'emu parade' just starting out at one end of the field to pick up all the lunch paper and other rubbish we could find.

"Kevin! Kev!" I could hear my Mum call, "come and get your shirt dear."

"Thanks Mum," I called back.

I walked over to her and she asked where I had gone in the afternoon.

"I just went for a walk around the island with the Policeman, Mum," I replied.

"Well you didn't come back with the others and I was a bit worried," she said.

"Oh, yeah, Mum, we found a dead fish on the beach and we went off to look at it," I lied.

"Oh, I bet that was smelly," she said.

I had learned to tell a few lies to my mother and other adults now that I was older. Not serious lies, but what I considered lies that were pretty harmless, you know, fibs to avoid the predictable interrogations that adults always seemed to think were necessary especially when it involved kids and fun stuff.

"Did you have fun dear? What did you like best?"

"I loved the races Mum. And the ice-cream," I said. "I love ice-cream, especially honeycomb."

"I know you do dear. I'll buy you one the next time we go to Nana and Grandpa's place."

On the way to the boat with the other kids, I thought that the very best part of the picnic for me was the secret trip down the steep bank to find a sailors hat. I planned to keep it in my locker, perhaps my Camp Box, and to wear it on special trips like, up One Tree Hill on Saturdays or to Waikaraka Park on Wednesday evenings. I relished the thought of wearing my hat up at Camp at Christmas time. Bobby wore the one I gave him last year and I thought he looked like a real sailor. But for now I said nothing of this to anyone and easily kept the secret to myself. There was something in delaying the gratification of my find that I knew would make it all the more delicious later on.

That image of myself at Camp with my sailors hat on at a jaunty angle and other kids wanting to take turns to wear it, kept popping up in my mind all the way back to Davenport and to Auckland on the ferry. I was excited by the events of the day. It wasn't often that us Home Kids were treated like this.

Anybody watching us on the ferry coming back from Devonport would have easily been able to tell that we had just spent a great day out. Constant chatter among our group with wild windblown hair and sunburned faces was enough to show that whatever we had done had raised our level of excitement.

" How many ice-creams did you have today Warren?" I asked.

"Two," he said, "they were so big I couldn't eat any more."

"I had four," said Carl.

"Guts," said Party.

"I would'a had more but we had to clean up," said Carl.

"Guts," I said.

"How many did you have Bobby?"

"Only one 'cos when I went to get my second one they were all out and they said that some kid with specs had taken the last scoop in the tub."

"Guts!" we all said looking at Carl.

The truck was waiting at the wharf when we walked off the ferry. Once on the back and snuggled in together we started off home. Before we even began to climb up Queen Street I had pulled the blanket tight around myself, laid my head to one side and fallen asleep. Everyone else did the same. Being early evening it had just begun to cool off especially in the open on the back of the truck. The Motuihe Policemens Picnic took its toll on small kids like me. Too much fun has a way of draining all of that kid-energy which hit its peak about the same time as we took the last lick of our free ice-cream. Tonight we would sleep well and dream a little.

"Kapai mates," said Bobby, "this Maori had a good day."

Tomorrow we would talk again about Motuihe and the Policemens Picnic. The details might fade over time but the memory of the fun would play like a movie in our minds for a long time.

One Tree Hill

On a cold wet and windy Auckland morning in 1853, Darcy Titmus crawled out of his grassy cave on the slopes of Maungakiekie and opened one eye to the weather. It had been raining most of the night and in spite of the fact that Darcy was under cover, he was shivering from the cold. He had a headache, dry throat and a general feeling of discomfort exaggerating his hangover from the previous evening of drinking.

He had spent the day before in the company of several seedy types just off a ship from Australia. Auckland's waterfront at the time had many small drinking establishments tucked here and there. They were hovels, and the one that Darcy and his mates ended up in was the worst. Once the first bottle of Aussie gut-rot bush whisky was finished, it only primed them for more. This was not the first time he had met up with his pals. His cousin Jake, a deserter from the Australian Bush Wackers, with his two mates Seamus and Terry, had arrived in Auckland from Sydney as crew on the ratty old cargo ship Adelaide. On each of their trips Jake had sought out his cousin Darcy while they were berthed in Auckland.

The Adelaide was loading up with a variety of produce supplied by Maori entrepreneurs who had begun a lucrative trade with Australia. The three had worked hard on the rough trip over the Tasman and were looking for some 'recreation' on their two days off. Of course, 'recreation' to them usually meant drinking any alcohol they could lay their hands on and there were numerous watering holes in Auckland that catered for this kind of appetite.

"This place'll do us Darcy my boy," said Jake when they had settled into the bar just off the Auckland waterfront.

"It's great to seeyuh Jake," said Darcy. "We've a lot of catchin' up to do. You're the only family I have down here at this arse-end of the world."

They settled quickly into a second and third glass of beer which would soon be supplanted by the whisky in no time at all. The talk seemed to go better that way.

"Darcy, this here's Terry and Seamus, me mates in Sydney. We signed on to the Adelaide as crew a week ago. Had to move quickly this time, eh boys?" grinned Jake.

The two men stood by the bar and nodded. "Move quickly" was an understatement, since the Aussie police were always looking for Jake after his desertion from 'The Wackers', the three moved more like lightning whenever the need arose.

Darcy looked the men over. They were big strong Irish lads who hadn't seen a barber shop in months. Cousin Jake was no looker either, sporting a thick beard and a craggy, pock-mark face. Darcy felt right at home.

"Great to meet some Irish lads and have a chance to put back a few Jamieson's and have a jaw," smirked Darcy.

"Sorry boy, but Jamieson's this ain't. Good old Aussie bush liquor does the same job though," slurred Jake. "Here have another."

"All the same mates, it's grand t' meet up with youse. Living here in arse-end New Zealand I never get a chance to talk to any Irish lads and the place is a regular rats nest anyway. Plenty of people comin' and goin' but not many jobs. Then there's all these Maoris who'll kill yuh quick as look at yuh."

"Darcy my boy," said his cousin, "why don't yuh cut yer ties here and make the trip back with us to Sydney. There's plenty of work there. And you want Irish to talk to? Well Sydney's full of Irish. So's any other place you want to go in Australia."

"Maybe I will Jake, maybe I will," said Darcy. "I'll think about it. What do I have to do to sign on to the Adelaide?"

"Yuh just have to be prepared to stay off the booze mate, and work hard while you're on board. And yeh, do as you're told by the officers otherwise you'll not make it to dry land. That's all," he grinned.

"Will I have to be liftin' much now?" Darcy asked.

"You'll be liftin' 'n pullin' 'n shovin' 'til you're sick of it my boy," said Jake.

"Well, I'll be thinking about it cousin, I'll be thinking about it."

"Don't be thinkin' too much Darcy my boy. The Adelaide pulls out on Friday at dawn so that only gives yuh three days."

Darcy sipped his whisky and digested this information. He saw the chance to leave this hell-hole of a country but he didn't relish the idea of having to work that hard to earn his passage to a new opportunity. Being no entrepreneur and not all that keen on a days hard work either, Darcy was not one to be attracted by so-called opportunities which he saw as an interference to his penchant for the bottle and the bed.

"That's enough serious talk lads," said Seamus speaking for the first time. "Let's drink to good-old Ireland and let's have another to good-old freedom."

Somehow, by the following morning, Darcy had made his way from the harbour to Maungakiekie and slept off his drunken stupor in the same cave he had slept many nights before. Necessity for a place to bed down had driven Darcy to the hill quite a distance from the waterfront core of the young city. Not being Auckland's most employable citizen since he had arrived from Sydney more than a year ago, he was usually without the means to pay for room and board and had scrambled from one place to another, one hedge to another, until he had found the relative security of this cave. It was temporary digs for sure, but at least he had somewhere to go.

After a night of drinking with his cousin, there was no way Darcy could remember how he got back to his cave. The distance from Auckland's port to Maungakiekie was greater than he could walk given his sad condition. Somewhere along the route he must have hitched a ride on a wagon or dray. Now on all fours, dirty, unshaven and reeking of his unwashed body, he peered out at one of the worst of Auckland's days the past week had offered.

He was cold. He thought of a fire to warm himself. He checked to see if the matches he had picked off the bar last night were still dry. They were.

Darcy grabbed an axe from the back of his hole-in-the-ground and headed off toward the peak of the hill not far from where he slept. When he was at home in his cave, foraging for firewood was part of his routine. Many a day, as was his habit, he had been out in worse weather than this collecting all the wood scraps he could find. And those same wood scraps is what he should have been collecting on this day. But for now he raised his collar and gritted his teeth as he stepped out. He knew that right at the top there was an old Pohutukawa tree large enough for lots of firewood but small enough to chop down and drag back without too much effort. It didn't cross Darcy's small mind that if he cut this lone tree down he would be left with monsters even further away to harvest on all the days after. He should have stuck to foraging for old branches and scraps. The sad fact is that by mid-morning Darcy, ignorant vagrant that he was, had cut through the trunk and changed the landscape on Maungakiekie forever. It was not the first time however, that this alteration had taken place at the summit of the hill. Nor would it be the last.

Trees had always been on Maungakiekie ever since Aotearoa erupted from the ocean and formed its present land mass. Some had forever grown near the summit and when Darcy Titmus cut down the lone pohutukawa he was not the first to do so but one of a line of people who had violated the foliage at the top. Some made their mark centuries before and a few did their damage in the years long after Darcy passed away. In those small morning hours people nearby might have heard the sound of the axe in Darcy's hands and thought nothing of it. But in present day Auckland, people still cringe at the thought that if they had only listened carefully not so long ago on that certain night in 1994, they just might have heard the sound of the lone Monteray pine succumbing to the savagery of a chainsaw in the hands of a certain Mike Smith. Once again the landscape on Auckland's most famous hill had been altered by man. Some things never change.

Looking far back to 1605, long before Darcy's white Pakeha ancestors arrived in New Zealand, Koroki, a child of the Ngati Whatua Iwi of the Isthmus, was born. According to legend, on the sacred hill of his birth, the stick, used by the Maori midwives to cut his umbilical chord separating him from his mother so that he could grow strong and tall, was tossed aside and lay on the ground for years. A Totara tree sprouted, fed by the nutrients in the umbilical chord residue and by the minerals in the rich volcanic soil on this hill destined for fame. Over the years the Totara grew among the Pohutukawa on the hill, their seeds spread by winds blowing cool off the harbour below. Among the Maori inhabitants of the Isthmus it was known as "Te Totara a ahua", the totara which stands alone.

All during the 1600's the Totara stood as a sentinel stands. Known and revered as Koroki's tree, it held a special status in Iwi storytelling. The legend of how the Totara grew was told over and over. But, over time, the totara too eventually died and was replaced by a Pohutukawa tree which seemed at once to inherit the stature of 'Te Totara a ahua'.

Maori called the hill 'Maungakiekie', the mountain which talks, and Maungakiekie it was to remain. It was one of a circle of volcanic peaks dotted throughout the Auckland Isthmus. When white people eventually invaded the land of the Ngati Whatua in the mid 1800's, the symbolism of this lone Pohutukawa was already well established in the consciousness of the people of the isthmus and volcanoes. That is, until our ignorant friend Darcy Titmus arrived on the scene.

About 1853, Dr John Logan purchased the farmland around Maungakiekie known already to the increasing white population as 'One Tree Hill'. Dr John was encouraged to purchase after he learned what damage one drunk could do to a beautiful landscape for the sake of self-gratification. There was no doubt that the Doctor was a good business man but he was also a conservationist at heart. In the spirit of the Maori forefathers, he felt moved to preserve the area from further possible vandalism from the likes of Darcy Titmus. In the wake of this damage, Dr John busied himself on his new property a week later, chasing Darcy and other vagrants away and planting Monterey Pine seedlings at the summit. He knew a thing or two about horticulture and felt certain that over time a new tree would grow in place of the unfortunate Pohutukawa. Time, it seemed, proved him right. The pine grove flourished.

On one of his walks to the summit 20 years later in 1875, Dr John selected a site above the pine grove to plant a Monteray seedling he had been nursing for some time. As he patted the soil down around its infant trunk he stood and blessed the tree and wished it good health to grow tall and strong like it's family on the edge of the crater below. His blessing hit home and his wishes were fulfilled. The tree grew strong for 125 years.

Citizens of the fast growing Auckland City, urged their government to build a memorial to a war they chose not to forget. They demanded that it be located at the summit of Maungakiekie or One Tree Hill as the pakeha chose to call it. It would look majestic right next to the lone Monterey Pine now full and strong in its maturity. Once the memorial was in place at the summit, an icon was born. The tree next to the war memorial was visible from all points around Auckland. An early edition of The New Zealand Herald proclaimed: "The hill has re-created itself through many ages from 'Te Whenua o te Ngati Whatua' (the land of the people of the Isthmus), to 'Te Totara a ahua', to 'Maungakiekie' and now to 'One Tree Hill'. All of Auckland's people, Maori and Pakeha, feel the spirit of Koroki and his birth, symbolic of the creation of the icon, residing in the collective imagination of all citizens of our wonderful isthmus."

"Come on Kev, pick it up mate. Wanna get to the top before dark," said Bobby.

"Yeah Kev," chimed Carl, " I could carry the sled if it's too heavy for ya."

"Shuddup Newman," I replied. "You'd be the last one I'd give the sled to. You'd probably drop it and forget where you did. Or smash it!"

"Yeah, Carl mate, leave Kev alone, he can carry his own sled," grinned Party. "But I can help if it's too heavy for you Kev," he added.

Warren looked over at me and smiled and I smiled back. It was always like this when the five of us were together as we were today on our way up One-ee for an afternoon of sledding.

Wood had arrived at the Home earlier in the week and by Wednesday we had started building our sleds. We put the finishing design touches to them earlier that same Saturday morning. At lunch, Frank Bickerton and Jim Palmer had announced that they would be leading any kids who wanted to go up One Tree Hill to have some fun for the afternoon. This wasn't news. We had been talking about it all week once the wood arrived.

"Jeez Kev, that sled you and Warren made's a beauty," said Bobby.

"Thanks, Bobby mate," I said. "You made a good job of rounding off those runners Warren."

"It's a beauty, Kev, and it'll be slippery, flying down One-ee like an eel in a stream."

"You blokes have a good slider as well, Bobby and Party," said Warren. "That's the biggest sled to come out of this wood yard in a long time."

"Yeah, well it needs to be," said Carl, " 'cos Parata's got the biggest bum at 109 Mt Smart Road."

"That's alright Carl mate, go ahead and be a cheeky bugger," said Bobby. "I might have a big bum but at least it's gonna have a seat to sit on. Where're you gonna put yours?"

Party grinned at this and said, "he's right, Carl, where's yours mate?"

Carl leaned over and picked up a board with two pieces of wood tacked onto one side. He held it up.

"That's it Newman?" asked Warren in shocked disbelief.

"Yeah, it's ok though and it'll go just as well as your bloody sled, Francis."

"Don't think so, mate," I said, "first bump you hit Carl, we'll be watching you go head over tea-kettle all the way to the bottom."

All this slagging didn't phase Carl one bit. He hammered one more nail into one of the runners on his board, tightened the rope he would hang on to, slung it under his arm and said, "hurry up you blokes. I'm ready." We finished up our building and headed off to lunch when the bell sounded.

"You kids who are coming up One-ee meet out the front after lunch," said Jim.

"And think about this, you blokes," said Frank, "we don't want stragglers this time. You've gotta keep together and not string yourselves out all over Onehunga like some of you did last time we went. Get it Little Davies? And you Lee brothers too. You blokes are slow when it comes to walking."

After leaving the front gate of the Home we headed straight toward the nearest fenced-off paddock on the slopes of One Tree Hill. It was short cuts all the way for us. As usual I was a bit of a slowpoke. My brother went by with Les Allen and Gordon Stretch.

"Hey Kev ," said Barry, "you'll need to walk faster than that if you want to make it up the hill today mate. I'll take your sled if you think it'll make a difference."

" 'S'ok Ba," I said. "I want to carry it myself."

"It's a beauty alright mate," he said. "Did you make it all yourself?"

"Warren and me," I said. "What d'ya think of the runners Barry?"

"Beauty mate, beauty," he said. "You two did a good job. Nice and smooth so it'll run down the hill real fast."

With that he patted my shoulder and was on his way.

"See you up there Kev," he said.

Kids were strewn back down the streets carrying their sleds. We kept an eye on Jim and Frank to notice any signal that we would be bawled out for lagging. Pretty soon we reached the first stile over the barbed wire fence.

"Hey, Parata, d'ya think Billy-Big-Balls will be among those cows over there?" asked Carl.

"I think I see him, way over there under the Puriri trees, Carl my friend."

"Better watch your back, Carl," said Party. "Last time he was at the Home you made him mad and bulls've got good memories mate."

We walked on through the field, hopped another fence, crossed the road which looped around One-ee on it's way to the summit, and headed up the grassy slopes which were now becoming steep. Sleds or not, if there were short cuts we took them.

"Hey you two Lees, Henry and Norman," said Jim, "stay away from that path and that old steel door. If you take off and work your way into one of those old tunnels we'll never find you again."

The two brothers snapped back into the group. They had been spotted trying to open the rusty old door set in a bank of the hill.

"I was just going to show Norman the tunnel," said Henry. "Jim, did you know that the tunnels were built into the hill during the 2nd World War?"

"D'you know why they were built Henry?" asked Jim.

"Yes I do," said Henry. "The New Zealand government was afraid the Japanese would attack Auckland and land here so the tunnels were built leading to small rooms where they kept secret documents and stuff. There's lots of them leading quite a distance under One-ee."

"Secret stuff eh?" said Bobby Parata. "I wonder if they kept my Koro's special hangi instructions and his plans for the world's fastest canoe in one of those rooms?"

"Hangi instructions Parata?" said Carl, "they weren't interested in any stuff you Maoris had. Secret stuff means plans where things are hidden and how to build things. That's what they wanted."

"Well Carl," grinned Bobby, "maybe you should mail the plans for your sled, 'cos I bet they'd want those."

Around noon we reached the summit of One Tree Hill and stood gawking up at the war memorial and the lone pine tree next to it.

One-ee, One Tree Hill, Maungakiekie

It was always a strange experience standing right next to the tree on the hill after living daily in its shadow. The tree and war memorial could be seen from miles away and from many different angles. Now to be standing next to it felt like I had intruded into one of those photos of One-ee you could buy downtown on Karangahape Road. Like being in a familiar spot but not sure exactly how I got there.

"Over here, you blokes," said Frank. "This is a good spot to have our sandwiches."

"Sandwiches!" said Party, "I didn't know we had sandwiches. Are they ham?"

We noticed for the first time that the older kids were carrying packs and out of them they now took wrapped sandwiches and laid them inside the circle we had formed.

"Hey, thanks Jim and Frank," said Warren.

"No problem, Francis," said Frank. "Now just remember you blokes, only one package each. Parata, down boy. I know all about your famous appetite."

We lay back and nibbled away, feeling relaxed but excited and somewhat nervous by the prospect of some fast and dangerous sledding. Sitting below the summit high on the top of an old crater, gave me a sense of being above the city even though I couldn't see it from this place. Our view was straight down a steep slope to the bottom of the crater. Sheep were grazing on the sides of the old volcanic pit. It was like a perfect cone tipped upside down.

"That's it I guess, Warren," I said.

"What?"

"That's where we sled down."

"Pretty steep," said Party.

"Not steep for me," said Carl.

We fell quiet, thinking about our sleds. Now that we were confronted with the actual hill the butterflies began flipping about. I thought, *glad Warren and me did a good job on our sled and made it strong. Hate to have one like Carl's.*

"Alright, you blokes," said Frank, "if you've finished your lunch you can hit the slopes. I'm going for a walk around the other side of the hill. You coming with me Jim?"

"Come on Warren," I said, "lets start on the other side 'cos it's a shorter ride over there and we'll have a good warm-up and get used to it."

Down I went fast and furious just like Tom Mix chasing an outlaw. My tummy was tight at the top but after I hit a few bumps and had to maintain control, I settled down to the ride. The first time down was always the hardest. Once I slid to the bottom, checked for grazes, I made a quick hike back up to the top to let Warren take his turn. My confidence was already up as I waited eagerly for the next ride.

"Nice one Kev!" said Warren. "Now watch this mate!"

Over the next half hour kids were flying down the slopes at all speeds and angles. Sometimes I made it all the way and sometimes I spilled off. Warren had a graze down one leg and I had blood coming out of both knees. Party had a big dark smear of sheep shit down the side of his shorts. There was no way any of us could avoid cuts and grazes with so much volcanic rock around. We accepted that it went with the territory.

"Hurts my bum," said Bobby. "Hitting all those ruts and rocks feels a bit like riding the tractor over my Koro's farm."

The sloping sides of each volcanic pit were groomed with little terraces making it easier for water to collect and grass to grow. There were thousands of red rocks about the size of tennis balls, some smaller, which lay strewn all over. Riding over those meant that it wasn't only Bobby who ended up with a sore bum.

Barry and Stretchy came by and watched us for a while. After one particularly fast run of mine, over all the noise of kids laughing and shouting, I heard Stretchy say to Barry, "Jeez Davies that little brother of yours sure can fly."

"Yep. He can ride that thing and he hardly ever comes off. Hey Kev, what's your secret mate?" Barry yelled.

"No secret Ba," I yelled back. "I learned from you remember? Last year you were flyin' down here on your own sled. I'm just riding like I saw you ride mate."

"He's good Stretchy, he's good," I heard Barry say. "I taught him everything I know!"

It felt good to have Barry's compliments coming my way. I loved it when he expressed that he was proud of what I could do. It made me feel like my big brother was looking out for me.

"Over here, you blokes," I said, "lets do the big slope." My confidence was up now and even more importantly, the sled was holding together.

"Hand me the hammer, Kev," said Bobby. "I don't want these nails digging into me."

We raced down every part of the slopes. The better the sled, the faster it went. Speed and danger made me laugh. There were enormous spills and end-over-end tumbles. My sides hurt laughing at some of the spectacular crashes.

"How's your sled holding up Carl?" I asked.

"It's ok," he said.

"Where are the runners?"

"Aww, they came off long ago but the board's still good," he said taking off on another slide.

After a yard, Carl stood up to remove a piece from the front of the board that had managed to dislodge itself, then sat on it again and went another yard or so. He did this all the way down, turned and grinned, "not bad, eh Kev?" and climbed back up the top for more fun. I shook my head and thought, *not bad at all mate. You know how to get some fun for yourself out of any situation.*

"Jeez," said Warren, "he's going so slow he may as well stay at the top."

I watched Warren put our sled through its paces down the slope. He fairly flew and was back up before Carl was even half way down. "It's a good one, Warren," I said after one particularly fast run. "I don't think it'll ever break."

We watched as Carl slid off again from the top and this time he chose a slope with less rocks. Half way down and going quite fast, his board hit a rut. The end jammed in, Carl flew off and landed face-first in some sheep shit. A couple of rolls later and he came to a stop.

"Jeez," said Warren, "our boy might have hurt himself this time."

We shot down the slope to check Carl out.

"Wipe that sheep shit off his face, you blokes," said Bobby, "then we can tell if he's still alright."

Carl looked up at us through obvious pain. "My glasses?" he asked feebly.

I looked about and spotted them ahead of his board.

"Here Carl," I said, "but they look a bit mangled to me and one glass is broken."

"Aww...now I won't be able to see."

"Come on mate," said Bobby, "try to stand up."

Carl struggled and then yelled, "my leg, my leg, I can't get up. I think it's broken this time."

"We've heard that before, Newman," said Warren.

"It's true! It feels like it's broken and it hurts like hell," Carl snivelled. "How am I gonna walk down One-ee with my leg like this? Awww..."

"Let's see," said Frank now returned from his walk and coming over to check what the fuss was about.

We stood back while Frank and Jim talked to Carl and checked his leg.

"Seems to be in a lot of pain you blokes," Frank said to us. "Don't want to take any chances that we might damage it more. 'Fraid you're gonna have to carry him down to the road where we can get some help. Warren, you and Bobby give him your shoulder on both sides and support him. Take turns you blokes 'cos it's going to be heavy going. And Carl, you're not to put any weight on that leg."

We lifted Carl into place on the shoulders of Bobby and Warren and all of us set off down the slopes of One-ee carrying our sleds and our now injured friend. Carl yelled in pain at first and then settled into a low moan with each step. I felt sorry for him and thought, *why do all these bad things seem to happen to Carl, especially at times when we're havin' fun?*

We came to a fence where we had to get Carl over the stile into the paddock. Way off in one corner were some cows. Warren and I took our turn supporting Carl this time and set off for the near corner of the field. I found it heavy going. To carry someone as awkward as I found Carl wasn't an easy thing to do. Just over half way along we heard a sound behind us and turned to look. A bull, which we hadn't noticed before, had emerged from under some trees and was giving us the 'hairy-eye-ball' just like we'd seen Billy do in our paddock at the Home.

"Jeez Carl," I said, "I hope he doesn't chase us."

"Looks like Billy Big-Balls," Carl said nervously.

Just then the bull took a step in our direction. Then another.

"Oh-oh you blokes," said Frank, "start moving. Fast!"

"Eh hoa, Kev," said Bobby, "let me and Party carry our boy. We've gotta move before Billy makes mince-meat out of us."

Carl groaned and moaned as a bit of weight went onto his leg in the change over.

The bull started into a slow trot just as we took off.

"Hurry, you blokes!" I yelled, "Billy's starting to charge us!"

For the next half fence line our group raced toward the stile in the corner hobbling along with the wounded Carl in tow. A quick check back and it seemed to me that Billy was closing.

"Faster, you kids, faster!" said Jim.

Party and Bobby were straining with Carl on their shoulders.

"Billy's gonna get us," whined Carl. "I don't want to die like this," he yelled, suddenly dropping his arm off the supporting shoulders and ran like the wind for the stile. Except for Bobby and Party, none of us in this particular moment noticed this amazing transformation in our friend. We scuttled down the fence line and over the stile to safety. I breathed a sigh of relief because I had to admit to myself I was really afraid that Billy was gonna get me and trample me all over the paddock.

"You bloody bugger Carl Newman," said Warren when we were safely on the other side of the fence. "There was nothing wrong with you at all especially after that run you just made. Your leg isn't broken and neither is anything else except your glasses... and your nose after I get finished with you. Bloody bugger!"

"E tama, Carl," said Bobby, "you're just a faker mate. Not sure I like you much right now."

"No no no you blokes, my leg was really sore up the hill and I was sure it was broken," whined Carl. "But after seeing Billy Big Balls all mad at us I got scared and ran without thinking about it. I didn't know it was alright before that. Honest! It's still really sore even now," he added as he struggled to his feet.

"Carl, you're a bugger alright," said Party quietly. "You'll have to walk home by yourself now, 'cos none of us is gonna carry you."

"What we should do Newman," said Bobby quietly, "is to put you in the paddock with Billy and tie you to a tree. Teach you a lesson to trick us like that, mate."

"Good idea Bobby," said Warren, "but let me break his nose first."

"Hey you kids," said Jim who had been standing to the side looking over the group and counting. Where are the Lees?"

"Dunno mate, maybe Billy trampled them."

"No, they weren't in the paddock. In fact they weren't even at the first stile with us."

Frank was thinking out loud, "I wonder if those two...... no they wouldn't do that.... well maybe......"

"What d'ya think Frank?" asked Jim. "What should we do?"

"I wouldn't be surprised if they've re-visited that old tunnel we came across while walking up. Remember we had to tell them to keep away from it? Let's walk back that way to check. I bet that's where they are. Henry's not gonna pass up an opportunity like that. You know what he's like. Over here, you blokes," said Frank.

When we arrived at the path leading to the entrance, the door to the tunnel that Frank had warned the Lees about was slightly open.

Frank said, "I bet those two are in there somewhere and if I'm right it's gonna be murder trying to find them in the dark."

"E tama, Carl first and now these two. What next?" asked Bobby.

"Come on Barry, Jim, lets see if anybody's in here," said Frank. "Kevin you come with us too in case we need a small bloke to get in small places. There's no telling what......."

"Keep your head down Frank," said Jim as we crept slowly into the dark of the tunnel. "It wasn't made for tall blokes like you."

Barry went after Jim and made sure that Warren was holding the steel door wide open at the entrance so it would throw some light into the tunnel for a distance at least. I looked in and was glad I was with the older kids. It was pitch dark up ahead. And scary. We walked very slowly for about 10 yards when I heard a noise. "Hey, can you jokers hear that? Sounds like some banging."

Barry quickened his pace and the noise increased.

"That's banging alright, Kev," he said, "like banging on a door. I bet that's Henry."

The four of us, now blind in the darkness, crept on in the spooky atmosphere.

"Yow," said Barry, "it's a dead-end up here.... but wait a minute the noise is louder now." He felt around with his hands . "It goes off to the right. Must be another part of the tunnel."

We walked carefully toward the banging. I had my hand sliding along the cold concrete wall for guidance and security.

Barry had stopped. "It must be here, like a door or something."

My eyes, by this time more adjusted to the gloom of the tunnel, picked up a very shadowy Barry three paces ahead. "Here it is," he said reaching his arms out in front.

The four of us grouped at his side. He had his head to the door side-on, listening. "Hey Frank," said Barry, "I can hear somebody calling faintly."

"Let me hear," said Frank putting his ear up against the door. "You're right Barry. That's gotta be the Lees. There's nobody else in here."

Jim took a moment to listen. "Heck, this door's gotta be really thick 'cos I can hardly hear. But we know someone's there by the banging. Let's get the door open you blokes." He thumped his fist on the outside to let the Lees know that someone had found them, if it was them. A flurry of thumps and bangs was the reply from within.

Barry tried it and said, "it pushes in so we're gonna have to shove, you blokes," and the four of us did. Slowly the door, which we now knew was not only thick but heavy as well, started to move away from us. All of a sudden the banging stopped and there was a loud "hey, you found us," in our faces. It was Henry Lee, unmistakeably.

"Henry, Norman, we found you!" I yelled.

None of us could make out anybody else very clearly but we all could hear Norman crying quietly. Henry said, "thanks for finding us... Frank... Jim... but somehow I knew you'd figure out where we were... Norman's been very frightened for a while now."

"Yeah, well, you two, we'll talk about this when we get out of here," said a very annoyed Frank. "Right now though, we better get moving."

Jim got us into a sort of big hug just so we could make contact with everyone at the same time. Just having some contact with the others was reassuring.

"You blokes with us, Henry, Norman, Barry, Kevin, Frank?" he asked.

"Here," I said followed by the others.

"Well thank God we found you two," said Frank. "Come on lets get out of here. Barry you lead the way and find the passage back to the door. Jim, bring up the rear and the Lees and Kevin, you blokes stay tucked in the middle. Nobody gets out of line."

The faint light of the entrance door eventually loomed and pretty soon I could make out Warren's familiar shape with other kids around him.

"Hey Henry and Norman, good to see you two," said Mathew. "For a while there I didn't think we'd see you again."

There were pats on the back for the Lees and a couple of comforting hugs for Norman who couldn't seem to stop crying. Everybody was talking at once asking Henry for details.

"E hoa Frank, ask these blokes what they got up to," said Bobby.

"That's right you two," said Frank, "now that we've got you out of there and you're safe, what did actually happen? Spill the beans now. Stop your blubbering first Norman."

"We just wanted to find out what was in there and to see one of those rooms people always talk about," said Henry.

"See the tunnels? See the rooms?" asked an exasperated Frank. "What the heck are you talking about. You can't see in there, it's pitch dark!"

"But I knew that, Frank, and that's why I brought my torch with me," said Henry. "I got it out of my campbox this morning and carried it in my pack."

"Shoulda known that, Mr Lee," said Jim, "of course you'd have a torch with you. What are we thinking Frank? This is Henry Lee the famous scientist we're talking to here."

"Why didn't you shine your torch to get us out Henry?" asked Barry.

"The batteries ran out when we were in that room," said Henry, "and I couldn't use it any more."

"So you went off by yourselves and got into the tunnel, found that room and pulled the door shut? Why pull it shut?" asked Frank.

"That's because we knew we were doing something wrong and didn't want you to find us out," said Henry completely open and honest in his relief. "I didn't think about the door being too heavy to open."

"Gee, funny you didn't think of that Mr Scientist," called Carl from the back.

"Norman and I are really glad you blokes found us. I was worried for a while. I'll remember about the door for next time Jim," said Henry.

"There won't be a next time," said Frank. "You two are not going into those tunnels again. D'ya hear me? Ever!"

"Yes, Frank, sorry."

"Next time up One-ee you two are to be with an older kid all the time. That way we'll know where you are."

"Could'a got locked in, Henry mate," said Bobby. "Anyway , most important thing is, what the heck did you find in that room? Secret plans? My Koro's drawings of his new canoe the army wanted? Or was it the navy? His secret hangi plans?"

"There wasn't anything in there," said Henry, "they must have taken everything out or people visiting must have taken it all away."

"Well somebody's got my Koro's canoe and hangi plans. I bet it's the army, or the navy, and one day you'll see a new canoe that can go faster than anything. He knew....."

Bobby said all this with such a straight face that the Lees and the rest of us were taken in. Warren, Party and me grinned at each other but Carl screwed up his face and blurted out "oh yeah Parata, I bet it won't go faster than the launch we went to Motuihe on for the Policemens picnic. No canoe can go that fast. And I bet that they're not interested in plans for a hangi. They have their own stoves for cooking in the Navy. What would they want with your Grandpa's hangi?"

"E tama Newman, you'll never know for sure will you mate, 'cos, as the Lees tell us, the plans have gone missing."

The sun was now behind the summit tree. The lower slopes of the old volcano where we were now gathered were mostly in shadow. With the excitement of the lost Lee boys now over, we walked on down toward the road into more sunshine. As we climbed the stile over the last fence some blackberry bushes attracted our attention. It doesn't take much to distract a group of boys sometimes and the prospect of a few juicy berries was all that was needed..

"If you blokes are gonna pick those berries, Kevin, we're not waiting for you," said Frank. "Bobby Parata, the Lees are with you so make sure they get home safe 'n sound."

"Yessir, Mr Frank," said Bobby. "They won't leave my sight."

So while the older kids walked down the road toward the Home, the rest of us became lost in berry picking. We took our handfuls to a patch of grass in the sun and sat contentedly eating the deliciously ripe blackberries. *There was nothing better,* I thought, *I always want to be able to do this with my friends after a great day out on One-ee. Couldn't be better.*

End Story

Homekids & Tony The Dog

It had been a difficult week for all of us. Not everything that happened at the Home during the year was enjoyable or play, but this past week seemed particularly troublesome. On Wednesday after school I was tussling with some math homework and becoming more frustrated by the minute. I recall that it was fairly basic stuff but somehow the concept had not filtered through into my understanding.

"Help," I called out. "This stuff drives me crazy."

"E tama Kev," said Bobby, "that stuff's not too bad mate. Even I can do that."

"Here Kev," said Warren, "let me have a look mate."

Other kids put their two pennies worth in but it was no good. Staff even got involved and just made things worse. The problem was that the math was so simple yet I was having trouble with it. I felt stupid. When Mum spent some time trying to comfort me the tears began, in front of the other kids. I'm not even sure that it was the math so much as my own frustration at realising that I was having difficulty with stuff that others seemed to find a snap. And of course, the more I tried to understand, the more difficult it became. I had not learned the trick of letting it all go, moving away from the problem and allowing it space to sort itself out. That would come later in life.

Warren had come back in a cranky mood on Monday from a weekend at his brother's flat to report that Malcolm had broken up with his girlfriend which put him in a foul mood. They hadn't gone to any movies and Malcolm had not even taken him out for their usual milkshake.

"Jeez, he didn't even take me for a drive in his new car like he promised," said Warren, obviously disappointed. Instead, they had lounged around the flat all weekend eating stale pies and reading old comics. His brother had bawled him out after Warren asked for the third time if they could go to see Auckland play Wellington at Eden Park. This was as big a game of footy as you could get but not even that could draw Malcolm out of his mood. Nothing worked out and Warren had come back to the Home feeling completely out of sorts.

Party, always the most placid among us, was on washhouse clean-up duty for the week, but had forgotten to turn up to do the job on the first morning and ended up sitting on the Pink Seat after school that day. By the time he made it to dinner in the dining room no amount of bantering was able to cheer him up. We just assumed that Fernsy had laid a few good ones on him.

"Anybody can forget," he sobbed later in the dorm.

Even Bobby Parata who never seemed to get into any sort of bother, fell afoul of this week's bad spell. Bobby's problem was connected with his daily duty, just like Party.

"I was on cowshed duty for the week," he said. "You know how much I love those cows. I'm pretty good at milking those girls just like my Koro showed me."

The good part was when Stretchy allowed Bobby to milk some of the cows all by himself for the first time. But the bad part was when one of the cows lifted it's back leg and kicked him fair in the shin sending the pail of fresh milk all over Bobby and the stall.

"Yeoww, that hurt mate!" said Bobby rubbing the lump on his shin. "And to rub it in, Stretchy gave me stick for upsetting the cow and causing her to kick," he complained. "You know I wouldn't do that."

He was not a happy farm boy sitting there telling us his story.

So, we were not a very cheery group at all during the week and couldn't wait for school to be over each day so we could just take our time walking home and let the sun burn off some of our pent-up feelings. For me it didn't help that at the start of my arithmetic class later in the week, my teacher decided I had not done my homework properly and rapped my knuckles with her ruler. No wonder I hated math for the rest of my school days. I didn't know what was worse: that, or the fact that the art teacher was on my case again for not taking her woodwork session seriously enough. To top it off though, on Wednesday, Warren and I were caught smoking high up in one of the trees at the Home before we were about to leave for Waikaraka Park and the track meet. There was hell to pay for that stupid mistake. The week was a mess! I would be glad when it ended.

By Friday, Carl's escapades went over the top and definitely took the cake. First of all, on Monday he was caught red-handed trying to steal a comic out of Mathew Lowen's locker.

"Hey Carl, what the heck d'ya think you're doin'?" yelled Mathew.

"Nothin', I was doin' nothin'," said Carl.

"Nothin' eh, you bloody little liar, Newman," said Les Allen. "I saw you sneaking that comic out of Mathew's locker and looking around at the same time to see if anybody was watching. I saw you mate!"

"Come on Carl," said Mathew. "Give the bloody comic back. If you wanted to read it that badly why didn't you just ask?" said Mathew. "I would'a given it to you mate."

Yeah, well, it's only a comic," said Carl. "Besides, you guys never lend me anything."

"You know that's a load of bull," said Mathew. "Tell you what Carl. You're banned from the front room for the rest of the week."

"Aw yeah? Who's gonna make me stay out?"

"I'm gonna, that's who Carl," said Mathew. "If I catch you in here, I'll kick your bum all the way up One-ee!"

"Oh yeah Mathew, gotta catch me first," taunted Carl.

Mathew glared as Carl walked out.

The rest of us looked on at this exchange not quite believing Mathew's obvious anger and Carl's quite stupid bravado.

"Hey Carl Newman," said Bobby in the dorm later. "Why'n hell did you take on Mathew? You stole the comic and he's the nicest bloke in the Home."

"Not so nice to me," grumped Carl. "Just a bloody comic."

Then, on Tuesday after school, Carl was seen in the staff lounge being talked to by my Mum and it looked pretty serious. We learned later he was reported from school having got into two fights that day, one on the school grounds and one on the way home.

"Something's not right for Carl this week Mrs Davies," said the Headmaster. "He's been in a bad mood all week."

After leaving the lounge, Carl headed straight to the washhouse to start on an extra clean-up job given to him by Mum as punishment.

Now, if all of that wasn't enough, on Friday, our boy Carl and a few other kids were found by Fernsy near the wood pile at a time when they shouldn't have been there. They all had swords in their hands and were in the middle of a battle-royal right up against the cream shed. They must have forgotten Fernsy's rule to keep our distance from the cream shed after Party and I had destroyed the wire mesh coverings in our Spartacus-spectacular a long while back. Now Carl and his troop of swordsmen with all their fierce scrambling around, caused clouds of dust to rise up from the red gravel, filter through the fine wire mesh and settle on top of the separating cream dishes inside the shed. Fernsy was livid as she flew out of the back door of the kitchen.

"Carl Newman and you others, get to the Pink Seat right this minute," she barked. "You all know the rule about playing near the creamshed."

Later in the dorm, Warren asked, "ok Newman, stop your blubbering and tell us what happened."

All the swordfighters had been given four of Fernsy's best, sent to bed early without dinner and told that the woodpile was completely out of bounds for everybody until further notice.

"Everybody?" I whined. "Does that mean all of us?"

"Yeah," blubbered Carl. "Nobody's allowed to use the wood for anything and we all have to keep away from the woodpile."

This was tragic news because we had all made plans to build more sleds to take up One-ee on Saturday. What were we supposed to do?"

"That's not fair," complained Warren. "What a piss-off! Carl Newman you bugger! Now you've gone and done it. Ruined our fun up One-ee."

Carl blubbered away so we went to talk to Fernsy but that was no use as she just said, "the punishment fits the crime Kevin and Warren. Carl and the others did something which affected us all when they raised enough dust to ruin our cream. The woodpile will be out of bounds until I say otherwise."

That, as we knew from past times, was that!

So, you can imagine how we felt about Carl and the other kids when finally Saturday morning rolled around. It was a beautiful sunny day, a perfect one for sledding down hills which we couldn't and that thought stuck in us like really thick porridge. At breakfast, Jim Palmer announced, "if you jokers are still up for it, the senior kids will be leading the way up One Tree Hill for a good tramp to the top and back. What d'ya think? Raise your hands if you're coming."

I don't think a hand stayed down. Even without the possibility to make new sleds and take them with us, we were still up for any fun on One-ee that we could get. Everybody in the dining room then looked over at Carl and his gang.

"Bloody bugger, Carl Newman," said Warren. "No sleds. Your fault!"

Out the front after breakfast, Jim was counting us so he could keep track. He remembered the time not so long ago when the Lees went missing. Frank appeared with Mathew Lowen and Barry at his side carrying a large cardboard box.

"Take a look in here what Mrs Davies and Pommy has made for us Jim," said Frank.

We craned our necks for a look. Inside the box were stacks of sandwiches neatly wrapped in wax paper.

"Good old Pommy," said Barry. "She knows what we like."

"You better say good old Mrs Davies too," said Mathew, "because it was her idea and she was in there working away with Pommy from the time the two of them got up this morning."

There were lots of grins as we all looked in the direction of the staff who were there to see us off. "Thanks Mrs Davies. Thanks Miss Pomeroi."

There was a silent gap of about 10 seconds before Bobby piped up. "Ah, a sunny day, a tramp up One-ee with my friends, a picnic at the top with the sheep. Ain't life grand?" said Bobby.

Frank and Jim split the sandwiches among those who had packs. Barry seemed to carry most of them. He loved to tramp with his pack. And now that the important stuff was taken care of, we set out for the day.

"Thank God that week's over," said Warren once we were on the road.

"You can say that again," I said.

"Thank God that week's......."

"Ok Francis, ok," grinned Mathew. " ' drive me crazy with your movie talk. I just heard Groucho Marx say that to Harpo last week at the State."

We walked at a good clip. Even I kept up which seemed to surprise Jim, Frank and my brother Barry.

"You've got lots of energy today Kev," he said. "Not lagging behind like you sometimes do mate."

It had been uneventful up to this point. We made it to the lower slopes of One Tree Hill without incident, even through the paddock where the cows and a possible bull were, way off, under the trees. Before long we started the climb up to the summit. All of us knew One Tree Hill so well by now we knew instinctively where to go.

"Stop a minute you blokes," said Jim. He began counting.

"The Lees are not here Mr Jim," said Bobby. "They're probably in that tunnel again looking for my Koro's canoe plans."

"What? Where?" Jim spluttered. "Oh yeah Bobby. Nice try mate. I can see you trying to hide those two kids behind you. Don't scare me like that. Henry, Norman, you two stay close. Got it?"

"Yessir Mr Jim," grinned Henry.

"Hey Frank, have you seen Carl Newman?" asked Jim. " Seems to be missing."

"He took off ahead of us," said "Barry. "He's headed over toward the monument."

Sure enough, when we reached the summit, Jim found Carl sitting on the stone wall waiting for us to catch up.

"What took ya?" was all he said. He seemed a bit distracted to me, even a little down. Something was definitely up with Carl.

"Newman, don't take off like that," said Jim. "I like to know where all you kids are. I still haven't forgotten what happened to the Lees that time when they took off. We were really lucky to find them. Remember that?"

"Eh hoa Jim," said Bobby, "Don't be too hard on our boy. It's been a hard week for him. Come to think of it though, it's been a hard week for us all."

It was hard to beat sitting up the top of One Tree Hill munching away on our sandwiches in the bright Auckland sun. It was about as good as it got, except perhaps, for a footy game with all the Home kids involved. Or, maybe even a good afternoon at the State watching a Hopalong Cassidy flick, or a Lone Ranger and Tonto movie. Then again, Guy Fawkes Day wasn't bad and neither was the annual Garden Party for that matter. Hard to beat the Policemen's Picnic for sure, or the Soap Box Derby races in Onehunga. The annual Farmers Parade was a good one as well. But the event that took the cake was Camp up at Maharangi Heads. Yeah! Now even I had to admit that Camp was better than a day up One-ee. Yeah, for sure.....

"What'ya thinkin' 'bout Kev?" asked Party. "I can always tell when you're thinking or daydreaming mate. Your eyes sort of stare off into the distance and you have a grin on your face."

"I was just thinking about all the stuff we do at the Home, Party. You know like being up here on One-ee. It's brilliant mate, don't you think?"

"Yeah Kev, it's great but it would be even greater if we had some sleds. Now that would be the best. If that bugger Carl and his pals hadn't....."

Just then a lump of sheep shit landed between us and cut Party off.

"Who the heck.....?"

Another clump flew in from behind us and hit me on the arm. I looked over and caught the backside of Warren and Bobby ducking down behind the bank.

"You buggers are gonna get it," yelled Party. "Come on Kev, lets chuck some sheep turds right back at 'em."

If one could get over the fact that you were handling animal waste, sheep turds were the best for having a fight with. The clumps are conveniently made up of little round balls about the size of marbles. It was as if the sheep knew that kids liked to have little battles like the one about to start, so they produced their crap in ready-to-throw sizes.

"Ssshhh Party, this way," I whispered. We grabbed a few clumps of our own, snuck left around the bank and came up on the blind side of Warren and Bobby.

"Now!" yelled Party, and with that, both of us scored direct hits.

"E tama Warren," laughed Bobby, "we've been rambushed!"

That was it. The battle was on and continued for the next 10 minutes. Balls and clumps of dung flew everywhere except near the senior kids because we knew that to hit one of them meant instant death. By the time Frank yelled "stop it you kids" all of us were marked in several places with dark round stains. But everybody was laughing, even Carl, who often got the worst of these fights.

"Yahoo, got you a beauty Parata," he said. "Right smack on your forehead. You look like you did the day I tackled you in that huge cow pie in our last footy game."

"Oh yeah Carl," said Party, "you must'a missed him cos I don't see a big mark there."

"You can't see it on Parata's face Party, 'cos he's so dark," said Carl.

"Is that true Bobby?" asked Warren.

One Tree Hill

"E hoa Carl Newman! I'm glad you can't see the shit on this Maori's face," grinned Bobby. "But you should see your ugly mug. Looks like you had your own private sheep, leaving it's trade mark all over. You look like one of those dalmation dogs mate."

"I don't, do I, Kev?" asked Carl.

"It's pretty bad Carl," I said, winking at Bobby. "You're gonna need a good scrub tonight mate."

The sandwiches and fun over, we made our way down from the summit of One-ee. I took one last look at the monument with the tree beside it, back-lit against the blue sky. That image at the top was burned into my mind. Mention One Tree Hill anytime and immediately the tree and the monument at the summit came up. Still does! What I didn't know at that moment was that this was going to be the last I would see of One Tree Hill for the next few years.

Down at the bottom of One-ee, near the road, we climbed the stile to take the shortcut through the big paddock.

"Hey Carl watch yourself mate," said Barry. "I think that's Billy Big Balls over there."

Carl ran off to the far corner stile as fast as he could and we all laughed.

Once over, Jim took a head count and said, "everybody's together for once. My, my, you guys are getting better and smarter. Not even the Lees are missing!"

"Yeah, but where's Carl?" asked Bobby.

"Billy got him. Spread him all over the paddock," grinned Barry.

"What are you talking about Davies?" said Carl, "I'm here. Jim, I'm here. Count me in."

We passed the small path leading to the fateful tunnel into the hill where the Lees had lost themselves and almost never made it out. The trail sloped on down toward the road and by the time we were over the final stile I knew it wouldn't be long now before we were walking back toward the Home. I was ready to get back and have a Saturday night dinner. I'd had a good day, but now I was hungry.

We arrived at the familiar small grass patch bordered by blackberry bushes and even before we got there I could see ripe fruit all over.

"Come on Kev," said Party, "let's get those berries before Bobby or Warren sees 'em."

"E tama mates, this Maori's too quick for you pakehas," said Bobby already at the bushes ahead of us with a few black stains on his fingers.

"Boy, are these ever ripe," said Warren.

"Come on Carl, get over here and get your share before Bobby eats it."

"Hey Kev?" replied Carl, "I thought maybe you would pick some for me and bring 'em over."

"Lazy bugger," snapped Warren.

He was having a hard day with Carl today. Hard day? I think it was the whole hard week catching up on him!

"Sure Carl," I said, "how many do you want and what size?"

We each picked our share and sat with our juicy handfulls on the grassy space. The sun was warm on us in this late part of the afternoon. I felt a lazy mood come over me now that the walk up One-ee was over and we were on our way home. It seemed a perfect ending to sit with my friends and taste each blackberry as I popped it into my mouth. When everybody had picked their share and had joined the group, Bobby said to Warren, "hey mate why don't you tell us about that last Pirate picture you saw with your brother."

How did Bobby know that this was the perfect thing to do: to get Warren talking so we could lie back in the sun, finish our berries and let our minds float away on his story. But before Warren could answer Carl spoke up.

"Hey, you blokes," he said, "I might be leaving Mt Smart pretty soon."

Warren started to say "Well who gives a........" but I poked him in the back and he stopped. He was still angry at Carl. The rest of us had put Carl's woodpile incident aside, so we listened when he talked.

"How come Carl?" I asked.

"My Mum's got a job and a place to stay and she told my sister and me the last time we were together that as soon as that happens and she gets permission from the Social Services people, we'll be moving in together. So it could happen soon. Hope so anyway."

"Think you'll miss us Carl?" asked Party. "I think you will."

"Yeah, maybe a bit. Not sure. But I really want to be with my Mum."

This made us all think of our own situations.

"There's a chance I might be leaving too in the next month or so," said Warren. "My Mum's out of hospital and my brother's helping her get a job and a place to stay. When I saw her last she said she'd like me to live with her when things are ready."

"Wow, Warren, that's pretty sudden. You didn't say anything about it." I said. "I'll miss you, mate, if you have to go."

"Yeah Kev, I'll miss all of you blokes too but I knew this would happen one day; that I would go to live with my Mum again. It was always our plan and when you have plans like that, people want to make them happen. My Mum doesn't like being sick and not working. She's been looking forward to getting me and my brother together again as a family. It's been a long time."

"Hey, but Warren, you'll miss all the stuff we do here at the Home won't you?" I asked. "Like footy, going up One-ee, going to the State, and just havin' fun?"

"Yeah Kev, sure I'll miss all of that stuff. Who won't? But it's a chance at a new life, with new friends and schools. Even a new footy team. My brother says I'm young enough and can adjust to new things in life. He says it gets harder when you're older."

I munched on another juicy berry and thought back to Scotts Beach at Camp when Party and me had picked a bucket of them and Mum had made blackberry pie for dinner.

"What about you Bobby?" asked Warren, "d'you have any plans to leave?"

"Dunno mate," said Bobby, "but you never know with my family. You bet they've been talking about getting me back up north and I'll go when they tell me to. Right now you're stuck with me here."

"D'ya think you'll like leaving the Home?" I asked.

"Nah mate, I won't like it but I'll get used to it. My Koro said we can get used to anything. The important thing is how we get used to it. What we're like when we have to go. He said that it's important to learn to say goodbye to some things in life, to let them go even if you like 'em a lot, because when you leave, they're behind you. Koro says that it's where you find yourself is the key thing, and what you do with your new situation. It's like movin' ahead and not staying stuck is the most important thing in life."

"It'll be tough though, Bobby," I said.

"E tama, Kev, toughest thing this Maori's had to do since I left home to come here. But I can do it even though I probably won't see you blokes again. But I'll remember you. All of you. Even you Carl Newman," he grinned. "How could I forget my mates at 109?"

I licked the last of the sweet black juice off my hand as my mind wandered over our conversation. This was sure bringing home to me my own talk with Mum about moving to Wellington. I didn't like the feeling.

"Hey Party," said Warren, "what about you mate? D'ya think you'll be leavin'?"

Party was silent and staring at the ground. "Not sure about that," he said quietly. "Dunno. Haven't talked to anyone in my family. Don't even know where they are and I bet they don't even know where I am. I'll probably stay here until I'm as old as Jim and Frank and then get a job and leave."

"Jeez Partridge," said Carl, "that's gonna be tough havin' to do all that stuff by yourself without family."

"Yeah, well, I have to do it don't I? Nobody else is gonna do it for me. Look at Stretchy, he's the same. He doesn't have any family and he's ready to move out by himself. He's got a job to go to. He's doin' it all alone."

"Jeez, I couldn't do that," said Carl.

"I'll manage when the time comes," said Party, "but right now I still have to put up with you blokes," he grinned. "Now that's really tough."

Me & Tony

It felt like the right time at this point for me to put my thoughts into words, so I did. "When Mum told me that my Grandpa had died a couple of weeks ago, she said we might have to move to Wellington with my Nana. I didn't like to hear that then and I don't like thinking about it now."

"E tama, Kev, that's not gonna be easy," said Bobby, "but that's your life, mate. That's where you'll find yourself when the time comes. Remember what my Koro said."

"Yeah, I know," I said, "but right now I don't want to leave the Home. I don't want to go to school anywhere else. I don't want to have to make new friends. I like it here at the Home doing all the things we do, havin' all the fun we have."

"But when the time comes Kev," said Warren, "you'll have thought about it and you'll find it a bit easier to say goodbye. You'll see, things'll happen that'll make it easier. Right now it seems like the last thing on earth you'd choose to do."

"Yeah Kev, it could be worse mate," said Bobby, "you could be movin' to Eketahuna or even some place down the South Island. Now that would be bad."

"It's not Wellington that I don't like," I said, "it's leaving the Home and all you blokes. I've been here a long time now and I have lotsa mates. You blokes are my family. I like the Home. I don't want to leave. I know I'm gonna have to face it when my Mum says it's time, but I'm not gonna like it."

"None of us are, mate," said Bobby. "E tama, Kev, we're all gonna find it hard to say goodbye. But as my Koro says, sayin' "goodbye" lets you say "hullo" to a new situation in life. And they're both hard to do. You need to get ready for that day Kev, 'cos it's going to happen to you just like it's gonna happen to all of us. Party too, even though he'll be on his own."

"Yeah I know," I said, "but lookin' at it right now I don't like it. I know I'll have to get used to it and I know you blokes will too. But it's sure gonna be different."

"Umm, excuse me, but don't you think we should be leaving now?" said Henry Lee, " 'cos it's been a while since the others left."

"You're right, mate," said Bobby, "let's go, you guys. Henry, Norman you two stay close to us all the way home. No more tunnels. Forget about my Koro's hangi for a while. Alright?"

"Yessir! Mr Bobby Parata," said Henry looking pleased with himself. His brother Norman beside him, was looking relaxed and was even smiling a little. He had grubby smears all over his face from the turd fight and was looking at his brother. *He's lucky to have his brother Henry,* I thought. *They look after each other.*

We walked along the road toward the Home. It would take us the next half hour to get there and in the meantime we thought about the great sled rides we'd had many times up One-ee. And we thought about our dinner coming up. Being a Saturday, I knew it would be a roast and I looked forward to that especially after working up an appetite climbing the slopes, getting mixed up in another major battle with the others and whetting my appetite on the blackberries.

"I could eat a pig right now," said Bobby, "especially one done in a hangi."

"Pigs don't eat pigs, Parata," grinned Carl. "That's being a cannibal."

"E hoa Newman, you know my family were cannibals in the old days. They probably ate your ancestors."

"Yeah well, 'wonder what is for dinner," I said. "Hope it's roast lamb. Love that lamb."

"Maybe mate," said Bobby, "probably be lamb 'cos it's Saturday night. But I know for certain there's silver-beet too Kev, 'cos I saw Pommy picking it from the garden and getting it ready in the kitchen. You know how much you love that stuff mate," he grinned.

Suddenly, dinner was not such the attractive thing for me at the mention of that dark green silvery spinach. I hated the stuff.

"Last time we had that I wouldn't eat it and had to sit there in the dining hall 'til dark and then Fernsy sent me off to bed. Jeez what am I gonna do if we have it tonight?"

"E tama, Kev," said Bobby, "eat the lamb and the spuds but leave the silver-beet and if they make you eat it, just refuse."

"I'll refuse alright, mate," I said. "Fernsy can send me off to bed early if she likes but I'll never eat that stuff."

"That's right! But they probably won't let you leave the dining hall until you do," said Bobby with a cheeky grin.

I thought about this.

"So that's your solution to leaving the Home, Kev," Bobby went on. "You won't have to, 'cos you won't be allowed to leave until you've eaten all your silver-beet and that means you've killed two birds with one stone: stayin' here with all your best mates and not eating the stuff you hate so much. Couldn't be better."

Bobby grinned at me with his wide Parata grin. He was looking very smug and proud as if he had just solved the greatest problem. Warren and Party and Carl had smiles on their faces too.

"You're right Bobby," I said, pleasantly relieved, "that's exactly what's gonna happen. I like that a lot."

Carl, Warren, Party, Kev, Bobby...Best Mates!